MW01711748

THE DECLINE

A NOVEL

CHRISTOPHER JESSULAT

The Decline

Cover photography by Bryn Robinson
Instagram: @brynphd

tellwell

Tellwell Talent
www.tellwell.ca

ISBN
978-1-77302-467-7 (Paperback)
978-1-77302-466-0 (eBook)

PROLOGUE

THE MID-MORNING SUNLIGHT PIERCED THE haggard canopy, bringing with it the vague promise of a warmth not known for months. While New Brunswick is known for its tendency towards harsh winters, this year the season had been unusually long and hellishly persistent – stubbornly refusing to yield to the warmth of spring. Record snowfall had punished much of the province, and it lingered in a pervasive cold that rivaled even its traditionally deepest months. While it was true the days were lengthening, there was little to show for it beneath the tree cover.

The leaves overhead whispered gently, resisting little as they shivered from the light moan of a chill breeze, as if the forest itself were yawning wide and trying to shake off the morning frost. In this particular stretch of the boreal forest, the usual dominance of the Canadian evergreen was conspicuously absent – birch, poplar and sugar maple grew in thick copses about the gently sloping terrain. It seemed as if the trees had capitalized on some brief moment, long ago, to seize their territory amidst the abdication of the typical monoculture imposed by the domestic lumber industry.

Perhaps it reflected what could have been had man and commerce never disturbed her.

Since time immemorial, the eastern forest had played host to a varied, vibrant ecology. Now, however, she felt ruined. No songbirds can be heard greeting the morning from their perches, and no signs of life reveal themselves on the canvas of snow and spotted earth. In simple truth, aside from the hardwood dotting the landscape, the forest could easily be described as barren. A mere shadow of its former glory, and a scathing testament to the world as we left it; pockmarked and scarred with industry and monuments to our own excess and achievement – a surface, still beautiful to regard, but boasting an underbelly that is empty and soulless.

Despite the slowly gathering strength of a now long overdue spring, the snow clung steadfastly where it lay. It was far from the picturesque and pristine white associated with fresh snowfall. This snow was dirty, full of grime and yielded only sporadically to afford spots of dank earth a chance to be seen and feel either shade or sunlight. The Maritime snow had come hard and early last year, and had doggedly remained throughout the preceding winter months; having trapped beneath it the shed leaves and scabbed branches of yesteryear, it partially preserved them in winter's mausoleum. Now, the smell of damp earth and fetid leaves overwhelmed the scent of the budding hardwood, which lent the forest overall a sickly-sweet cadence; still familiar, though somehow completely foreign, like a flicker of recognition hastily buried beneath the weight of dementia.

A particular downed maple, its flesh brown and graying from enduring several seasons of rain, frost and thaw, lay strewn across the path. The wood and once protective bark offered little objection to the deliberate stabs and incisions of a modest fixed-blade hunting knife, being driven into it and shifted gently so as to carefully pry open the innermost layers. The desiccated wood crumbled under the assault, preferring instead to surrender and fragment, piece by failing piece. Perhaps it bargained with the assailant, desperately pleading to sacrifice a portion of its holdings to retain the rest, somehow affording itself a grim pact to continue along its own slow path to ultimate decay.

The knife came down measuredly, repeatedly, albeit with no particular rhythm, working the wood from about the midpoint of the trunk downwards towards the fulcrum of the break. The dull thud of the blade's tip probing the fallen maple was the only sound beyond the meandering breeze. He was looking for something, anything that could constitute wealth in this world within the depths of that trunk. As each small segment of wood fell away, the wound was scrutinized for any signs of movement, any subtle scurrying that would betray the presence of insects or some other protein-rich food. In truth, he had been looking for signs of carpenter ants – at least, insofar as he knew, what were commonly called carpenter ants – but the simple fact was he had no idea whether or not such fare could be found given the recent climate.

A thin, grim smile crept its way across his chapped lips as the most recent section of the tree's flesh peeled away to reveal the presence of a handful of small, white grubs. Their bodies writhed, visibly uncomfortable at being exposed to daylight and the open air, bared to the elements for the first and final time.

A meager meal, but a meal nonetheless.

Chapter 1

THE OUTBREAK WAS BOTH SUDDEN AND FEROcious, and is now measured by the weeks since the "First Wave" broke. Its approach was much as you'd likely expect – the occasional news report, buried under something sensationalized, likely pertaining to pop culture, celebrities or politicians misbehaving. The occasional headline, alluding to a resistant strain of something wholly uninteresting and unable to be packaged in a way it could readily be sold to the public. Scattered reports of some instances of civil unrest potentially associated with whatever it was the news report was about.

The exact point of origin was unknown.

The exact cause of the infection was unknown.

The exact date of the first event was unknown.

Truth be told, the above became increasingly irrelevant details; all just minutia. After a few short weeks, it really didn't matter to the masses if it was a natural mutation of something viral, microbial, fungal; the ill-gotten gains of scientific research, intended as malicious or benevolent; the desolation of bioterrorism; or the undiscerning wrath of a truly vengeful god, finally coming to terms with the realities of a failed creation – aborting this attempt in favour of starting civilization anew.

What mattered is that it had spilled into the streets outside your door.

The early stages of infection were relatively docile with symptoms most closely resembling the flu. Hospitals were filling up with patients complaining of fatigue, fever, sore throat. As it progressed, tremors and involuntary movements would shake the extremities, blood pressure would rise to the point where vessels in and around the eyes would burst, a general inability to swallow or keep food and water down. Whereas most patients were unable to eat or drink, rehydration was driven through intravenous drips, though even they couldn't seem to slake the body's thirst. It was almost as if the organs themselves were parched and arid, being overclocked and guzzling exponentially more water to fuel their frenzied function. As the dehydration deepened, the "shakes" became more pronounced, and the fever escalated sharply.

A combination of strains simply burned you out from within.

While the time between the onset of symptoms was not fixed and notoriously difficult to forecast, it was generally accepted that once you exhibited symptoms, mortality experience would be certain within ninety-six hours. When the hospitals were still running, there were numerous attempts to refine the understanding of the pathology's patterns – subdividing the infected through representative demographic samplings and forced observation under guard – but the studies didn't yield conclusive results. The infection made no distinction and had no conventional pattern amongst the young or old, men or women, the fit or the sedentary. It was seemingly random how long a given patient would survive the internal assault, but invariably... brain function would cease and the organs would fail.

But that wasn't the end.

It didn't take long to learn that there was a second stage, post mortem. In every traditional sense, the body had died; the heart stopped beating, the lungs stopped pumping, and the brain was lifeless and without spark. Official observation reports varied, but in as little as an hour, something profane and defiling.

A perversion; a twisting of our collective natural order.

Reanimation.

This new state was aggressive and predatory; categorically primal, driven by only the basest of instinct.

The insatiable desire to feed.

Ravenous, the recently reanimated would swarm the living, rend and consume their flesh. Though perhaps not as lithe in their raised state as they had been in life, the first few days or weeks of reanimation were when the dead could be described as the most "active." Ultimately, the flesh would turn necrotic and tighten, progressively withering to decay.

As the days and weeks progressed, the reanimated would begin to slow – whether this was from the advancement of infection or the gradual degradation of the flesh was unknown. The First Wave of the outbreak was now largely in this segment, still deadly and incomparably violent, but not near as agile as the more recently succumbed.

Small mercies.

* * *

Anders surveyed the grey waste that surrounded the compound, straining his already tired eyes in an effort to scan the empty streets between scores of abandoned buildings.

He had drawn this duty on several occasions, but honestly didn't mind it. Being perched atop a weathered building seemed as good a vantage point as any for the end of days, he mused.

While ordinarily serving the role as spotter would be relatively dull, on some occasions it proved frantic. Anders wasn't yet convinced either way if he preferred the lull or the chaos, but having something to focus on did ease his mind – even if only intermittently – as it kept his thoughts from straying away from duty. In truth, Anders had been fortunate to find himself here, much more fortunate than most.

And he knew it; that knowledge drove him.

On the surface, the prospects for survival in a small, unassuming place like New Brunswick, Canada were halfway decent. The landscape was largely rural and, for the most part, densely forested aside from three hubs of population.

Anders lowered his binoculars and shut his eyes tightly, vainly trying to combat their fatigue. The wind was fierce today; he could feel traces of windswept tears clinging to the outermost corners of his eyes. He knew he'd find no relief until the shift was over and he found himself back inside the relative warmth of the congested corridors and stale dormitories. Opening his eyes again, he sighed almost imperceptibly and turned his gaze away from his charge to where he now called home.

Anders had found himself in Canada for what should have been a brief stint on an exchange program, meant to foster heightened cooperation and consistency amongst nations potentially interested in joining the NATO alliance. His native Finland, in light of recent tensions between Russia and the European bloc, had renewed debating the subject of NATO membership despite years of thinly veiled Russian protest and posturing.

Anders took a deep, contemplative breath and considered his surroundings.

He looked about as threatening as a kitten; cherubic features, fair skinned with light hair and soft blue eyes. His appearance readily betrayed his Scandinavian heritage, and his accent ensured he was not mistaken for a local.

He was a long way from his birthplace, and held no illusion he'd likely see its shores again.

At least the winter was familiar.

As was customary, each spotter was paired with a sniper – one team for each of three nests about the compound. He'd never served an assignment with this soldier before; some grunt whose name he didn't remember from the duty roster, and who clearly had no interest in breaking bread. It was just as well – Anders was seldom one to connect easily, even without the language barrier. While his English had improved dramatically since his time with the exchange program, and even further now in the narrow confines of the compound's quarters, Anders had never been comfortable in initiating conversation with someone new; even less so away from home. He often felt his command of the English language inadequate, preferring to leave others to their own device in any event. Nevertheless, Anders was generally liked – the survivor's enclave appreciated his work ethic, and he was always ready to pick up a shift somewhere on the duty roster. It didn't matter if his reasons were to stave off his own boredom or because he was ultimately selfless – his time along the wall was noted.

Turning his back to the ruined city, Anders sat, rested the binoculars on his lap and blew into his hands, trying to chase away the stinging numbness in his fingers. Any reprieve from the chill would be short lived – his shift in the nest still had plenty of time remaining. Though spring would be on its way soon, the air remained bitter cold when being whipped by the sharp winds on the harbour, even moreso amongst the rooftop vantage points.

The city of Saint John was nestled on the coast of the Bay of Fundy, which boasted the highest tides in the world. The deep water port was ice free year round and made the harbours here particularly valuable for military and commercial application. The Coast Guard site was one of several designated safe zones dotted throughout the city proper, though at one point its borders stretched out beyond the confines of the base itself to include two neighbouring cruise ship terminals. It had extended southwards down the peninsula to encompass the better part the eastern half of the harbour. Whereas the west side of the harbour was largely zoned as heavy industrial, it wasn't suited for much else than unloading large container ships before the outbreak; thus, the official response had put their focus into fortifying the length of the east waterfront and inland a few streets as its primary conduit for extracting survivors. It was meant to serve as a beachhead for future military support arriving by sea or by helicopter, but it wasn't meant to be. There was a time when the west side of the harbour seemed occupied, and occasionally they would spot attempts to signal with flashlights, smoke or something reflective.

Now it only appeared desolate, defiled.

One by one, the outposts, checkpoints and camps throughout the city became overwhelmed by the swarms of infected and the response had little option but to abandon their inland posts. Recognizing the east harbour as being the last line of defense, they kept collapsing back to the waterfront with the aim of holding the port and their lifeline. The discipline and professionalism of the military was evident – they had fallen back in good order, executed their plans almost to the letter.

The "best laid plans," and all.

The line was thin, and the stations woefully overcrowded. Once the infection was inside, the terminals – designed for herding tourists through an assaulting array of tour guides and tacky souvenirs – simply weren't designed for any meaningful tactical purpose. The outbreak ravaged the camp, and the satellite guard stations watching over the hopeful evacuees were overwhelmed, literally swallowed whole by the surging crowds, equal measures of the dead and dying.

The infected had driven a catastrophic wedge into the very heart of the response. When the line finally broke, the harbour was effectively cleft in two; some fled to the Coast Guard site, while the rest broke for the city barracks at the southern tip of the city's peninsula.

That was a dark day.

The compound itself was previously used as a staging area for training exercises and for the collection of meteorological data. The site was in the process of being decommissioned, and even before the outbreak was largely stripped of most of the man and material that once called it home. Rumour had it the municipality had been pursuing negotiations with the Federal government to acquire the site in order to repurpose it into commercial development for several years. As discussions progressed, the Coast Guard saw little reason to invest in its upkeep, believing it clearly destined for another fate. While the compound's position was indeed ideal for its purpose with the Coast Guard – it occupied a prominent position on the waterfront – it stuck out awkwardly against its renovated, tourist-friendly neighbours.

A strange relic of an era past, seemingly aware it had no place in the future portrait of the harbour.

Almost half the site's natural borders were waterfront and jutted sharply into the Bay. The areas not protected by the water were almost completely wreathed in a chain link fence that was crowned with barbed wire. The survivors sheltered here had been productive during their charge, and had taken to reinforcing their walls by cannibalizing fencing from elsewhere within the compound; given the nature of the disease and the aggressive, violent disposition of the afflicted, having an already erected barrier to scab on to would prove invaluable. The site also featured cleared space for a helipad, and with the combination of a landing area for helicopters and docks to load and unload ship-borne cargo, resupply and rescue seemed probable; in the event the site was compromised, necessitating extraction, they had options.

Largely of brick construction, the aged strength of the masonry offered some strange comfort to Anders. The compound proper contained four significant permanent structures, each repurposed into the variety of services required to support the colony, and a garish sheet metal monstrosity that housed the enclave's stores. Command and control, a makeshift infirmary, an armory and workspace, as well as respective quarters for the civilians and soldiers alike were carved out of the compound and arranged between buildings as efficiently as possible. Sniper's nests – like the one Anders found himself in – dotted several roofs, while a hastily erected shooting-platform-slash-guard-tower offered cover along the various approaches.

Piecemeal checkpoints were built at the front gate, and a temporary registration tent had been set up in the front parking lot between the fence and the command building, though now they served no practical purpose. Whatever hopes there may have been for an orderly approach to the situation were long since abandoned. The registration tent now only housed bleak coffee and hot water to those on patrol and guard duty, and the main gate's checkpoints would only be manned in the event someone approached the gate to be granted entry.

It had been several days since the compound had encountered anyone that was breathing.

At least, breathing in the conventional sense.

Some of the facilities were powered by diesel generators, but largely the compound would be considered dark. Some battery powered lanterns were used to light rooms and provide a psychological lift for the occupants, and command did have a few smaller, portable gas generators to power individual rooms or modules, but fuel was in short supply. It was cold and dark, though as unwelcoming as it was, it was preferable to the alternatives.

Overall, the cluster of buildings was tightly packed; with scarcely five feet separating the street frontage fence and the structure where you slept, its claustrophobic nature was keenly felt. It required constant patrol and chronic vigilance, and this became infinitely more taxing as the numbers of trained personnel dwindled and provisions rationed. There was plenty of space towards the back of the complex, but it wasn't feasible to try to change the facilities.

No, this was as good as they were going to get.

Looking down now at the compound, Anders couldn't stop himself from thinking that while the site was defensible, its geography was hardly ideal as a fortress besieged by a tireless, ravenous enemy. While it was a conclusion Anders reached several times while manning the nests, the realization lingered just a shade longer today.

Glancing up to see his spotter had been staring blankly in the wrong direction, the nameless grunt kicked Anders' boot. Snapping back to reality and remembering his post, Anders raised his binoculars and turned back to face the wasted landscape.

Chapter 2

THE COMMUNICATIONS ROOM AND CENTER planning were off limits to all but the official response and their supporting staff. Any communiqués meant for wide dissemination were posted in the mess of the civilian living quarters next to the day's duty roster.

Otherwise, if you didn't need to know, you didn't.

What was widely known, however, was the conspicuous and complete absence of resupply and relief the response had promised. The realization that whoever survived and wherever they now found themselves would be on their own for the foreseeable future was a troubling thought. Many simply couldn't accept it, or otherwise weren't equipped for the realities they now faced.

Unable to cope, many sunk into despondency.

A stifling, malevolent hush permeated the very air; it clung to the dormitory walls and to the skin as if a stale cigarette, idly smoldering. The world was both cruel and apathetic in even the best of times, but this new order... this was truly sadistic. Barbarous and bestial, it would be destined to change you.

* * *

Lying in bed, Isaac stared fiercely at the ceiling, ostensibly intent on burrowing a hole through the aging tile. Not much reward for the effort, but the congestion in the sleeping quarters was bordering on the claustrophobic; the confines were cramped and constricting, the minimal sleeping space on ration just as everything else. Having a cot or makeshift bed was a welcome amenity, but somehow the sleep just wasn't as restful knowing it would only be yours for your apportioned eight hours a day, shared with at least one other person during the remainder.

Imagining a sky, a vast starlit canopy overhead – however dull and overcast – gave him some degree comfort.

Isaac was thin – standing but a modest height, he scarcely tipped the scales at 140 lbs., even before the rationing. Truthfully, his appearance was rather unremarkable. Being neither fast on his feet nor considered strong for his size, he'd never have been thought particularly athletic, even without the black framed designer glasses and the awkward gait. But he had always been clever – clever, and ruthlessly pragmatic. It had served him well in the world before the outbreak, where he enjoyed a successful career as an analyst with a national telecommunications company. He loved numbers, loved both the challenge and the reward of attempting to dissect and find opportunity in the ever-changing figures. Despite how taxing the last few weeks had proved, his face didn't yet betray his age – the only thing that would give away his actual years was the presence of a strip of stark white whiskers on his chin when he wasn't able to shave.

Ignoring the many shortcomings of their current accommodations, Isaac knew their worth. Almost at the outset, he and his fiancée Keeley had found themselves in the Coast Guard site.

Keeley was a sweetheart, not at all meant for a world like this, and how she and Isaac had ever come to be would prove a mystery to most. She was an absolute free spirit, selfless to a fault and full of life – diametrically opposed to Isaac, whom many would consider a bit of a "buzzkill," even if they would never admit as much. She had spent several years working for a major chartered bank and had progressed through the ranks of working as teller through to being one of the top financial planners the bank had to offer. She excelled at working with people and had a genuinely buoyant spirit; people couldn't help but like her. She was small and light, not even reaching a full five-two, and even when wearing her customary high heels she could seldom look Isaac in the eyes. Her hair was a deep and lustrous brown and she had dark, obviously kind eyes. Despite her small stature, she walked with purpose and had a surprisingly heavy footfall for someone otherwise so graceful.

Keeley had served as one of the bank's First Aid attendants for several years; this coupled with her natural likability had her frequently drawing duty rotation in the infirmary. Medical skills, even fundamental training, were highly prized at the compound, and she wasn't afraid to get her hands dirty. She would often pull double shifts and otherwise was called away regularly. Keeley always strived to maintain a strong façade, as often as possible, and consciously made an effort not to display the fear and anxiety boiling under the surface.

Keeley was blessed with the ability to flip the proverbial switch and function on autopilot when need be, but after the adrenaline dump, she couldn't always shake the memories. She understood the challenges facing the enclave, and the realities of her post. The infirmary couldn't take chances, especially inside the walls. The more recent the infection, the more deadly the patient; the early stages were both the most dangerous and had the highest probability of being communicable.

Keeley always preferred the term "euthanized" to the more guttural sound of "putting them down." Although she understood the necessity, she was thankful the guards didn't force the infirmary staff to watch the infected being lined up on the pavement outside.

Isaac and Keeley lived and worked in the Uptown core of the city, each had offices within walking distance from their home. When the calls came out for survivors to get to shelter, they were blessed to have found each other in the chaos, even despite their proximity. Isaac had emptied their bank accounts, believing he might be able to buy them safe passage to the best defended facility they could get to – reasoning at best he'd successfully secure safe passage, and at worst the money wouldn't be worth anything anyway. In any event, he was able to barter their way as far back as the last line of defensible terrain, the dormitories of the Coast Guard site. He was even able to ensure they shared the same room, albeit stacked up with several other refugees.

Isaac had never shared that information with Keeley.

As far as she knew, things just worked out.

Isaac spent most of his time working the nests or out with the scavengers. His father – an excellent marksman and an avid outdoor enthusiast – had taught him to shoot alongside many foundational camping and survival skills. While not as gifted a shot as some, his aim was reliable, and he had logged trigger time with a variety of firearms;

even went so far as to pursue a restricted permit. Isaac didn't appreciate the lessons as much in his youth, didn't care for the simple life as much in his early years as when he was aging and craved the escape from the hustle of corporate life. In any case, he'd proven himself to the response and as a good soldier; none of the officials questioned his position, and no one doubted his loyalty.

Since the night the line broke, Isaac preferred being outside the walls.

Isaac and Keeley tried to avoid talking about their shifts, which led to the majority of their evenings being spent in silence. Through everything, she was convinced there still had to be a plan, a grand design. After all and against all odds, they were together, and they had found shelter.

She had always believed in miracles, and he wouldn't tell her any differently.

* * *

Lynn was finishing her shift in the civilian section of the command building. She had experience in administrative support and had worked a number of summers with the city cashier's office, and had been in the final year of her Business Administration degree at UNBSJ. Most people would have described her as attractive – she was young, blonde and charming – though few would have considered her as much else. She wasn't street smart and no one would have mistaken her for being well read; but she never needed to be. She had the unmistakable air of someone who had gotten by with their looks alone, and never concerned herself much with the nuances of hard work. The fact she was near completion of an undergraduate program was a shock to most.

Lynn mostly made coffee for the officials in the building, took notes and the like. While her official capacity was limited to the most menial of tasks, it didn't bother her; she enjoyed the prestige, the entitlement of being part of the "inner circle." She rarely paid much attention to the chatter around her, except when it came to the three-day duty roster. Smiling smugly at her self-importance, she relished in the sense of being so close to the action.

Putting on her jacket and turning the collar to shield her skin from the winter air, she started back out in the cold and headed towards the living quarters, stopping only briefly to look at the supply shed. She always scanned it on the walk back after finishing a shift; seeing both the size of the structure and the stately guards posted outside gave her comfort. With stores that size packed with provisions and the ever improving prospects of springtime, as long as the walls held they'd be well looked after.

They could do this.

* * *

Quinn stared into his stale, black coffee, patently underwhelmed by it but determined to find some brief distraction. Quinn had command of the facility and the movements of its occupants, but little desire to lead; he loathed the weight of responsibility on this scale, cursed the day the crown had fallen to him.

Quinn wasn't a bad choice for command. He'd served with distinction in Afghanistan – two tours – as a First Lieutenant integrated with an armoured unit, and was himself a Maritime transplant to Petawawa; he was born and bred in Moncton and thus knew most of the province's terrain. He had seen sustained combat against an unconventional enemy, and had been wounded in service to his country. Furthermore, Quinn understood the burdens and the realities of leadership – he understood the need to make tough choices, and how to live with the consequences. A career soldier, he was only days away from his promotion to Captain when the First Wave hit and he was thrust back into service.

It would have to wait.

Most of his current capacity circled around the duty roster and managing the facility's remaining inventory. Though he had advisors and people whose counsel he valued, instinct was his true compass.

That instinct was telling him that they'd be on their own.

Since communication broke down, he had plenty of time to consider the math. The Federal response would invariably be concentrated in the nation's major population centers. All the Maritime Provinces combined – with Newfoundland and Labrador thrown in for good measure – wouldn't equate to the population of Toronto alone.

Quinn leaned back in his ragged chair, sipping the faintly metallic-tasting coffee and tapped his pen against the whiteboard. The administrative work bored him, but it allowed Quinn to make sure he had the pieces where he wanted them. A true utilitarian, he would devote however long was necessary to be wholly satisfied with the efficiency of his lineup – sleep be damned.

The things outside never slept.

Upon assuming command, Quinn had immediately canvassed the survivors for any marketable skills; anyone with medical training, however rudimentary, was deemed critical complement and reserved for the infirmary. Anyone with military, police or general firearms experience was earmarked for patrol, scavenging and defense. Those with construction or mechanical backgrounds were assigned to facility maintenance and upgrading, and were responsible for developing lists of priority materials for the scavengers and salvage missions. Everyone else was deemed more-or-less non-essential and relegated to general labour; cooking, cleaning, sanitation and the like. There were a few orderlies and laypeople running about – but for the most part they made up the supporting cast of the unspecialized.

Quinn needed to keep the survivors fit and wasn't afraid to work them, and his soldiers were loyal and would enforce his edict. He also understood the dangers of having too much time on one's hands, especially when tired and hungry. When no better option presented itself, and partly in compensation for the onslaught of snow and freezing rain, he would assign shifts outside clearing snow throughout the compound and along the perimeter walls. He would ensure the pathways were traversable and guarantee the site was highly conspicuous against the backdrop – especially for a trained recon or relief team. The bare pavement would shine as a black beacon against the otherwise snow covered landscape; it would be unmistakable the site was occupied, or at least had been occupied since the last snowfall. Clearing the snow and ice around the border fencing was of paramount importance as well; if the snow drifted against the chain link and froze, it could provide easy access to the compound for an unwanted guest, or the intrepid dead.

His approach didn't make friends, but quite frankly, it didn't have to – in any event, Quinn didn't care. He needed to drive maximum utility out of each and every limited resource, and with their supplies continuously dwindling, labour would prove the most readily available asset. The cost for this labour was simple, but it was high – food, water, warmth and shelter – and in light of current weather patterns, Quinn was forced to scale back the commitment to scavenging. To compensate, he instituted a tighter rationing plan. It was widely unpopular amongst the population and led to sporadic unrest; it even led to occasional violence. But he reasoned it served two purposes of equal importance – one, it extended the life of what little stores they had left. Two, it temporarily spared Quinn the necessity of an otherwise very public admission that their stores would soon be exhausted, as were the remaining complement of trained soldiers at his disposal.

Urgency meant Quinn had to step up scouting activity as well, and part of him was banking on a big score; they were out there, and he knew it. The problem was the commitment of man and material to go for the high value sites, especially whereas the roads were largely impassable for the limited vehicles on hand. The implications of failure, both in terms of the lost resources and public perception, weighed heavily upon him, but Quinn had to maintain order. The conditions were dire, but only the upper echelons of command knew exactly how dire things had become. He could sense his grip on the situation was slipping. Tenuous as it already was, he couldn't abide the possibility of public sentiment swinging to despair.

Generally speaking, Quinn didn't trust his civilian militia for much but working the nests and scavenging, ultimately preferring what little company of military and veteran presence for scouting, patrol and maintaining order.

But there were a few civilians he could count on to do what needed to be done.

Polishing off the remainder of the ghastly coffee, Quinn rubbed his weary eyes and ran through the duty rotation again.

His hand would be forced soon, and he knew it.

Chapter 3

KEELEY AND ISAAC WERE BOTH ON THE DAY shift this morning, and woke before the reveille to eat breakfast together before parting ways. Keeley would find herself in the infirmary whereas Isaac had drawn a scavenging placement, the details of which were unknown; the briefings, when applicable, were seldom more than a few hasty minutes in advance of departure.

The mess hall was a makeshift space, but it served the purpose. Whereas the duty rotation accounted for shifts throughout each twenty-four hour period, there were always survivors milling about – either those just finishing a shift, those about to begin, or those otherwise too agitated to rest. While many faces were recognizable, Isaac mostly kept to himself and could truly only claim to know a handful of refugees in the entire compound; mostly fellow scavengers, a handful of the guards, and Keeley's cohort in the infirmary.

Isaac didn't want to know anyone else.

Hell, glancing around the mess, he didn't want to know as many faces as he did now.

Breakfast this morning was lackluster and consisted of boiled oats in water – there were so few flakes of oat you couldn't rightly call it oatmeal – served alongside a weak tea and packets of sugar; both the dairy and powdered milk had long since run out.

They ate quietly.

Even without an appetite, Isaac would finish his ration; Keeley ate like a bird in general.

Isaac looked worn out. As he scraped the bottom of the metal bowl for his last few apportioned calories, he inexplicably became distant and fixated on the empty vessel. His breathing was regular but shallow, his lungs barely inflating.

He wasn't the same. Before the world ended, Isaac could make her laugh, but since his time on the wall and the night the line broke, he was constantly preoccupied. Keeley wasn't sure if it was the result a long, gradual slide or something more sudden and specific, but she saw a change in him.

Keeley reached across the slender table and placed her hand on top of his. Isaac snapped up, eyes fixed to hers in a severe glare, neither knowing her face nor processing his surroundings. A flicker of recognition and his demeanor softened – he even managed a weak smile and a deep breath before averting his eyes back down to the bowl.

'Good morning,' came a friendly, albeit unexpected, greeting from behind them; you could hear the smile in the voice. Neither had noticed the approach and Keeley shifted in her seat, startled by the sudden address.

Looking over Isaac's shoulder, Keeley recognized Daniel. She returned the smile and motioned him to join them. Daniel was a fourth year nursing student at UNBSJ, and as such frequently worked the infirmary with Keeley;

he must have pulled the morning shift as well. He was tall and athletic, dark eyed and obviously the descendant of distinguished African pedigree.

Daniel had moved to Saint John from his native Nigeria several years previous to pursue an education after the untimely passing of his parents. He had some siblings but they were outside of Canada; he'd been making it on his own since his late teenage years. His birth name wasn't actually Daniel, but that's what everyone called him – he had given up trying to teach the locals how to properly pronounce his name while still a student at the university. Nevertheless, he liked his adopted moniker. He was kind, educated and intelligent, always willing to lend a hand, and never seemed to be cracking under the stress.

Despite his best efforts to the contrary, Isaac liked Daniel from the moment they met.

Isaac seemed to find himself in the moment again.

'Hey, man. Pull up a chair.'

Keeley smiled subtly and fiddled with her engagement ring, finding some reassurance that Isaac was still in there somewhere.

* * *

Keeley and Daniel began making their rounds in the infirmary, getting their instructions from the attending physician.

The night shift had been cataloguing supplies and running inventory at the instructions of command, and being short staffed it was now up to the morning rotation to change soiled bedding and replace IV drips.

Most of the patients here were suffering from dehydration, but a few of the survivors had more chronic disorders of varying severity. For the most part, triage was geared to determining first if a patient exhibited signs of infection, second how to make them comfortable. Occasionally they would need to treat something more traumatic – accident victims and those who may have been hurt while scavenging – but for the most part, they were wards against the spread of infection. Check for fever, signs of broken blood vessels in the eyes, rash, swollen glands in the neck, then proceed with treatment as applicable.

The infirmary was shabby at best, being an improvised space in what was intrinsically a rundown warehouse. You could dress it up and soak the place in bleach and disinfectant, but it still carried with it the faint musk of an old building that sat vacant for too long. Hardly sterile, but the floor space was the most accommodating to their needs.

Keeley went about verifying the IV bags and checking temperature of the patients while Daniel read over the makeshift charts to get a handle on what medications may have been administered overnight.

She detested the responsibility of checking for fever; admitting anyone was running a high temperature was a fatal condemnation. The response wouldn't take a chance with anyone running the symptoms of the infection, and the acknowledgement of its presence was a death sentence. Anyone feverish would be brought outside, laid on the pavement, and shot.

Those were the rules, and they were absolute.

In the cramped quarters allotted to them they ran twenty beds, all full, with charts scribbled on scraps of cardboard and tacked wherever possible. When necessary, additional patients would be slumped over and laid out anywhere they could find the space. IVs were hung from whatever they could rig. The infirmary was powered by generator, being one of the few facilities earmarked for such privilege. The lights hummed out a dull, yellow light which somehow emphasized the worn interior. The response had also afforded them a couple of gas powered heaters, similar to the ones that contractors would use for new home construction, which at least made it more comfortable to work and partially regulate the core temperature of the patients.

Being a former warehouse, the infirmary also had a couple of large bay doors which in the spring could be opened to allow fresh air in – but for now, the elements ensured they would need to stay closed, and the treatment area would be forced to wallow in its own stagnation.

As Keeley worked her way about the room, Daniel watched her go. She had remarkable bedside manner, natural and effortless, and genuinely cared for the people here. Daniel did too; he was at the top of his class and that dedication was evident. Still, looking about the facility and assessing the state of things, he couldn't help but feel a bit of doubt… the creeping tide of defeatism.

Sometimes these shifts felt more like vigil.

* * *

Lynn strolled in to her shift at the administrative centre a full twenty minutes late. The response paid her no heed – in truth, if it weren't for the fact she was pretty and made a drinkable cup of coffee, she'd scarcely be noticeable. They were almost oblivious to her presence anyway; there was much to do in the heart of the colony to keep the compound moving.

Lynn ran her fingers through her blonde hair in a vain attempt to give it some lift. She wanted the attention of a few of the soldiers. She had contemplated the implications of the compound falling – she would be helpless on her own; the things outside the walls terrified her. Once she arrived at the Coast Guard site and it became common knowledge a duty rotation would be established, she made sure everyone in uniform, everyone even remotely official-looking, knew she had an administrative background. She carefully worked it into conversation, trying to ensure her assignment to the main building, believing that to be her safest bet.

Now and then, though, her thoughts occasionally turned to planning in the event of absolute disaster – what if the command centre was overrun? What if the compound was altogether lost? Even with the razor wire tops, those fences were only so high, and there were only so many soldiers left in the compound.

Scanning the room for any likely marks, she took stock of the official presence.

She would trade sex for protection.

If she played her cards right, she might even be able to secure some lonely soldier in a position of authority, maybe someone able to work some additional privileges for her.

The officials in the compound wouldn't have noticed Lynn at all in their presence, but she was attractive and flirtatious; that was her weapon. She could play the part. She'd done it countless times before.

They certainly wouldn't have noticed her for her work ethic.

Or the coffee.

* * *

It was briefing time. This assembly was noticeably bigger than any recent runs Isaac had been part of. Checking the faces present, he recognized only a scant few out of the dozen or so gathered, with only one soldier in particular he had worked with before.

She was corporal Cox. Isaac didn't care for her. He found her too cocksure and too assertive, the type that didn't play well with others. Out in the wasteland, though, she was talented – results focused, a steady shot, and all business. Isaac considered her 'high up' and a favourite of Quinn, and Isaac believed her to be counted amongst his trusted few. She had dark eyes and a fair complexion, about the same height as Isaac though a dozen pounds lighter. Her hair was jet black and always pulled back into a tight ponytail. She may have been small in stature, but she was built solid and didn't mince words.

To Isaac's recollection, it had been a while since the scavengers were out with one of Quinn's inner circle. A representative from the armory oversaw controlled load-outs for everyone participating in the mission.

Hm... this run must be important.

Isaac started to settle in to the briefing, and felt a fool for his behaviour over breakfast. He glanced down to catch a glimpse of his wedding band – he wore it even though they hadn't officially been married as yet. He bought it online in preparation but the world went to shit before they had the opportunity. It was a simple band of black titanium, still surprisingly reflective given the abuse it had taken from life in the compound.

Thankfully Keeley was always quick to forgive his shortcomings.

Isaac had drawn the assault position with his team. He'd be outfitted with a Remington 870 as his primary carry and a Norinco knockoff 1911 for a sidearm. Being assault, he'd be first through the door once it was breached. Of all the positions to be assigned, Isaac was most apprehensive to the assault role. He'd done most of his pre-outbreak shooting at the range – he'd never fired at an animal for sport in his life – so the bulk of his experience was target shooting at distance with a long rifle. He had shot some skeet before on a couple occasions, but it was never a focus for him. Isaac's real apprehension stemmed from the fact the assault post had the highest likelihood of getting up close and personal with the infected, and being of a small stature didn't lend itself well to hand-to-hand combat with an enemy that wouldn't tire and wouldn't go down without severe brain trauma. He didn't have the strength to kick down most doors in one shot, and this mission was going to take them into what was a dense population zone and through tight corridors. Considering the porters would probably be kept at the back with the professional soldiers, it really should have come as no surprise he'd find himself in this predicament today.

Isaac was passed two clips for the pistol and a pocketful of shells.

They were ultimately to be split in two teams. They'd move out as one unit and push several blocks northeast towards St. Joseph's Hospital. *Ground fucking zero,* the assembly collectively thought at once; it was almost audible. Isaac allowed himself to survey the expressions of the group and get a feel for the room. Most didn't flinch, but the eyes of the several scavengers Isaac didn't recognize grew wide with a pang of fear. Even if Isaac despised Quinn, he knew that command would only take a calculated risk; he was sure the brass wouldn't have tapped anyone for this mission that wasn't game… so he let it pass from notice.

Fear was healthy, after all.

It meant they were at least smart enough to know the hell they were about to walk into.

Quinn wouldn't risk a medical attendant to accompany the run itself, so he had the infirmary prepare a list of priority items and their associated descriptions. The goal was intravenous solution, IV bags and the like, respirators, bandages, surgical instruments; any pills or drugs you could find. Soap, disinfectant, toothpaste, bedding, assorted toiletries...

From the sounds of it, they'd take anything.

Without a trained attendant, the salvage team would have to rely on the smash-and-grab style for anything that resembled the items described. In and out, no need to linger, and no reason to probe the halls of the hospital any deeper than need be. Take mental notes and remember any opportunities you couldn't get to, but no unnecessary heroics. There had been an official presence at St. Joseph's at the early stages of the outbreak, so there was a very real possibility of recovering ammunition and weaponry as well as miscellaneous salvage of value.

Quinn's scouts had been floating around this part of the Uptown at his specific behest, trying to determine if a big play like this was feasible. While the scouts individually never got into the hallways of the hospital, the site reportedly looked promising, and most of the reanimated dead had meandered off in the time since the site was abandoned.

Once they neared the target, they were to breach an adjacent building with a clear line of sight and split up. A seven man fire team would move in to the hospital while the scavenging team holed up awaiting signal. Whereas Quinn fully expected the fire team to find itself in close combat, he didn't want them carrying anything that would give the ghouls a handle with which to grab on to and haul them down, so he instructed them to move in with nothing but weapons and ammo. The salvage team would use that time to mark the cleared building and reinforce it insofar as possible.

If this run was successful, and if the hospital was as rich with salvage as suspected, Quinn would want to be back.

The three designated porters would be carrying side-arms and improvised melee weapons, but their primary purpose was stocking their 65L packs. They would be covered by two babysitters, both sporting refurbished surplus Russian SKS 7.62mm's with bayonets affixed. They would lay low, remain out of sight and keep the porters covered while the team gained entry. If things went to shit and the fire team needed an exit, they would provide a base of fire for retreat. If all went according to plan, the two gunners would hold the building adjacent while the rest returned their supplies to the compound. They would brief Quinn on what materials would be needed to establish a more permanent outpost and – hopefully – a supply line. Their relief would come as soon as possible.

It was a good plan; had contingencies and was forward thinking.

Isaac turned the shotgun over in his hands, getting reacquainted with the weapon. He had carried this piece before, and he trusted the feel and weight of the 12 gauge. He preferred his Mossberg, but the Remington was a fine choice. The Norinco was every bit as reliable as the authentic Colt version, and the .45 caliber model had a manageable, balanced recoil. Isaac also always carried with him a fixed blade knife he had found on a previous run – he had owned one just like it; a Gerber *Bear Grylls* survival knife. It was hokey and marketed to city boys camping at National Parks moreso than the true outdoorsman, but the 4.8" blade was tempered cold steel, full tang and partially serrated, and it came with a sharpener and fire starter built into the sheath to boot.

It was ghastly, but effective.

Isaac was passed a flashlight to affix to the rails on the 870; he'd need it to check rooms on the way in. It was surprisingly light, but even the scant few ounces it represented would slow his ability to react with the shotgun. Still, he'd prefer the ability to see his way around, and rationalized the ability to see where he was going would more than compensate him for the slightly delayed reaction time.

Isaac was, however, much less enthused with covering fire being provided by the SKS. They were common guns, he'd see them at the range from time to time; he'd even personally put a few rounds through an SKS or two. They were easy to get a hold of, though still somehow collector's items. They were loud – deafening, really – but they boasted serious stopping power.

But really, if the shit hit the fan, the noise wouldn't be his primary concern.

Content with their assignment, the team suited up. Isaac racked the slide on the shotgun a couple times before loading it.

He loved that sound.

Chapter 4

IT WAS AN UNCHARACTERISTICALLY CLEAR day; the recent weeklong cloud cover had finally broken to afford the morning sun an opportunity to shine through, and the wind was not present but for a light breeze.

Anders took a deep breath, filling his lungs to capacity. It didn't matter that the air was still cold – this was as sure a sign as possible that spring had not yet completely forsaken them.

And it felt good.

He was once again stationed in the nest above the civilian living quarters, scanning the landscape. The natural light and absence of flurries and freezing rain would mean he might be able to do some proper surveying today.

A salvaging team was setting up at the main gates for departure; Quinn must be using the break in the weather to try and scrape something together. It was a good size crew heading out, as well. This morning Anders was smart enough to remember to bring a cup of that weak tea up with him to the nest, something warm to keep the mobility in his fingers for at least a little while. He had also smuggled a few extra packets of sugar with him for an extra little boost of caloric intake.

Yes, he thought, managing an awkward grin for his benefit alone.

Today would be a good day.

The salvagers headed out and shut the gate behind them. Not surprisingly, the scavenging team set off north, up the hill between the two large retail complexes whose names he could never keep straight.

One of the buildings had a strange assortment of carved statues outside, hewn from rough timber. They were effigies of people, frozen in time, arranged to be cheerlessly facing outwards, an eternal silence between them. Waiting for something that'd never come, they stayed while others left.

They lingered.

There was something deeply unsettling about them.

The two complexes were raided through already and there wasn't much left to be found inside but the scattered infected. There was a pedway system that the compound had once held as a conduit for supplies being pillaged from the mall and the city market, but once it was determined they had picked it clean there was little incentive to maintain a permanent presence there.

Couldn't spare the manpower.

Couldn't spare the bullets, either.

They had barricaded the exits and marked it as a "No Entry" building as best they could and left it to rot.

The streets immediately adjacent to the east of the compound had probably been picked over already, and the southern tip of the peninsula had been thought largely burned out weeks ago – the nests had spotted the smoke and flames. For a while there was concern the inferno would build and storm its way towards their position on the harbour; it would appear the fires came to a line of brick period homes and waned until exhausted. Though the great fires were out, steam and white smoke billowed amongst the remains of the charred and skeletal structures.

No one truthfully knew how the fires started, but there were a host of theories about the compound, ranging from natural gas tanks to other pockets of survivors wielding improvised weaponry, like Molotovs. Most of the buildings in that part of town were old and of wood construction; it wouldn't have taken much to set the place ablaze by accident.

Or deliberately; whichever.

Anders knew there was once a refugee camp, very similar to the compound he now found himself in at the tip of the landmass, but he couldn't get a good bead on it with the relatively poor magnification of his binoculars. He had seen it once before when making landfall the first time in Canada. It was an immense stone construct – it should have survived the flames.

Anders allowed himself to hope.

Some slight movement caught Anders' eye from the street stretching southwards. He turned his binoculars along the loop towards the roadway access of the barracks safe zone. Looking through the aperture he spotted two figures, a pair meekly shambling on the snow covered road, ambling about without purpose or direction. They were dead, and he knew it without having to study them. He reckoned they were a solid four hundred yards away.

No point telling the sniper he was with – the same mute grunt from last shift.

Anders doubted he could hit the targets at that distance anyway.

* * *

The salvage team would start north and climb a hill until they made it to an office complex called the Mercantile centre. There they would slip around the structure and make their way down the parking access along the rear of the building. They'd continue a few hundred yards until they hit the first four way intersection, where they would hang a left for a couple blocks and then break right towards their destination. Once outside the hospital and able to assess the scene, they'd determine which building would serve as their outpost.

It was a long and circuitous route, but would allow the team to avoid the denser residential housing prevalent along the more direct paths. It would also ensure they travelled through or alongside as much open space and parking lots as possible. Not to say it wasn't without danger – this pass would take them treacherously close to Harbour Station, the city's primary sports complex and large event destination. It was converted to an aid station in the early days of the outbreak, before the true catastrophe of the infection was fully understood. While they would be overlooking it, the team would never need to get down to street level alongside it. Well over a thousand people would have been treated there; hundreds of volunteers.

And the overwhelming majority of them would have died.

Those among them not fully consumed by the dead would have reanimated.

This was an area where angels would fear to tread.

So long as they moved quick and quiet and didn't fire their weapons without absolute necessity, they should be able to slip by, sight unseen.

Only one short stretch would have them uncomfortably exposed.

* * *

Quinn tapped his middle finger against his temple, listening intently to the rhythmic static being played for him.

The communications room was always closed and guarded; Quinn had to control the dissemination of any messages, or the complete lack thereof. He sat at a plain wooden desk with his resident improvised comms expert. Andrew, he thought his name was.

Didn't really matter. This kid wasn't much of a soldier.

Andrew was short and portly, hardly a physical specimen. He'd spent his days pre-outbreak playing computer games, and judging by his pallor and somewhat sickly demeanor, he devoted far too much time to them. He telecommuted to work daily and was asthmatic – probably hadn't seen real exercise for months at a time. His hair was shaggy and unkempt, like the rest of his appearance, and his posture was overtly flaccid. But he had a head for electronics and was obviously an intellectual; Quinn valued that skillset, even if he was socially stunted.

He couldn't help but judge Andrew as being lazy and withdrawn.

He was soft, doughy.

Still, when the world fell apart, Andrew stepped up and volunteered his service, such as it was.

By Quinn's estimation, that counted for something.

Andrew was stationed at the radio, broadcasting a scripted message and periodically trying to rig it any way he could to boost a signal either in or out. He had successfully altered a few of the two-way radios, but batteries were becoming scarce and Quinn needed to ration those as well.

Andrew had been at this for days with no sign of progress, and those frustrations were plainly written on his face. With the break in weather, he had hoped the signal would have less interference; Quinn meant to make the most of it and correctly believed he would need to prod Andrew to keep him on task.

'Keep trying,' Quinn instructed, standing from his seat.

'There's no one out there,' Andrew began, looking like a puppy that had been kicked too many times, 'at least no one who can respond.'

Quinn studied the boy. He wasn't accustomed to people questioning his orders.

Turning to leave, Quinn stopped only long enough to force eye contact and flatly state the obvious.

'Keep trying.'

* * *

The salvage team had just crested the first hill; they had advanced without incident on the first leg of the journey. No movement aside from their own.

The unit crossed the intersection as one and hugged up against the Mercantile as they snaked their way to the back of the building. The snow had drifted up against the structure and made the fencing easy to climb over. It was fortunate as climbing in snow gear and heavy boots could prove a challenging task.

One by one the team would hop the fence while the others scanned the surroundings.

Isaac leaned his back against the building, waiting his turn. It dawned on Isaac that he had actually worked in this building at one point. He had an unceremonious office on the ground floor; the team literally walked under his former window to get to their current position.

Now, he was standing in the cold with a team of masked strangers, holding a shotgun, outside his former workplace.

Unsure of exactly why, Isaac found it hilarious. He stifled a laugh at his own expense, shook it off and rotated his shoulders forward to bring himself back to game focus.

Slowly, deliberately the team moved up the slight bank to where the rear parking area would be.

Cox would be in command of this mission. She carried the Canadian Armed Force's standard issue Colt C7 with tactical rails, choosing today to mount a flashlight for illuminating the expected deep darkness of the hospital's corridors. She motioned the team to sit tight while she slid up the rest of the embankment. Raising her rifle, she leaned into the aperture and scanned the streets ahead with careful intent. The team waited, breath filtering through their various masks as plumes of ragged vapour in the crisp morning air. Content their path was open, she turned back to her team and silently mouthed the order –

'Let's move.'

Cox kept the porters in the middle of the pack; they were the purpose of this mission, without which the team would be stuffing whatever they could into their jacket's shallow pockets. Those packs were a lifeline for everyone back in the compound, and Quinn had entrusted their success to her.

The team had to reach the top of one last gentle incline before they would be able to level out, this little hill along the ridgeline culminating in the ultimate view of Harbour Station. Once they got past this stretch, they would have building cover to exploit from its line of sight. For now, they would be against the horizon with the morning sun in the sky behind them. They could potentially cast silhouettes against the overlooking ridge if they weren't absolutely perfect in their positioning.

It may have been unlikely, but she wasn't going to risk it. There was no guidance on how keen the eyesight was for the infected. They could smell you and they would be drawn to sound, and Cox reasoned if corpses had any vestigial sight it would be capable of processing either motion or light; she didn't want to chance disrupting the skyline.

She had the team advance in pairs and in orderly fashion, evenly spaced and timed, running like clockwork. Wherever possible she kept everyone to the right side of the street, away from the ridge, and used the buildings to regroup in cover before scanning the path ahead. Cox brought up the rear only because she was using her scope to scout the road in front, and in the event shit erupted around them, she would cover their withdrawal.

Isaac noticed one of the porters – a big, burly, bearded man – was already beaded in sweat, wringing his gloved hands around the grips of an aluminum baseball bat. Otherwise, everyone looked relaxed.

Good sign.

With the rest of the team in position, Cox sprinted up to catch them. The team had almost reached the crest of the incline and she could plainly see the roof of Harbour Station. It had partially collapsed under the weight of the ice and snow and showed the telltale signs of soot; she couldn't see the street level. She knew from this position they had to make it three blocks ahead and then carve a path to the left.

Cox peered around their cover at the corner of the building to get a glimpse of the road ahead.

Fuck me.

* * *

Andrew couldn't stop thinking about how futile this pursuit was.

He had been repeating the same script for days, pausing every few hours to tinker with the radio and consider how he could possibly boost the signal.

He always came up empty, and each time he did he lost a little more interest.

Andrew was often left alone in the communications room, sporadically visited by Quinn to check on progress. Occasionally the comms room was host to closed-door meetings, but Andrew was always ushered out for those, leaving him to stand awkwardly in the command centre. He didn't know anyone's name out there, and while no one made any effort to learn his, he was starting to recognize a few faces.

He definitely recognized the blonde administrative assistant.

Jesus, she was a hot little number.

Andrew had never been blessed with social graces, but he shut down completely around her. Though he didn't speak much to begin with, she stole the words from him, and along with it any sense of mental faculty.

Andrew shook his head and tried to reorient himself to the task at hand. He reached for a screwdriver and once again turned the radio around to remove the protective casing.

* * *

Quinn was being briefed by a civilian administrator about complaints being levied by a group of the survivors.

William.

A fifty-something litigation lawyer.

Quinn had little respect for the legal trade in the world pre-outbreak; he had even less use for it now.

William was tall and thin, with features that most closely resembled a fox. Covetous and angular, he seemed at once both scavenging and predatory.

Without his monthly touchups at the stylist, his hair was steadily shedding its colour. The once slick and suave salt-and-pepper aspect fast eroded to the addled gray that more honestly reflected his years. Despite now being bereft of his accustomed wealth and status, William clung fervently to the idea of his elevated worth amongst the rank and file of the survivors.

Still, this man was intelligent. He had legitimate finesse with words.

Conniving, manipulative, he always sought to box Quinn in.

It was infuriating.

They were complaining of the tight rations and the heavy workload, difficult and cramped conditions in the living quarters.

After a while it all just blended together for him.

Not that Quinn was callous; he did care for the people in his charge. He didn't take the command lightly and knew he would be faced with difficult decisions.

He had weighed his options and set his course, believing them always to be for the greater good. He would do what was necessary, whether it was comfortable or not; this was nothing he didn't expect. Obviously tighter rationing of the food and water, let alone "comfort" items would be unpopular, but the banality of this was starting to set Quinn on edge.

He took a deep, calming breath. If a few moments of his time to indulge this administrator's concerns would help comfort their constituents, he would find the time for it.

* * *

Cox turned back from the corner and leaned flat against the wall for support.

'We've got company.'

She counted at minimum five of the reanimated bastards milling about the entrance to a structure on the opposite side of the street. It had been a correctional facility of some type, maybe storing prisoners for transfer. Didn't matter; the building itself was right up against the ridgeline Cox needed to avoid casting shadows by.

Cox cleared her throat.

'We need to do this quiet and we need to get them on this side of the street. I don't want to be anywhere near the top of that embankment on their side of the road,' she paused to make sure her orders were understood. 'Around this corner is a pair of raised concrete platforms, we're going to move ahead – quick and quiet – and we'll determine how to engage from there.'

The dead didn't notice their advance and continued to fumble about up the street. The team huddled in tight behind any cover they could get. The dead were little more than the road width away. From this distance, the signs of serious frostbite were evident – decrepit skin, blackened by the frigid cold.

It was a marvel the things could still move.

Cox signaled the group – this encounter would be settled in close quarters. 'Six targets, porters go last.'

Isaac unhooked the binding on his knife which he had tied to the side of his right leg.

The bearded man with the bat closed his eyes, took a deep breath and issued a prolonged exhalation through his nose.

Everyone ran through their own little routine to make ready.

Cox whistled sharply, but was conscious of how far the sound could carry on a clear, mostly still day like today.

The dead responded.

* * *

Anders continued to survey the streets looking for signs of life; signs of anything, really.

The grunt next to him slept soundlessly, wrapped around his C14 Timberwolf as if it anchored him to the earth itself.

Far off in the distance over the Bay he could see a cloud bank forming, but it wasn't gathering quickly and didn't appear at all menacing.

The pair of ghouls he had spotted earlier was still staggering about down the road and hadn't moved any closer nor further away from the compound, though it appeared a few more had joined them. Anders would turn his eyes to them every so often, just to ensure the congregation wasn't swelling to an unmanageable number while he was occupied surveying other parts of the town.

After a few moments spent fruitlessly scanning some of the other streets, Anders needed a break from the sun's reflecting glare. He turned from the wasteland to face the compound. He fumbled in his coat for a moment, sifting through his pockets for one of the little packets of sugar he had pilfered away from the mess.

Anders always had a bit of a sweet tooth; even if this was just a paltry serving of refined sugar, it would brighten his mood. In the world before the outbreak he could eat a chocolate bar faster than most would be able to unwrap one.

Through an amazing feat of self restraint, Anders patiently allowed the sugar to dissolve on his tongue without swallowing it.

You need to take time for the little things.

The things that make you feel human.

Looking down at the compound, Anders' gaze fell to the blue and green storage shed. It was always guarded. He knew provisions were finite, and Quinn controlled every aspect of the enclave's rations. The scavenging teams hadn't been able to mount a serious effort in over a week due to the weather, and every day supplies were being used at what must have been an alarming rate.

Anders suddenly felt a little guilty for helping himself to the sugar packets.

Still needing to rest his eyes against the snow covered streets, Anders raised the binoculars again to spy the soldiers guarding one of the entrances to the stores. Two soldiers, a male and female, stood taut and at alert.

While he didn't know either of them, he couldn't help but think they looked agitated. Something in their posture, the way they held their weapons; fingers resting on the trigger guards despite being deep in the compound and far from the fences. They were wound up, tight as a spring.

Anders couldn't shake the feeling that something wasn't right, believing this went beyond his usual distaste for military rigidity.

He could feel it in his bones.

* * *

The dead advanced on them, and when they were about halfway to the group's position, the team emerged.

It was hardly elegant.

The burly man, running on instinct and ignoring Cox's order to hang back leapt forward and swung his bat wildly at the lead ghoul, annihilating what was once its skull; it crashed to the snow in a heap. On the uneven terrain, the big swing had thrown him off balance, and he stumbled – the next ghoul in line lunged for him, and it would have had him had one of the other survivors not come in with the butt end of their rifle. The blow didn't take the creature down, but it did knock it back long enough for the rest of the team to enter the fray and the two survivors to find their footing and square to the oncoming threat. The combined weight of their blows finished it off.

Isaac didn't like the melee; it was unpredictable. He preferred deliberate and concerted action, and he hung back a bit to find his moment to properly engage. He tightened his grip on the shotgun and studied the carnage.

Cox made short work of her target. She isolated a ghoul on the fringe of the group, slipped her blade neatly underneath its chin as it clumsily groped the air for her.

The SKS gunners had both cleanly taken down targets with their bayonets before they ever got within reach. With such a clean dispatch, it was obvious to Isaac they were both well seasoned in the wastes.

One of the remaining porters dove in headlong, rushing past Isaac while brandishing a tire iron. He brought it down hard and struck the monster's clavicle, closer to where the neck meets the shoulders. The blow cracked the bone audibly but didn't phase the reanimated corpse in the least. It shambled forward as the porter raised his weapon arm for a second strike, latching on to him at an awkward angle before wrestling him down to one knee. The arm wielding the tire iron frantically struggled to keep the snapping jaws from finding their intended mark.

Isaac subconsciously unsheathed the dagger and dropped the shotgun to the snow, stepped forward calmly and buried his knife to the hilt in the hairline of the ghoul. It went immediately limp and the porter wriggled from underneath its weight. Isaac wrested the blade from the skull and wiped the ichor on the corpse's clothes.

Everyone took stock of the situation. Not their best work, but it did the job.

Isaac was studying the clothes being worn by the corpses when he was shoved hard from behind, knocking his glasses off kilter and almost spilling him into one of the lifeless bodies on the ground.

'You *fucking* coward!'

Isaac wanted to snap, and he wheeled around to face the porter who had shoved him, who was now being restrained by Cox and another gunman. He was carrying a crowbar and evidently had crosschecked him with the metal implement.

If you only knew the shit I have done for that compound.

'Waiting until he was almost down to step in like that, what the fuck is wrong with you?'

Cox settled the porter down. 'You're lucky he had hung back. If he had rushed into the pocket the way your friend did – ignoring my orders, I might add – he wouldn't have been in position to help that simple bastard.'

Cox never wavered; her glare was cold.

'Besides, I didn't see *you* rushing in to his rescue, either,' Cox emphasized her point by jabbing her finger into the man's chest.

The last remark hit home and shut the aggressor down.

'Forget it, let's move on. We have a lot of ground to cover,' one of the SKS gunners offered, voice slightly muffled through his charcoal grey balaclava. Seeking to ease the tension, he wiped his bayonet clean by piercing the snow with it.

All the ghouls were wearing simple clothes; one of the riflemen patted them down and checked their pockets, but there was nothing of use.

Cox took a look around their position. She didn't think they had made too much noise and they had maintained a wide berth away from the ridge overlook.

She was pleased. That could have been much worse.

Isaac didn't bother meeting anyone's gaze. He collected his shotgun, sheathed his knife, and fell into line.

Chapter 5

ANDREW WAS RUNNING OUT OF IDEAS.

Replacing the protective casing on the radio system, he could feel his frustrations welling up inside. He knew a fair amount about computer hardware and electronics, certainly well above average, but was beginning to realize his affinity for gadgets wasn't infinitely transferable.

After tightening the last few screws, he turned the radio to face him and gingerly flicked the switch on.

He was greeted anew by the same droning static he had been listening to for days.

Andrew was growing concerned; he didn't know how Quinn or the others would react to his continued lack of results.

He didn't want to find out.

Andrew had always been a creature of comforts; he loved take out, fast food, and his video games. He barely left his gaming chair but to pay the delivery guys. The radio room was a good gig; it was heated, and he was left alone. He had space here, unlike the dorms.

But if Quinn ever thought he had outlived his usefulness, or that the power being devoted to the radio had become a waste of resources, he would undoubtedly assign him elsewhere in the complex. And few places were as safe and accommodating as the communications module.

Shit, what if he sends me outside?

Andrew's heart rate spiked. He knew he would never make it in the infected wasteland.

Suddenly, it occurred to Andrew – nobody else seemed to know anything about the radio, or about computer hardware.

Why else would he alone have been entrusted with the communications?

A mocking smile crept its way on to Andrew's face.

Therein lay Andrew's opportunity. Quinn was clever, but Andrew knew that Quinn didn't have a head for this kind of thing; this was *his* arena. The other soldiers in the command module all looked like serious combat vets; a couple grease monkeys in the lot, but none that struck Andrew as being particularly tech savvy.

Aside from Quinn, the highest ranking soldier left is a corporal.

All the administrators seem qualified to do is take notes and make shitty coffee; all Andrew needed to do to retain this comfortable posting was to ensure Quinn believed no one else was better suited to the job.

With a renewed sense of purpose, Andrew picked up the receiver and started mindlessly rolling through his script.

It felt good to have an angle.

* * *

Cox had taken point and led the team up the street.

They were moving steadily away from Harbour Station and had plenty of cover to obscure their line of sight.

By her estimations, the most dangerous pass of the journey to St. Joseph's was behind them. As long as they kept quiet, they shouldn't attract attention from whatever may be roaming around the streets below.

At each intersection, Cox would take the team to cover and make sure the streets running perpendicular to them weren't swollen with the dead. The biggest obstructions were cars long since buried in snow and ice; nothing that would slow them down. She did spot a few scattered infected, but they didn't seem to notice their presence. Cox wanted to get the team to their destination as quickly as possible to ensure they still had daylight with them for the return trip.

The second intersection had them hugging against a brownstone building and staring across the street at a fieldstone church. Cox checked the streets again running down towards the Uptown area; looked clear enough. She scanned across the street and noticed the red wooden church door was slightly ajar, likely forced open in the wind and the snow accumulation held it there.

Cox considered her options. If there were infected inside, it was a big structure; no telling how many it could be housing. She didn't think the door was open enough for the dead to force themselves through.

Believing it to be more trouble than it was worth, Cox signaled the troupe to keep moving.

They made quick time to the major intersection where they needed to turn. Cox led the team against the side of a corner building and peered around the edge. Several vehicles were frozen in place, and several ghouls milled about. One corpse lied next to an abandoned grey sedan, half buried in the snow about a dozen feet from the corner where she stood. Across the street there was a grey apartment building with what looked to be a large alcove for off street parking behind it. Several of the corpses seemed to be congregating near the entrance to the alcove, and from her vantage it appeared to have offered significant cover against the wind and snow drifts… it almost looked bare.

She turned to address the gunner who had spoken up earlier. 'Sully, clear that corpse and get a line up the street. I want to know if behind that building is swarming or not.'

Not saying a word, the man slunk around the corner, advancing surprisingly quick for someone on the move while crouching. The corpse noticed his approach as he drew near, but could offer little resistance. It turned, feebly raising its head and the one hand not buried in the snow, rasping out a growl from its desiccated lungs. Sully could tell this one had mostly been consumed before it reanimated; still deadly, but no risk of sudden movement.

He deftly silenced it with his bayonet before settling into position behind the vehicle. He rubbed the passenger side window and checked the car for any unseen occupants. Satisfied it was empty, he went prone and crawled towards the backend of the vehicle.

After peeking across the street, he rolled to his back and held four fingers up to Cox, waiting for her acknowledgement.

Cox nodded. She pointed to three of the riflemen and then to the porters. 'Stay here, cover them. Isaac, you hook up with Sullivan behind that car. Once you're positioned, the rest of us will run across the street. They should see us and start moving on our position. Once they pass you on the street, come out behind them and take a couple down; we'll get the rest.'

Cox slung the C7 over her shoulder and drew her knife; a wicked instrument that looked a bit comical in her small hands.

Isaac nodded his agreement and slipped out to take his position alongside Sully and relayed the instructions. Sully smirked.

'She's a bitch, but no one I'd rather be on a run with.'

Isaac considered the endorsement.

It was true; she was damn effective in the field.

* * *

Anders had been studying the guards outside the storage shed for some time now, trying to glean anything from their behaviour that might give him an indication of why they seemed so disturbed. Whatever it was continued to gnaw at him; he was convinced something was amiss.

The nameless sniper continued to nap, blissfully unaware of the crisis of conscience his spotter was undergoing.

Anders rubbed his knuckles, eyes darting nervously about the complex as he chewed on his lower lip. A flood of possibilities took their turn toying with him; he wasn't able to fully consider any before some new speculation would dominate his thought.

The mutinous pace of his theories enveloped him, and in his compulsion to rid himself of their various implications, he had wholly neglected his post for the better part of an hour.

Anders hadn't noticed the wind had begun to pick up, and the temperature was subtly starting to shift. The cloud bank over the Bay was spreading, stretching its fingers out and consolidating strength.

Nor had he noticed the streets were getting crowded.

* * *

Cox adjusted her ponytail and made sure the elastic held tight. Nodding to those accompanying her, she led the charge across the street.

Sully and Isaac remained still and watched as the four reanimated corpses hissed in guttural alarm and shambled towards Cox. Isaac laid the shotgun on the snow, opting to rely solely on the knife.

Sullivan whispered to Isaac – 'I'll get second from the end, you get the closest to us.'

Isaac turned the knife over in his hands and waited for the ghouls to pass their position behind the car. The dead cried out and their pace quickened; this must have been the closest they'd been to a meal in days.

As the infected were nearing parallel to the driver side wheel, Sully and Isaac emerged from their hiding spot. So intent on their plainly visible quarry from but a moment ago, the ghouls failed to notice the two assailants creeping up from behind.

Sullivan rammed his bayonet with such ferocity through his target that it collapsed a portion of the rear of the skull. The weight of the blow reverberated with a heavy shudder throughout corpse, crumpling it to the snow. At near the same instant, Isaac grabbed the tattered hood of the coat worn by his ghoul as though a leash. Giving it a stiff pull, its posture stiffened as he slammed his blade sideways through its temple.

As their targets slipped off their blades, Cox and her contingent sped around the corner, quickly dispatching the other two.

Isaac retrieved his Remington as Sullivan rifled through the ghouls' pockets; nothing but keys, a wallet and a smartphone with a shattered screen. Knowing that the phone or its components might still have some practical use, he tucked it into his jacket and looked to Cox for direction.

Cox motioned to the rest and they moved quickly up the centre of the street. She was feeling confident; they were making good time. Two blocks in this direction and the hospital would basically be within their line of sight.

Cox once again took point. She had switched back to the C7 now and was scanning their path through her scope. They had good cover for this block and were lined with buildings on either side. As they neared the next intersection, she saw the open expanse of the hilltop parking for Harbour Station. It was fenced in by chain link and the decline led all the way down so that the main entrance of the arena was visible. Standing now at the corner of the building, she couldn't help but look down to the streets below.

The entranceway was burnt; signs of fire damage covered the brick façade, and a significant proportion of the windows had blown out. They were on the side of the building where the section of roof had collapsed, and from this angle it was plain to see fire had ravaged at least that part of the building. Several military transport vehicles and ambulances were abandoned in the streets below – it was almost serene, like the moments immediately after a car crash when everything comes to rest.

But there was movement down there, stirring in the otherwise calm. Raising the scope to her eyes, she confirmed her suspicions.

Dozens of infected were milling about outside the structure. Even taking a brief moment to scan the wreckage, she could estimate at least thirty in plain sight, and that ignored whatever the arena itself would hold.

So fixated on the dead at the base of the hill, she failed to recognize the more immediate threat.

* * *

Lynn was working hard.

Digging deep into her arsenal, she put emphasis on her baser, more physical charms. She even added in the occasional bit of incidental physical contact – selecting the most form fitting clothing available, she'd casually brush her body against the servicemen in the command post, place her hand on their arms during conversation, play with her hair and giggle, bat her once delicate eyes.

Play the innocent type.

The servicewomen couldn't stand her; Lynn knew their female intuition sensed she was working an angle. Probably just thought she wanted to get laid; most likely never would have assumed something more subversive than that.

In fact, they probably believed she wasn't clever enough to orchestrate anything more complicated.

Lynn didn't care.

Fuck them.

She earned her attention, and she relished in it – especially when stealing it from the uniformed women – but it wasn't progressing according to schedule.

* * *

The dead roared with a sound reminiscent of grating stone as they rushed against the fencing.

Cox was startled as she removed her eye from the scope and noticed two infected recklessly throwing themselves against the chain link fence surrounding the parking area. These weren't like the last few they had dealt with; these were much fresher. While their skin subtle signs of abuse from exposure to the elements, their flesh wasn't yet necrotic. Decay had yet to claim their features. Trails of blood, dried and frozen, still clung to their faces.

They had both been men and were both clean shaven.

They couldn't have been dead longer than a day.

They pounded their fists and pressed their faces against the chain link, desperate to rend and tear into fresh meat so tantalizingly close, crying out in unnatural hunger. The fencing rattled and strained beneath their frenzy.

The more recently reanimated were virile, fast; especially if they were largely sheltered from the elements. Not much smarter, but they were nonetheless significantly more dangerous.

'Shut them up!' Cox whispered sharply, and Sullivan and the other SKS gunner crossed the street to put them down. Cox raised the aperture back to her eye and scanned the streets; no sign the creatures at the base of the hill had taken note. She allowed herself a moment to steady her pulse and calm her nerves.

As Sully and his partner drove their bayonets home and silenced the two forever, they strained their ears; there was another sound present, something dull and throbbing.

Several of the cars scattered throughout the parking lot were occupied. The dead contained within, awakened by the fury and the commotion, pressed their blighted faces against the windows and struck the glass with their fists and feet.

In the hush of the late morning air, it was almost rhythmic.

A morbid chorus announcing their presence.

Sullivan considered the scene. These two were recently turned; they were probably here searching through these cars only yesterday and somehow got careless in the process.

As Sully knelt to study the facial features of the corpse he had just terminated, he couldn't restrain a disapproving frown. He felt no pity when dispatching the older, more decomposed dead from the First Wave; but dispatching those they had presumably 'just missed' always struck a chord of guilt in him. He would never hesitate – in any him-or-them scenario, it would be him. But he treated the task differently, almost delicately. His hands were guided by necessity and not malice.

Maybe it was the realization that there were so few people breathing that were left. Maybe it was the fear he would be condemned to the same restless fate.

Best not to dwell on it.

Chapter 6

COX PUSHED THEM ON. SATISFIED THE SEA OF corpses at the base of the hill weren't aware of the stir they were causing above, she motioned everyone to fall in and get to the next intersection.

One of the other riflemen put his hand on her shoulder. 'Shouldn't we clear those cars first? There's a pile of infected.'

Cox glanced over at the dead occupants of the vehicles, pressed awkwardly against the glass and thrashing against their prisons.

'They're not smart enough to work the doors, and we can't spare the time.'

Isaac considered the arguments; both were fair.

But this was Cox's show.

Looking back at the dead faces he wanted to end their suffering and silence their fanaticism.

He fell into line and the procession was on the move once more.

* * *

The meeting had come to an end; a line of officials emerged from the office space, leaving Quinn alone in the room. He sat pensively in his chair, head in his hand, seeming thoroughly bereft under the anemic yellow hum of the lone overhead lamp.

The faces of the column exiting the session ranged from cold stoicism to the lingering heat of vestigial anger.

Lynn wasn't able to make out any of what was said from where she was sequestered with the others, but it was obvious the tone of their discussions had been grim.

That sense of urgency was even more real now, more palpable.

Between the figures leaving the meeting, Lynn could make out Quinn as he sat forward in his chair and lowered his hands to his knees. He stared at the floor a long while and slowly clenched his hands into fists.

The door swung slowly, closing of its own accord as the last official left the office.

* * *

They had made it.

Staring up the final street they could see their prize – St. Joseph's Hospital.

The signs of the former aid station were obvious. Abandoned vehicles and the remnants of temporary facilities in the streets stood empty. The tatters of tarpaulin covers fluttered, meekly whimpering in the faint breeze.

The team fanned out and picked their route, always careful to clear a vehicle for unseen occupants. Many of the vehicles and buildings lining the street bore evidence of stray small arms fire. It was clear the infected had overwhelmed this safe zone from without as well as from within.

There were bodies everywhere, strewn about and buried in the snow and ice to varying depths, but none stirred as the team worked its way to the central site. Most were indistinguishable, long since feasted upon and petrified solid in the frost.

Sully and Isaac walked point with Cox close behind, occasionally stopping to prod the frozen corpses with their boot or the muzzles of their guns.

It was a wasteland; bleak and uninviting, leaving no doubt that the dead had long since claimed this place.

As they neared the final hub, Sullivan tucked in behind a truck and raised a closed fist; the team reflexively knelt. Cox signaled everyone to stay still and shuffled to the head of the column to join Sullivan and Isaac.

Sullivan directed their attention to the north wall outside the main entrance to the hospital. Several conspicuous mounds were at the far end, wreathed by what seemed to be an abnormal amount of ice. A dozen or so feet away there was an overturned ambulance, isolated and derelict.

'Probably cleaned out already, but could be an easy score,' Sully began, motioning to the ambulance.

Isaac sat silent.

Cox surveyed the site. There were several buildings in decent standing with unobstructed lines of sight to the hospital. The front of the building was north facing and in perpetual shade – they'd be able to signal with a flashlight through the windows. The far side of the central hub showed no indication of activity and no additional signs of promise or threat; just the same forsaken tarpaulin structures and ruined vehicles.

Checking her options, she settled on a brick two storey building opposite the entrance to urgent care that looked like it had been home to some commercial space. The ground level windows were small and there was a sign hanging indicating office space for lease.

'Check it out; we'll be setting up shop right here.'

Sully and Isaac crossed the clearing towards the mounds as Cox motioned the rest of the team to the building. The riflemen kept watch over the porters as they set to work on breaching the door with the crowbar. Cox took Sullivan's position behind the truck and raised her rifle, keeping watch over he and Isaac as the rest worked to gain access to the building.

Isaac put his ear against the roof the ambulance and listened for sounds of movement inside; satisfied it was empty he worked around to the cab. Sullivan peered around the flipped vehicle to get a better glimpse of the strange mounds.

It finally dawned on him what he was looking at.

Bits of blackened limbs and burnt clothing jutted out from beneath the snow. The odd prevalence of ice concentrated around the mounds was evidence the pyre continued to smolder for some time after it was lit.

Sullivan's breath was stolen from him.

Rounding the vehicle, Isaac noticed Sullivan's distant expression.

'Come on, let's check the ambulance,' Isaac offered flatly.

The spell was broken and Sully instinctively gripped the handle. The latch required a few heaves before the frost covered joints yielded and the door swung open.

The inside of the ambulance was rancid; blood spatter covered the walls and ceiling. Isaac lit the flashlight and checked the corners of the cabin. No bodies, but most everything had evidence of blood spray on it. The gurney was overturned and the bedding was clearly soiled beyond salvage. A small case of surgeon's implements was upturned and spilled throughout the compartment, glinting in the artificial light between bits of gore and material. The compartment's drawers were strewn about.

Someone had already been through this; whether recently or as the response fled the site was unknowable.

As Sully held the door open, Isaac climbed into the back of the ambulance and sifted through the debris. He managed to come up with a couple sealed packets of gauze and a bottle of prescription pain medication, but the rest was tainted. The cab wasn't in much better shape; the dash and console were each torn to shreds. Isaac popped the glove box and found a small Maglite flashlight and a protein bar, but nothing else of note.

Climbing back out of the ambulance, Isaac stuffed everything into his pockets except the Maglite which he passed to Sullivan. Sully shut the ambulance door quietly, as if in reverence for the tortured spirits within.

Sliding the flashlight into his jacket, Sully turned to rejoin the others working the door on their proposed outpost.

'Hope the hospital's in better shape than that.'

* * *

It was approaching noon, if not shortly past when Anders had caught sight of a line of officials leaving the command module and parting ways without speaking a word to one another. One of the officials immediately went over to the guards on either side of the storage shed, and whatever was said was met with some protest that was quickly silenced.

As the official finished briefing the soldiers, their agitation was even more pronounced. Anders subconsciously lowered the binoculars as the theories ran rampant in his head.

The sleeping sniper had finally started to rouse. Fearful of being chastised again for his wandering mind, Anders quickly turned himself to face the wasteland. Anders didn't want to betray his suspicions to the grunt, and refused to be scolded by someone who had slept away the first few hours of their watch.

It was in that moment that Anders realized exactly how inattentive and preoccupied he had allowed himself to become.

The length of the Bay was now a formidable cloudbank and the sky over the horizon was ever darkening. Now that Anders was propped up and turned to face the city rather than hunched over and surveying the compound, he became aware the temperature had dropped several degrees and the wind was picking up against his exposed skin.

The weather off the coast was beginning to look as unwelcoming as the streets below.

Anders' eyes darted nervously about as the sniper sat up. Conscious to the risk of their betrayal, Anders raised the binoculars in order to conceal his face from the grunt's immediate view.

Anders arbitrarily scanned the streets, hoping the awakening soldier would assume he was in the midst of surveying his usual circuit. As his gaze turned southwards, his eyes locked on where the pair of ghouls had previously stood.

Anders felt as if the blood had been drained from his body.

* * *

With a final thrust, the locking mechanism yielded.

Isaac was first inside and clicked his flashlight on. The door opened unto a thin corridor with several rooms coming off it at irregular intervals; the ground floor had little natural light aside from the slender front windows. The walls were covered in a rich brown wainscoting that ran about a third of the way up to the ceiling, the remainder being wallpapered in a garish navy-blue-on-cream motif.

The floor was yellowed hardwood, recently refinished but still maintaining the vintage look. While it retained a faint trace of polish, it was evident it had been well travelled since. Despite Isaac's deliberate effort to make minimal sound, the boards creaked and groaned in protest of the intrusion.

Isaac stepped slowly, purposefully before advancing, scanning every darkened corner and focusing his sense of hearing for indications of movement. Cox and Sullivan were close behind.

Empty.

The ground floor was barren. Nothing here but some dingy furniture.

Confident the first level was clear, Isaac turned his attention to the stairs at the back of the building. They were covered in red carpeting, not terribly soiled but not entirely clean; they muffled his footsteps during the ascent.

The next floor was more of the same; an odd arrangement of office space, mostly vacant. As Isaac worked towards the front of the building he noticed dark spots and the telltale rings and tendrils of water damage on the ceiling above him. The roof must have been leaking; water was running down the walls and spoiling the wallpaper, which drooped pitifully as it peeled off the plaster. Water had pooled in spots and the hardwood warped along the front of the building. The entire second floor smelled of mould and the musk of fouled adhesive.

The team set up shop. Cox directed the scavenging team to set about shifting furniture into a more defensible arrangement as the gunners took positions at any windows that offered a good vantage over the courtyard. The porters rifled through the desks and bookshelves for anything worth taking.

Sullivan pulled an overturned chair to his post and sat down. Removing his balaclava, he ran gloved fingers through the curl of his ruddy blond hair; he clearly came from Irish lineage. He was blue eyed and a perpetual five o'clock shadow framed his square jaw. He was built like a farmer – stocky and powerful, with a nose that had clearly been broken at least once in some previous misadventure.

Probably a tale of youthful indiscretion, retold with a roaring laugh over a pint.

The crooked nose was probably well earned.

He laid the SKS on his lap and casually folded his arms. The other gunner leaned against the water stained wall near another window overlooking the central hub and pulled a pack of cigarettes and lighter from his jacket. He offered one to Sullivan who waved them off without speaking.

Content the building was secure, the team afforded themselves a moment to regroup and renew their focus on the task at hand.

* * *

Andrew was rattling through his script completely on reflex at this point, hoping the monotony of the repetitive task would allow him to achieve thought on some higher plane.

He had racked his brain all morning for some believable techno-babble he could spout to subvert Quinn. Some jargon he could use to parlay himself into a position of import and solidify his comfortable placement, but had nothing yet to show for his effort but a hoarsening voice and the unabated company of perpetual static.

Andrew wasn't sure why, but he doubted he could trick Quinn. He had never had to lie before, at least not with such exceedingly high stakes. Somehow he was certain no matter how convincing it was Quinn would see right through the deception.

He continued to blankly roll through the script, pausing a few moments after each sentence to see if any of his attempts garnered a response.

Plaintively depressing the button to broadcast, he began again.

'Mayday, mayday, this is Coast Guard site broadcasting to anyone within range. If you can hear my voice, please respond…'

Andrew released his hold and attended to the empty airways.

Greeted by the same dead air.

Weary of the same taunting static, he raised the receiver again. Andrew licked his dried lips and was about to begin.

Before he could launch back into his script, the hush was briefly punctuated.

… … … … … krrrshtzzz … … … …

Andrew's eyes went wide and he nearly dropped the receiver.

What the fuck was that?

'Hel… Hello?'

Chapter 7

IT WAS TIME TO MOVE.

The fire team broke off from the porters and hustled across the courtyard.

The structure looked intact; some of the glass windows were broken or missing altogether and it bore signs of small arms fire all along the brick façade. One couldn't help but notice the bullet holes were concentrated around the entrances – residual evidence of the exact moment the soldiers outside realized the site was compromised and turned to stem the tide of infected pouring from within.

The main entrance was frozen shut behind the drifting snow, and the team would be forced to gain entry through an adjacent window. The windows along the ground floor offered little insight to what was within; minimal natural light pierced the veil of grime and condensation coating them.

Never hesitating, Cox blasted one of the windows out with the butt end of her C7. The glass splintered and spilled inside onto the cold linoleum, a shrill twinkling as it skipped across the floor. The team held their breath waiting for sounds of shuffling feet or the rasp of dead lungs, but there was only silence.

Nothing but the deafening quiet of a mausoleum.

Isaac took one look skyward, savouring the last sensation of sunlight on his skin before clicking his flashlight on and accepting a boost into the building. He dropped down to the floor heavily and heard the crunch of glass beneath his boots. Coming to his feet, he raised the 870 and scanned his surroundings, trying to get his bearings despite the absolute blackness within.

The conical beam of the flashlight scanned rows of empty waiting room seats, and caused strange shadows to dance in the gloom about the perimeter of the emergency room. Despite several missing windows, the air was thick and stale. The temperature dipped sharply at the immediate loss of sunlight.

The room reeked of anguish, and it only compounded the sense of despair.

Turning to scan the entrance, the torchlight revealed a grim canvas. A wide expanse of blackened and long since dried blood emanated from an uncountable tangle of bodies, piled upon one another and heaped at the exit. The mass of flesh, almost singular were it not for the bits of limbs and recognizable scrubs and clothing, sat still. The remnants were old and decrepit, with much of the meatier morsels having been eaten away some time ago. Isaac studied the pile for a moment, allowing his flashlight to lament over the snarl with the hope that if any were still capable of movement it's beam would register somehow with their vestigial senses.

None among the sorrowful mess reacted.

Strangely satisfied with the stillness, Isaac banged the wall beneath the window with his fist to signal the others outside. The team popped in one after another and each took a moment to acclimate to their surroundings. More flashlights came on and pierced the bitter darkness, their beams throwing more shadows against the walls. They fanned out in silence, sifting between rows of waiting room chairs, the weight of each step forcing shards of splintered glass to gnaw into the linoleum.

As if a single organism, the team scoured all the adjacent offices and behind the reception desk, coming up with little beyond further evidence of antecedent carnage. Nothing but picked clean and half consumed corpses, scattered papers and stationery amidst various signs of struggle. Shell casings littered the floor in places but there were no weapons and little else of use.

Isaac and another rifleman whose name he hadn't learned had worked straight back towards the far wall. Isaac had been in St. Joseph's before the world had ended, and knew this to be a moderate sized room subdivided for triage and diagnostics. The rifleman looked back to Cox for permission to proceed as Isaac bent around the corner and illuminated what he could with the flashlight.

Cox had hung back by the window, surveying the movements of the group. As her gaze turned to the rifleman with Isaac she nodded her accord with their entry to the back room. She snapped her fingers a couple times to get the attention of the rest and motioned them to stand their ground before she advanced to take the position of the rifleman. The rest of the fire team took cover around corners and kept watch on the various halls leading away from the emergency room.

Isaac and the rifleman stepped into triage in unison, each taking a side as Cox monitored their movements from the doorway.

The dark in this room was even more pronounced than the main foyer. There were no windows, and the air was heavy with the smell of iron and rust. A long corridor ran perpendicular to the entrance and was subdivided into several rooms. Many of the sheets that separated the individual beds were torn from their tracks along the ceiling, the rest hung limp and pitiful. Blood spray and smeared handprints, still a brilliant red despite their presumed age, stood in stark contrast to the turquoise sheets. IV units and various pieces of medical instrumentation were strewn about and trampled on the once white tile, now sullied in a jumble boot prints and spilled saline. Isaac and the rifleman worked their way down the row and scrutinized each compartment.

The rifleman had some luck; a small trolley was in the third-to-last room. It had a series of polypropylene IV bags and a number of packets of syringes, gauze and several vials of miscellaneous medications; far too much for him to stash in his pockets.

Not a bad start.

He motioned to Cox who relayed the info on to the rest of the team. One of those remaining in the main room signaled out the window for a porter, and the burly man with the bat ambled across the courtyard and set to work emptying the contents of the trolley into his pack.

Satisfied the rifleman and the bat wielding porter could handle their job, Cox bounded up to address Isaac.

'There's got to be a store room down here,' she whispered, and pointed further down the corridor.

Isaac and Cox moved almost back to back as they systematically cleared the individual chambers until they had finally come to the end of the row. Where they expected another bed was a small alcove leading a few feet off the main corridor.

It had a large, official looking doorway at the end.

A wry smile crossed Cox's thin lips, as if she couldn't contain her excitement at how clever she was.

Isaac and Cox advanced to the side of the door frame. The door was clearly heavy and had an electronic key swipe to get in. It was mounted to swing inwards and would have been magnetically sealed, but whereas the power had been out for weeks it would offer little objection. The door had a partial glass window in it; the type with the wire mesh within designed to thwart an attempt to shatter it.

The room was pitch black, an absolute void.

Isaac looked to Cox, and pounded on the door twice.

A moment of silence before a thud came in response; the unmistakable sound of a body throwing itself against the door. A coarse cry of hunger issued from within, a foul and severe drawling.

Cox considered their options. Judging from the size of the door and the placement of the room, it would likely be little more than a closet.

'Okay, on the count of three we shoulder the door together; send this corpse flying,' she began. 'Then you go in and knife it.'

Isaac didn't like it; far too uncertain. But they needed to get in, needed to be quiet, and the door only swung one way. Nodding his accord, he leaned the 870 against the wall and unsheathed his knife.

Pressing their bodies against the door, they could hear the anguished cries from within; a few tantalizing inches were all that separated it from a long awaited meal.

Cox led the count and they both stepped into the door with all the power they could muster. It exploded into the room, crashing into the corpse on the other side and sent it sprawling to the floor. Isaac pushed the door open the remainder of the way and rushed in with knife in hand.

As Isaac stepped into the room he was beset by another ghoul within. Stretching outwards, it clawed at Isaac's arms and torso as he struggled with it. The shambling corpse towered over Isaac; it stood several inches taller and dramatically outweighed him despite its obvious decomposition. Isaac backpedalled at an awkward angle as the ghoul lunged; he tripped against the door frame and tumbled to the floor.

The ghoul had found a grip on one of Isaac's arms, trapping it under its weight as it came down on top of him. Isaac had managed to frame his forearm under its chin as they collapsed together, desperately using it to create distance. As he struck the floor, the air was blasted from his lungs under the sheer girth of the attacker. Its eyes fixated on his, wild with vulgar hunger. He struggled to keep the gnashing teeth from tearing into his unprotected face. Thin wisps of what little hair remained on the assailant's head hung against Isaac's skin as the teeth snapped the air feverishly. The jaw opened absurdly wide between bites, the necrotic flesh stretched taut about it.

In that moment, Isaac's gaze met the dull mirrors of his assailant's eyes; he could recognize nothing but the imminent void in their reflection. There was no memory of humanity therein. He squirmed frantically, bridged his hips and tried to free his trapped arm, but the weight was insurmountable. His lungs couldn't draw breath, and without oxygen his strength would fail.

In horror, Isaac's arm began to buckle and the sinister jaws crept ever closer, spurred on by the primal recognition of its tiring prey.

A sudden jolt and a wet sensation; something viscous and vile spilled onto the side of Isaac's face, thick and foul as spoiled molasses. The creature on top of him went strangely limp as its head lolled to the side, its lusting hunger extinguished. Isaac twisted his body and managed to slip out from under the dead weight. As the door swung closed he saw Cox had laid waste to the other ghoul before it had recovered its footing.

Isaac sat up and wiped the blackened blood and ichor from his face, careful to brush it away from his eyes and mouth, and took a gasping breath. Through his crooked glasses he watched Cox as she brought down the stock of her rifle repeatedly into the pulverized remnants of the corpse's skull a few extra times for good measure.

Scavenging was messy business.

Satisfied at last that her handiwork was finished, Cox turned back to regard Isaac. He seemed calm despite the close call; she reasoned he must have emerged unscathed.

Checking the room around her, it became apparent they had hit pay dirt. Though several shelves were bare, they had found a veritable trove. Maybe not everything on their list, but the storage unit had medications, bedding, and a variety of implements.

And now, no one to object to their taking.

She turned to Isaac.

'Get that porter in here, we hit the jackpot.'

Isaac sheathed his knife, wiped his gory hands onto his pant legs and rose to his feet. His ribs hurt and one of his shoulders was tweaked; he had probably hyper extended something, but he was mobile. He recovered his 870 and stepped back out to the triage area to instruct the burly man.

Cox called after him – 'Get the other runners over here, too.'

* * *

Sullivan stared from his perch at the window where the fire team had gained entry to the hospital. They hadn't been gone long at all and one of the porters was already summoned.

Maybe this was going to be an easy win?

Neither Sullivan nor his counterpart had spoken much, and the remaining two porters stood and shuffled their feet awkwardly as they tried to hold their nerves off. Occasionally they whispered to each other, but Sullivan paid them little mind. Aside from the scuff of someone's boots as they paced nervously, the only consistent sound was the other gunner as he sucked on his cigarettes. The acrid smoke didn't do much to mask the smell of mould in the room, but Sullivan liked it all the same. It reminded him of the days before the outbreak, back in the days when you could settle in somewhere for a pint and light up in the bars.

Despite never having a taste for cigarettes himself, he regarded them with a fond familiarity these days.

They'd been used as currency amongst other survivors – he'd seen them bartered for wares smuggled in by scavengers, the ones who didn't feel like truthfully accounting for all their spoils when returning from a salvage mission. It wasn't just the vices that had a place in the enclave's tiny illicit economy – though alcohol, cigarettes and marijuana were highly prized – but other, less sinful items like toothpaste, books, and various foodstuffs were also easy to trade.

Any of yesterday's comforts.

Sully had always turned over everything he had found to the authorities when he came back. Whatever he found out there, he figured someone else would appreciate it more than he did. Whatever he needed, the universe would provide.

He was a glass half full kinda guy.

Sullivan had a couple of step brothers, quite a bit younger than he after his father's second marriage. They were both away at college when the First Wave hit, halfway across the country on athletic scholarships. Sullivan was sure that, wherever his brothers were, they were alive and looking after their people, just as he was doing.

Sully had always been an athlete himself, but wasn't interested in immediately pursuing a postsecondary education. With an insatiable desire to not be tethered to the small town of his birth, he opted to travel some of the world and focused on amassing life experience.

Good thing he had; no one was traveling for fun anymore. He was thankful he had afforded himself the opportunity.

His eyes caught some movement again. The fire team called for the remaining porters.

Sullivan leaned back in his chair and turned to the runners.

'Looks like it's your turn, fellas.'

* * *

The burly man was filling his pack with everything that looked useful in the storage closet as the other two porters filtered in to the main chamber. Each loaded their packs with everything from bedding to bandages.

Cox left them with two riflemen as they sorted through the storage room and the list the infirmary had provided them. She and Isaac rejoined the rest. Cox wanted to push on deeper; the spoils had been well worth the effort thus far.

'You look like shit,' one of the other gunners said, addressing Isaac as he and Cox stepped back into the lobby.

'I've had worse.'

Cox gave her orders. Two guns would hold the emergency room lobby and their exit. She, Isaac, another gunner and the remaining porter would continue on. Immediately adjacent to the emergency room was a hallway with elevators and a staircase; Cox wanted to see the second floor.

Isaac's shoulder throbbed and he could no longer take a deep breath comfortably; he was sure nothing was broken but knew he was more banged up than he wanted to admit. He took out the prescription painkillers he had taken from the ambulance and popped a couple, then tossed the bottle to the accompanying porter who slipped them into his jacket.

With everyone aware of their assignments, Cox led the four out towards the stairwell. As they lined up outside the staircase entry she flashed her light further down the corridor and paused to listen. Nothing but the same dereliction; some overturned gurneys, windswept paper and shell casings scattered across the floor, bullet holes and blood stains on the walls. In the distance she thought she could hear a faint rumbling, but their goal was upstairs; the corridor was long and dark and full of debris.

She grabbed the door handle and gently opened it. The beam from Isaac's flashlight lit an empty staircase. He peered inside, checked the corners and started in. The team followed suit, each slipping by in single file. Cox was last to enter, and she latched the door behind them.

An oppressive darkness crowded around them, keenly aware of their trespass. The encroaching black was punctuated only by the thin beams of their flashlights as they wove up the stairs.

In the tight confines of the stairwell, every footfall was amplified. Comically loud, the sound resonated off the walls and climbed the stairs ahead of them.

Isaac couldn't help but feel they were making entirely too much noise.

Chapter 8

ANDERS LOWERED THE APERTURE FROM HIS eyes.

What have I done?

The streets were now milling with the dead; he estimated almost three dozen shambling about. While they were yet a fair distance and he knew they'd be able to thin the crowd substantially before the ghouls ever made it to the walls, he cursed his childlike obsession with the imagined intrigue below.

He was being counted on. The spotter's role was critical.

He had to take initiative or be thought completely daft.

Anders slapped the shoulder of his sniper who woke with a start. Anders motioned to the streets below. The soldier sat up and peered through his scope.

'Holy fuck, you didn't think to mention that?'

'They gathered faster than you'd think.'

'Fuck you they did,' the sniper replied, dripping with cynicism. He cycled his sights through the hostiles.

Anders raised his binoculars again.

'They don't notice us; they're not coming closer.'

'I bet they aren't getting further away, either.'

Anders felt defeated. Had the soldier been looking directly at him, his attempt at deception would have been plainly painted across his face.

The storm continued to mass over the Bay. Judging from the dimensions of the cloud bank, it hadn't lost any severity; the horizon was darkening and its corruption was spreading towards landfall.

Guilt swelled inside Anders, and he could feel a cold sweat bead on his forehead.

'What do we do?' Anders offered sheepishly.

The sniper lowered his rifle and turned to scowl at Anders.

'Alert the guard,' he spat. 'And tell Quinn you're a fucking moron.'

Anders wanted to protest the insult – *that self righteous prick had slept his last two shifts in the nest* – but ultimately thought better of it.

No sense in alienating him.

They might need each other soon.

* * *

They had come to the second landing.

The door to the second floor was solid metal; no window offered the troupe a glimpse at what this level would hold.

Isaac was still sore; the pills hadn't had a chance to kick in yet. It hurt to shoulder the Remington and he didn't want to deal with the recoil, but he knew the discomfort would be a small price to pay.

In any event, he knew none of his present company would give a shit about his complaint anyway.

The team held their breath outside the door, taking turns to press up against it. There wasn't a sound to be heard, but the unmistakable sickly scent of decay was ever present.

Thick in the air, it was palpable.

Intoxicating.

Cox pushed against the door and it swung open, Isaac and the other gunner immediately stepped into the corridor with weapons raised.

Their torchlight splayed across the chaos.

Wires and tubing hung limp and lethargic from the ceiling panels, plastic coverings for the lights and shattered fluorescents covered the floors. Bloody boot prints smeared the tile. Gurneys and desks were overturned in the hall. Several partially consumed bodies lay strewn about, some in uniform, some in scrubs.

The life within was long since spent.

Cox and the porter surveyed the scene and began canvassing the uniformed dead for salvage; Isaac and the other gunner scanned the hallways leading away from this clearing.

The rifleman snapped his fingers and the rest wheeled to face him. The beam of his flashlight was fixated at the foot of a nondescript door where three ghouls lied. He held them in his beam and nothing stirred in the glare; the rest moved up to the doorway. Cox gave them a nudge with her boot, but none of the corpses offered a response.

It was obvious they wanted in there; less obvious what happened to them.

Cox turned her attention down the corridor. All the doors looked the same. Several had furniture or hospital beds placed in front of them.

An ominous feeling they had overstayed their welcome swelled inside her.

'Alright, this room and we're out.'

Isaac and the others were surprised by her apparent change of heart, but no one offered an argument. The hospital was big – four scavengers plumbing its depths alone seemed foolhardy.

Cox shifted the door slightly, and needed the other rifleman's help to shoulder it open. Someone inside had slid a small desk up against the doorway as a barricade. This signaled immediate danger to the seasoned veterans – whatever had walled themselves in hadn't managed to wander back out.

Isaac used the widening crack in the door to shine his flashlight in. Surely the shifting desk would have stirred anything inside; as soon as Isaac had the space to fit his frame, he squeezed through.

It was a small room with a single bed. The windows were textured glass and muddled the only bit of sunlight that pierced the dreariness. The dividing curtain was drawn around the patient's bed, but otherwise the room was unremarkable.

Isaac advanced slowly, blood thundering in his ears. An overwhelming sense of malaise called to him from behind the curtain. Isaac ducked down and raised the covering with the muzzle of his shotgun. It revealed a corpse, tucked in to the bed neatly and with fresh linens. The face was covered with a white cloth, but long hair was evident beneath the covering and upon the pillow. She had been treated with a great deal of care and reverence – whoever had arranged this had cared deeply for her.

A better fate than most.

Isaac circled around the foot of the bed with the muzzle raised. The remains of a uniformed man were slumped awkwardly on the floor, an obvious exit wound through the side of his head; the walls were splattered with the self-inflicted trauma. Lying at his feet were a pair of sheets, each as neatly arranged as the woman in bed, separated by a white and blue vase that held a withered floral arrangement. The linoleum between them was littered with wilted petals shed from the crumbling stalk of whatever breed of flower it once held. The sheets were bloodstained from where he assumed the heads would have been oriented, only these two were small… much too small to have been adults.

Isaac's shoulders dropped and the Remington lowered as he realized what he was looking at.

The other rifleman was shimmying through the door when Isaac waved him off. Isaac bent down and collected the .38 revolver from beside the slumped man's boot. As Isaac turned over the dead man's pockets, he met its sorrowful gaze. Tearstains left tracks on the grime covering his face, visible now even in the decomposed state. The man would have been handsome in his day; fair haired and well groomed.

Isaac sat back on his heels, stood the shotgun up on the stock and leaned the barrel against his shoulder.

Poor bastard.

He continued to study the man's features, such as they were now. In the dim and woeful light he couldn't help but pity him.

Isaac felt a strange kinship with this man.

He did what needed to be done; made the only choice there was to make.

Isaac had failed to realize how engrossed he had become with the soldier; several moments had passed with him vacantly staring at the dead man. Isaac had seen a great deal of death since the world ended, and had done more than his share of killing. But something in this corpse resonated within him. Ordinarily he would step over the dead without a second thought, but this one was different.

He wanted this one to find the same peaceful rest as his family.

Using the shotgun as a prop to help him rise, Isaac stood and took stock of the room. A small closet was next to the lavatory; inside there were a number of towels, but no linens. Isaac took the largest towel he could find and he started back towards the dead soldier. Before he made it, Isaac stopped in his tracks.

Something had caught his ear; muffled, but unmistakable.

An alarm.

* * *

Sullivan and the other gunner froze in place.

A wisp of smoke curled from the cigarette in the gunner's mouth, twisted obscenely from the sudden interruption in his draw.

'What the fuck is that?' Sullivan cursed as he came to his feet.

The sound was coming a few blocks away, back the way they came.

And it was blaring.

'Jesus Christ, is that a car alarm?'

The two stared incredulously at each other. Neither had heard a car horn in weeks.

Now was not the time to appreciate the nostalgia.

'We need to go,' the other gunner spat as he abruptly threw the cigarette down. The cherry flared as it struck the stained boards and sent bits of embers dancing along the floor.

Sullivan nodded his agreement and the two grabbed their gear before rushing back down the stairs to the main level. Their heavy boots and hurried strides thudded on the hardwood and reverberated throughout the abandoned building; they cared little for the racket they made.

Speed was of the essence now.

The alarm continued to wail down the street.

They came to the entrance they had breached and Sullivan peered out the doorway. He couldn't see any movement in the streets, and he couldn't see anyone from the salvage team.

'Stay here and keep a close eye,' Sully ordered his companion. 'I've got the streets the way we came; I need you to keep your sights trained on the opposite side of the complex. If there is anything over there, it'll be heading this way.'

The young gunner nodded solemnly and fell into a prone position, fixated on the far corner of the building.

He looked composed; Sullivan felt the confidence in his colleague surge.

Sullivan sprinted from the entranceway and skidded down behind the ruined truck in the courtyard. He shouldered the SKS and scanned the streets from where they came.

The sound was a block or more away, but it would draw a crowd.

They couldn't stay here.

* * *

Anders had turned to signal the other nests. Ever since Quinn had confiscated the two-way radios, the teams relied on basic hand signals to communicate with each other over distances.

He felt foolish as he admitted the approximate count; the repetition forced him to articulate his ineptitude.

Over the next several minutes as the information was circulated below, the complex transformed into a beehive of activity. Soldiers took position and lined up along the wall, their regular patrol routes abandoned to shore up the southern fencing.

Only the constructed shooting platform had a line of sight that would accommodate firing in this direction, albeit from an extra thirty yards. The nest on top of the command module wouldn't be able to get a bead around the living quarters.

Soldiers were in short supply, even moreso skilled shooters at range. The sniper that was in the command nest came up to join Anders and the grunt; if they needed to thin the crowd he rationalized they'd be better off with two from this vantage point. He brought with him a mostly full box of .338 Lapua Magnum. Taking a position next to the other grunt, he spoke –

'How did you manage to let that many bunch up on our doorstep?'

The grunt Anders was vaguely familiar with briefly took his eye from his scope to address the other soldier. He twitched his head and quickly shot a piercing glare back at Anders.

'*That* fucking tool.'

Anders again wanted to protest the accusation on the grounds that the grunt was asleep, but kept his mouth shut.

It wasn't a particularly compelling argument.

The new sniper rolled his eyes in contempt and shifted in his seat as he searched for a comfortable firing position.

'Who's covering the middle approach?' Anders asked, trying to regain some modicum of respect.

Neither soldier turned to look at Anders.

'We need to deal with the problems we know about, first,' the new sniper stated flatly. 'Besides, we have a decent line on the main drag from here, in the event we need to redeploy.'

Anders didn't like dividing resources like this; he was deeply unsettled with the knowledge the command nest wasn't properly manned.

And it was his fault.

Of course, he realized not only that it wasn't his call – but also that nobody present cared about his opinion anyway.

The two snipers practiced cycling through the crowd of infected, grimly rehearsing their pecking order.

Anders stammered to find something meaningful to say, but only stumbled over himself.

He sagged down into his seat and almost lost the will to breathe. He felt it best to sit in downtrodden silence, lest he screw up again and further compound his miseries.

Anders sulked in this new isolation, a biting loneliness gnawed at his innards as his memory turned to home and his people there. It didn't matter if across the Atlantic was faring any better; he'd likely never see the familiar shores of Finland again. He'd never see his parents, his sister, or his friends… assuming any of them were still alive.

He wanted to slink off and crawl into a hole.

Anders rolled his head back on his shoulders and he stared into the sky. Closing his eyes for a moment, he allowed himself a brief fantasy that none of this had come to pass. The breeze was brisk and it had stirred the surf; the sound of the waves as they thirstily lapped against the pier transported him back to the cold harbours of Kotka, his hometown.

The illusion was almost complete when his eyes shot open.

He sat up immediately and noted his present company heard it, too.

A siren of some kind; car horns.

The two soldiers exchanged a somber look. The sound was coming from somewhere off behind them, it bounced between the buildings and through the inescapable wastes.

Anders leapt from his seat and instinctively raised the binoculars, trained them southwards at the congregation of the dead.

Shit...

They heard it, too.

Chapter 9

COX KICKED EVERYONE INTO GEAR.

'Let's go, we're out of here.'

Recognizing he didn't have time for the dignity he meant to afford the soldier, Isaac bounded over to the dead man and threw the towel over his shattered form.

Cox led them back down the staircase and they slammed through the doors. The rest of the team had regrouped in the foyer and anxiously awaited Cox's return. In the relative silence of the lobby, the sound of the wailing car alarm was more pronounced as it filtered through the bullet holes and missing windows that peppered the hospital's ground floor.

But there were other sounds announcing their presence amongst the darkened hallways.

The hammering of fists and limbs as they pounded at distant doors and barricades.

The hoarse rasping of dried lungs as they stirred from an unnatural slumber.

The shambling march of an army of teeth.

The narrow beams of tactical flashlights punctuated their nervousness as they darted about the adjacent corridors, their rays hungering for the silhouettes of movement.

Cox and her small group came into the centre of the foyer as two riflemen maintained overwatch at the hallway. They madly scanned the corridors.

'We got what we came for, we're leaving,' Cox offered and motioned to the window where they came in, 'Porters first.'

The porters threw their packs out the window and the burly one climbed out first, then helped the other two. The fire team was lining up for extraction when one of the guards at the entry opened fire.

The report was deafening inside the structure.

The second rifleman wheeled to face the direction of his colleague and he snapped off a round into the approaching storm.

Both had bolt action rifles; they cycled the actions one more time before firing again into the advancing fray.

Cox called out, 'Fuck them; let's go!'

Isaac was next out the window and passed the Remington through the opening. The burly man and another runner grabbed his arms and heaved him up. The strain on his shoulder was intense, but worse still were his ribs being drawn over the window frame. Isaac swooned and his vision darkened as he crashed unceremoniously to the snow. He started to scramble to his hands and knees when he was grabbed by the collar and hauled to his feet.

Isaac had found his senses again; he realized how much he had missed the feel of sunshine.

The gunner stationed opposite the central hub opened fire with his semi auto, but none of the fire team could tell the direction or the intent of the shots.

They definitely recognized the thunder of the SKS, though.

Still inside the foyer, Cox crouched down and brought the scope to her eye.

As the two riflemen fell back from the hallway entrance toward the window's lifeline, she squeezed a few rounds into the advancing ghouls. She was utterly disheartened to find her aim was off – the rounds didn't fall anywhere near her intended mark.

The earlier melee must have dislodged the scope.

She cursed under her breath and hurried the others on.

The jumble of dead advanced steadily, but hadn't yet made it to the foyer entrance.

Cox slung the C7 over her shoulder and bolted for the window, easily reaching it ahead of the other two.

The burly man caught her outstretched hand and effortlessly hauled her slender frame through the window, his natural strength exponentially supplemented by the fires of adrenaline.

Sullivan glanced over his shoulder and saw most of the team was out of the hospital now. As badly as he wanted to rush over and rejoin the group, he kept his post and surveyed the streets on his end. He knew his colleague had rattled off a few rounds and suspected the troupe would need to head his way for the run home; he would do his duty.

That damned wailing continued.

Cox found her footing and turned to help the next rifleman out of the window. She couldn't see the swarming dead inside but guessed they had to be close now. She reached in and found his frantic hands.

As they hoisted him out, the panicked expression on the man's face said it all. His feet kicked fervently as he tried to propel himself to the salvation of the open air.

The burly man brusquely threw this one aside and started back to reach for their last mate when the screams poured from within. He bent to glance through the window to the foyer but only witnessed a sea of hands and faces, a great clutching wave of hungry corpses as it broke against the hospital walls and smothered the unfortunate man trapped inside.

Even if it weren't for the horrible screams, there was no doubt he was lost. The burly porter stepped back from the window and swallowed involuntarily.

More shots rang out from across the courtyard.

Things were getting dodgy.

'Get your shit; we need to go, now!'

The porters collected their gear and everyone fell in. Cox spotted Sullivan by the truck, positioned to face their original approach and guessed the other gunner fired at the opposite side of the building. They collapsed back to Sully and shouted for the other gunman to converge on their position.

The alarm continued to scream down the road.

The SKS gunner was the last to hook up with the unit. He crashed over to the group.

'We just made a pile of friends,' he blurted sarcastically as he fiddled with a fresh clip. 'There's more coming from that side.'

Cox had a general sense the alarm blared from near the top of the hill where they had stopped and scanned the streets below around Harbour Station. By this time, no doubt the majority of the infected she counted about the entrance had crested that hill.

'What set that off?' one of the porters asked.

'We must have riled them up pretty bad, maybe one broke a window from inside the car it was trapped in?' another suggested.

'Doesn't fucking matter,' Isaac retorted. He stared at the ground. His ribs ached.

Cox agreed. Maybe it would have been prudent to clear some of the cars, but retrospect was worthless.

They couldn't go back the way they came, and they couldn't go around the hospital.

They'd need to find an alternate route.

Sullivan chimed in. 'Look, we gotta go – I don't care where, but we can't sit here. These streets are going to be swarming with corpses soon.'

A pair of ghouls wandered into view from the other side of the parking lot, irrevocably drawn towards that blasted horn. The SKS gunner rose and shouldered his rifle when Cox grabbed his pant leg.

'Save the rounds,' she commanded.

'We're going to need them.'

* * *

As if they responded to a single consciousness, the ghouls staggered forward in blind pursuit of that damned alarm.

Somewhere in the distance, Anders thought he could hear traces of sporadic gunfire.

'Look alive,' jeered the original grunt, who managed a grin at his clever wordplay. 'We're about to be busy.'

Anders didn't even have a weapon; his impotence astounded him.

Both the snipers focused through their apertures and chattered about their preferred targets as the wall of dead approached the compound. They settled on their plan of engagement and set a landmark to begin firing.

Anders raised his binoculars.

The storm over the Bay was closing fast, stretching to envelop the southern tip of the peninsula.

The earnest horde wallowed forth in its thoughtless hunger.

'Here we go…'

As the dead reached the appointed place along the street, the Timberwolves cracked to life. The .338 Lapua Mag were devastating rounds – a hit most anywhere on the withered corpses would fragment their ruined bodies and cause them to burst. The report roared from the muzzles and echoed through the wasteland; Anders covered his ears for the discomfort.

The snipers set about their work with grim precision. The C14's were bolt action, but neither shooter needed more than one round per target. Neither fired with unnecessary haste, and each only fired when wholly satisfied with their bead. The dead were mindless and moved in an almost straight line – there was no need to rush their shots.

Anders had to admit, despite the predisposition to sleeping on the job, his nameless partner was operating with near mechanical efficiency.

The crowd of advancing dead was thinning fast, the snow covered road stained with their blight as they were cut down in their tracks.

Both snipers dropped their spent mags, clicked new ones in and cycled their actions.

Capitalizing on a chance to redeem himself, Anders collected the two discarded magazines. He tipped the box of .338 into his hands and loaded the clips again, ready to swap them out for spent ones.

Anders counted their bullets. Based on his initial estimate of the ghouls congregated in the street, Anders figured they'd have just about the perfect amount to wrap up; maybe even a couple rounds to spare.

The rifles continued their deafening anthem.

* * *

Andrew could hear the shots split the air outside the command centre.

He had been working on the radio at a furious pace in a vain attempt to raise whatever had interrupted the static before. His frustrations mounted. He fiddled with the knobs in the futile hope of improving the signal clarity. His voice cracked as he forsook the script altogether and freewheeled whatever pleas for assistance came to mind.

Nothing but the droning, inescapable static.

He wanted to smash the radio for its taunt, scream into the receiver.

The shots outside continued to echo throughout the complex.

Desperate, Andrew called for Quinn, all thoughts of subversion abandoned.

Quinn burst into the room.

'I… I just heard something, someone maybe,' Andrew bleated. 'Something interrupted the static.'

Quinn's eyes widened and he rushed over to stand near Andrew's chair.

'What did it say?'

'Nothing, really…' Andrew stuttered, who now felt very foolish at his hysteria. 'Something clicked, like someone was trying to respond to my signal. Or someone picked us up. Squelch, maybe?'

It wasn't much to go off of, but it was the most success they had enjoyed yet from the radio.

Several more shots pounded outside; fear was written all over Andrew's face. Quinn could see Andrew struggled for something else to say.

Quinn didn't have time to coddle the boy.

'Get them back,' he reiterated, turning back for the door. 'That's an order.'

* * *

Cox and her team sprinted down the only other street open to them, away from the hospital and on the other side of the Y intersection they had taken to the ruined courtyard. Buildings lined the street on either side and offered some cover as they ran.

'That fucking alarm has got to shut off at some point,' one of the porters wheezed as he struggled to keep up.

They meant to break left at the first intersection, dart away from the cacophony of the blaring horn, and then cut down through some of the mixed residential streets until they were more or less due east of the Coast Guard site. From there, they'd come out along the main drag and be within sight of the shooting platform.

Further down the street the group could see silhouettes of the shambling dead, thankfully oblivious to their presence as they sought only to converge on the source of the alarm. Cox motioned them all to hug up against the corner of a large, beige brick building behind her, where she leaned out and inspected their proposed route.

In their quest for the blaring horn, several of the reanimated creatures were climbing the hill towards their present position.

They would need to fight their way through.

'There's nothing for it; we've got to go now. We can't wait. Don't fire your guns unless you absolutely have to, at least until we get to the bottom of this street. We want that alarm to be the only sound now, hope it keeps drawing them away from us.'

Everyone steeled themselves, prepared for the melee.

Cox crouched down and tapped Isaac and Sullivan on the shoulder.

Without hesitation, the two slipped around the corner, followed after a few short strides by the rest.

The dead roared.

A large, bulging ghoul was first in line. Its heavyset frame was scarcely contained inside a weathered, thoroughly grease stained brown winter coat. The few wisps of its black hair yet remaining were matted and patchy. Wide eyes bulging, its fat grey fingers floundered in the air as it stretched out for its intended prey, its scowling face twisted in pain.

Sullivan was the faster runner of the two, and slowed his pace to match that of Isaac's. As the fat corpse lunged forward, Sullivan kicked at its knee. The dried bone buckled at the joint and the thing collapsed to the ground. Isaac seized the moment and buried his knife into the side of its skull. As the massive body shuddered into stillness, it crumpled backward and pulled Isaac along with it.

Sully saw Isaac fall to the snow, but was confident he had dispatched the corpse first. He squared himself to the street and the oncoming attack as the rest of the team poured out from behind the corner to join him.

The chaos was absolute.

There was no semblance of formation now, no discipline in their ranks. They struck wildly.

Sullivan saw no option but to pick a target and take it down.

Isaac finally wrenched his blade free of the skull it was trapped in. As he went to stand his ribs pulsed with fresh pain. The melee wasn't a good place for him, now less than ever. He managed to get to his feet and stumbled a few paces towards the team to see they were now besieged on all sides.

Clutching his ribs, he staggered on.

The burly porter was berserk. He swung with all his might and stepped in to each flailing arc of his bat. He didn't notice his brutish style was pulling him farther away from the body of the group and he became beset on multiple sides by the ghouls.

Isaac watched helplessly as a decayed hand found a hold on one of his straps and used the pack to haul him down. He continued to thrash with his bat as the corpse tore into him. A second ghoul dove into him headlong and he was buried under their combined weight.

The screams were terrible.

Another rifleman was tackled from behind by what looked to be a janitor as he drove the butt of his weapon into the head of a teenage girl. The blow knocked the girl back, but it didn't finish her; she joined in the feast as well.

The battle was going poorly.

Caution be damned; Cox drew her sidearm and started firing rounds indiscriminately. Seeing her lead, Isaac drew his Norinco as well, trusting it infinitely more than his current capacity in close quarters.

The horn continued to blare in the background.

Sullivan had just finished off his second target when he heard the shots behind him. Turning to the shooters, he realized just how badly things had gone.

Cox had exhausted her clip and let it fall to the snow. She slammed another one in.

More dead spilled into the streets from the buildings around them. They crashed through windows, splintered doors and emerged from unseen corners.

It didn't matter, they were fucking *everywhere*.

Sullivan hustled to the downed porter, but was blocked by his former partner.

'He's got the bag!' Sullivan protested, intent on pushing through and recovering the purpose for their sacrifice.

'Doesn't matter, it's lost,' the gunner retaliated as he attempted to restrain Sully.

Another hand reached over Sullivan's shoulder and pulled him back.

'We will be too if we don't get away from here,' Cox professed.

Sullivan knew it to be true. The screams and thrashes of their comrades were subsiding. Were it not for the grim feasting, they'd have been overwhelmed.

They had carved a break in the middle of the street, calm as the eye of a hurricane.

Many of the corpses filing in to the street growled in hatred for those yet living, but most seemed content to stoop for the easy meals rather than pursue the survivors.

There was still plenty of road ahead.

Chapter 10

ANDERS MARVELED AT THE EFFICIENCY OF THE two snipers.

Only a handful of the dead remained now, and they were nowhere near their walls. While the team had been patient in picking their targets, they were active in taking them down. The few scant ghouls remaining were still a solid hundred yards out.

The Timberwolves continued to hammer their report as the dead pressed on.

Anders fumbled about the nest as he collected the spent casings, zapped his fingers a couple times by picking up the searing hot brass. He sat back and fiddled with the box of .338 as he returned a handful of the empty shells to their placeholders. Anders had read somewhere that casings from most calibers could be successfully reloaded and recycled; he wanted to ensure those powerful C14's had every opportunity to stay in service.

One of the snipers dropped out his clip and turned to Anders, whom he expected to extend him a fresh magazine.

Anders looked at the soldier and realized maybe he had miscounted after all. He checked the box and the floor of the nest for any unspent rounds that may have escaped his notice.

The soldier turned to his colleague who never took his eye from his aperture.

'No matter,' he breathed before he squeezed another round off. 'There are only four of them left, and I've got two more in the mag.'

The sniper cycled the action smoothly and chambered another round. The jettisoned casing clinked playfully as it collided with another spent cartridge.

'Someone at the wall can finish the last of them off,' he mused, clearly more satisfied with himself than he ought to be.

Anders smiled wide as he slumped back down against the wall and returned his gaze skyward. He breathed his silent thanks to whatever god had watched over their little commune.

Though it felt an instant, Anders knew they had been firing for several minutes. He shifted his weight as the sniper took another carefully placed shot, and elongated his back into a luxurious stretch. Now that the action had passed, Anders took stock of himself. His ears rang terribly and the fresh air was replaced by the pungency of spent gunpowder. The tips of his fingers stung from the heated brass; he realized he'd likely be without his fingerprints for a few days.

He cracked another smile as the soldier cycled the action to chamber his final round. He could have covered his ears for this one, but he didn't care. He welcomed the deafening report, the solemn affirmation of their deliverance, and at least another day of their communal survival.

'It almost isn't even fair…,' chuckled the sniper as he scanned through the few available remaining targets.

He seemed intent on identifying the perfect final kill; this shot wouldn't be for just any ghoul.

The other soldier grinned as he removed his rifle from the ledge and stood it up on the butt end. He gave it a once over and brushed some of the snow clinging to the stock with a single finger.

Anders started to sit up, meaning to profess his sincere admiration for their efforts. He even meant to chance a pat on the back to his new mates – after the final shot was expended – but he was stopped short.

It was so unexpected, it almost didn't register.

A shot echoed from somewhere below them.

In complete confusion, Anders froze in place. The two soldiers stiffened slightly, almost imperceptibly, as each cocked their ears and strained them towards the sound. None of the nest mates had anticipated a shot aside from their own.

'What the hell … ?'

The rifle slowly lowered from the ledge as the soldiers exchanged dazed glances.

Another shot from below.

A flurry of recognition set the lot of them to motion. The shots were originating from the shooting platform at the other corner of the compound.

Anders started to rise and orient himself towards the sound, but instead crumpled awkwardly as he was shoved down by one of the soldiers as they scrambled to overlook the compound. Off balance, Anders scarcely caught himself before he fell flat on his face in a tangle of slush and spent casings.

Two more shots, this time in rapid succession.

Muddled cries of alarm.

It was unquestionable now – the shooting platform had a bead on something. The three could only make out indistinct shouts from below, though even at this distance their panicked pitch was plainly evident. Men and women scurried like ants over the snow and slush below as they splintered in every direction like smashed glass.

'Jesus Christ… what now?' bleated the first soldier.

Another shot rang out.

'What the fuck are they shooting at?' the other replied.

Though they couldn't see what threat the platform responded to, based on the muzzle smoke from the last round, it became apparent the platform was firing elsewhere. As Anders was righting himself the sniper brusquely yanked the binoculars from him.

'Talk to me…,' the sniper breathed between clenched teeth.

'Damn it, I can't see shit past that corner,' the soldier spat as he lowered the binoculars and surveyed the scene beneath them. Several survivors spilled from the central structure and ran for the fences. The typical guard frantically redeployed themselves and headed to shore up the wall.

'How many rounds do you have?' the sniper stammered.

'I'm spent.'

It occurred to the sniper then that the central nest was unmanned.

'Fuck me…'

The sniper picked up his C14 and shifted his sights towards the same firing line as the shooting platform.

Not that it mattered much; he had but a single bullet remaining.

'Are we sure we're spent up here?'

It took Anders a moment to realize this was basically his department. He swam his hands through the slush and the brass casings. When he came up empty, he tore open the box of .338 and spilled its contents.

The empty metal cylinders clinked cheerfully as they mocked his every effort, laughing above the wet smear of the grimy snow.

Two more shots pounded from below.

As the realization dawned on him, Anders slumped back on his haunches.

It was a wasted exercise.

He knew they were spent.

'Give me some good news, man ...,' the sniper pleaded.

Utterly bereft, Anders collapsed on his heels.

'We're out.'

* * *

Quinn was busy directing traffic when one of his civilian guardsmen threw open the door to the command module. Quinn had sensed something wasn't right – the shots were coming faster than he expected, and their hurried pace set his teeth on edge. He knew his men were generally disciplined, especially those in the nests; their shots should come slow and deliberate. They each knew how scarce ammunition had become – every round was important.

Something outside was testing their nerve.

Instinctively, he produced his favourite sidearm from a desk drawer and had already mindlessly loaded a spare clip when the door almost came off its hinges.

The guardsman gasped for breath.

'... the fucking wall!'

With the door open to the elements, the report of the rifles was all the louder. Quinn knew immediately the direction of fire had changed – these weren't rounds being snapped from atop the civilian quarters.

That meant a new front had opened up.

Quinn turned to his troops. The module normally had a dozen or so military personnel and a variable civilian presence; he had a full complement.

'Get runners to the armory, the barracks and the civvy quarters,' Quinn stared fiercely at the guardsman as he considered what pieces he had available, though he had no interest in speaking with the man. 'Get me a firing option from the central nest; I want two damned useful shooters up there *now* and I need close combat ready to deploy. If the wall is going to be tested, I need options.'

The runners broke for their assignments and rushed past the stunned civilian guardsman, who stared blankly from the doorway.

Quinn drew a solemn breath and scanned the room.

'I want two with me and two to the infirmary,' he began. 'Everyone else, lock this place down. Get everyone settled in until I know what we're dealing with.'

Quinn paused for emphasis, though it was unnecessary.

The unshakable stillness in his voice only emphasized his authority.

Two soldiers fell in to flank Quinn on either side.

Quinn checked his mag and chambered a round.

Quinn turned to one of the remaining soldiers. The words were calm, but his tone was ice cold.

Motioning to the radio room, he added, 'That kid with the radio doesn't stop broadcasting or there *will* be hell to pay.'

* * *

Lynn watched nervously as Quinn gave his orders. She couldn't make out everything he was saying but she was confident she could guess the meaning. The panic of the guardsman had clearly signified something wasn't right. Even though she was no soldier herself, she could tell the gunfire's direction had shifted.

Lynn's eyes began to tremble uncomfortably, scanning the room without finding focus on anything at all, half taking in the scene as it unfolded and half searching through her subconscious. The soldiers present were gathered around Quinn while several of the administrators shifted about; they busied themselves to deflect the tension.

What am I going to do?

For all her physical persuasions, she hadn't managed to land a protector.

And this might be it.

She began to feel utter loneliness set in.

She had felt this before, before the end of the world.

Lynn had always hidden from her insecurities through physical pleasures. She was attractive, and men wanted her; it didn't matter if it was superficial.

In many cases, it was preferable. She was a superficial creature, feigning depth as a means of getting what she wanted.

In truth, she was empty, and she felt the sting of it now.

Two of the uniformed men moved beside Quinn as he checked his pistol. Whatever was happening outside, he clearly meant to meet it head on.

Lynn felt the hopelessness dam up her throat. Her tongue felt like sand in her mouth.

If there was one person in this god forsaken place that made her feel safe, it was Quinn.

With or without a handsome soldier as a bodyguard, if he was killed today – they'd all be lost.

Lynn shut her eyes as tightly as she could and prayed they'd last another day.

Chapter 11

HE STOOD MOTIONLESS FOR SEVERAL MINUTES and considered his surroundings.

Shoulder pressed against the partially burnt out wall, he peered through a smoke and grime stained window and scanned the streets beneath him.

He struggled to hear, but was now convinced that somewhere downwind he could make out the report of gunfire. The wind was working against him, and the jutted, burnt out buildings muddled the echoes, but he was confident of it now.

He hung his hatchet in one of the loops on the hip support of his pack.

There was some urgency to move quickly; he had made out the signs of a storm closing over their position in the southern peninsula earlier in the day. They had made it this far by scavenging daily for food, water and supply through the neighbouring ruined buildings, but with a storm rolling in and the confirmation of commotion in the distance, he didn't want to be caught away from his charge for any length of time.

Certainly not for the night.

He was being forced ever further out from their shelter; each day he would cover a greater distance to keep their little band functional. That meant each day he would leave earlier and be gone for a longer stretch of time, and each day he ran a greater risk of being pursued and unable to retrace his steps home.

He could deal with a few ghouls. In his youth, Jacob had spent time training with an Air Cadet unit, 527 Simonds Squadron. Like many of his cohort, he had never taken the majority of it seriously at the time, but he always enjoyed the survival training. That enjoyment had carried forward with him throughout his early twenties in a love for camping and the outdoors in general. He could move comfortably in any surrounding, and was blessed with a keen sense of perception. Perpetually alert, he could process a scene quickly, infinitely quicker than the dead could react to him.

No, what worried Jacob most was the living. He knew they would be out there in the wastes, and he knew first-hand of the evils that some men could do.

Still, he found some solace in the knowledge someone, somewhere nearby still had some fight in them.

Jacob turned away from the window and set his attention to the task at hand. He still had another unit to canvas in this building and hadn't properly swept the kitchen in this one. He shot one last glance to the grey wastes of the streets outside before he turned and stepped over the bodies of two dead ones he had just put down; the shattered remnants of a young couple.

The apartment bore all the telltale signs of being young and in love. Sparsely furnished with that cheap, shitty 'some-assembly-required' furniture, walls decorated with tacky framed photos of happy times together, and the kind of hand-me-down dishes and flatware that parents offload on their children as they finally leave the nest.

Likely this was their first apartment.

Likely they had just started their lives together.

He had split both their heads with a hatchet just moments before.

Now they both lie, smitten and emaciated on the dirty hardwood, their tattered hair matted with thick, viscous blood from deep splits in their skulls.

Lifeless eyes upturned to the ceiling, staring endlessly into the void.

He didn't allow himself to dwell upon it.

These people were dead long before he found them here; there was no saving them. He had people who counted on him. While the business was unpleasant, their continued survival was all that mattered to him, and he was the only one in any position to do something about it anyway.

The apartment air was stale and smelled thickly of smoke, faintly punctuated by spoiled food and the musk of wet plaster as it disintegrated off the lathe underneath, falling from the walls in clumps.

This would have been a swanky apartment once, a period home from the early twentieth century. Its vaulted ceilings and beautiful crown moulding were cracked and blistered throughout from the onslaught of the elements, heaves of frost and rapid expansion from the heat of flame.

A bowl of rotten fruit sat rancid on the countertop and there were signs of rodent feces throughout the bottom row of cabinetry. Jacob shifted boxes of tainted cereals about and caught sight of a few mice as they scurried back through the holes they had chewed in the mildewed walls.

The drawers had cutlery but the knives were flimsy; maybe useful for cooking, but worthless for defending yourself.

Discouraged, he frowned slightly and turned to the fridge.

The scent of putridity assaulted his senses, and Jacob partially recoiled to acclimatize. Several plates of leftovers were loosely covered in saran wrapping, now blackened and spoiled. A pizza box, a carton of eggs and some milk weren't worth examining. But there were a few cans of soda; the calories wouldn't hurt, though he knew it would ultimately only compound their thirst.

As he removed his pack and collected the soda, he revealed a couple familiar blue-and-silver cans.

It almost didn't register.

Turning the can to face him, he couldn't believe his luck.

Beer, and shit… even his brand.

Locally produced, union made, and part of a long lasting legacy of the ruined city.

Jacob had spent so much time focused on salvaging survival supplies that he seldom allowed his head to turn to the comforts of the world pre-outbreak. He stared at the can for a long moment, turning it over in his hands and realized he had started to salivate amongst thoughts of barbeques, bonfires and better days.

Finding little else of immediate use, he produced a pen and notebook and took stock of some other non-critical goods that might be useful at some point. He flipped to the page that pertained to the address he was currently probing and jotted down a few notes. To keep the weight down while scouting, Jacob would only take critical items – food, water, weapons, medical supplies.

He had to account dearly for every ounce he carried.

Leisure and comfort would come later.

If they were lucky.

The muffled sounds of distant gunfire continued outside.

* * *

The group pushed on.

Cox and Sullivan headed the column while the rest struggled to keep pace. Isaac was keeping up, but his breathing came more and more labored with each passing block. He continued on without complaint, but knew if they were beset again, he wouldn't be useful at all in close quarters.

The car alarm was a distant memory now, and the team had made good time in gaining some distance. They were now filtering through the abandoned streets and were within a few kilometers of the compound. Thankfully they had met only sporadic resistance; one or two ghouls at a time, easily dispatched. With the loss of the medical supplies, the realities of a lack of discipline and taking undue risks now weighed more appropriately on the band.

Something in the air was catching their attention, though. Sounds in the distance, but not the car alarm; these were sudden bursts, punctuating the breeze.

Gunfire, and lots of it.

Coming from the harbour.

'Jesus, is that us?' one of the porters blurted.

Cox motioned everyone against the side of a building adjacent to a square, near the crest of a hill.

Isaac slumped against the brick building and tried to prop himself up to retain some modicum of respect. One of the porters gave him a shoulder to lean on.

Sully and the rest looked to Cox for direction.

Cox peered out from around the corner. She could see the entrance to the city market; it connected through a series of pedways and underground corridors to the mall almost next to the Coast Guard site. The compound had largely picked the shopping centre clean of useful provisions and had abandoned it as the costs to maintain the sprawl vastly outweighed the benefits of keeping it. It was an option, but they'd need to contend with the deep darkness of the mall, an unknown number of infected and barricaded exits at the far end.

Alternatively she could run the group hard and fast, right down the hill on the home stretch. Presumably anything hostile in the area would be moving towards the report.

Coming in behind them should give us the advantage, she reasoned. *And it saves us another crawl in the dark.*

'Alright,' Cox began. She slung her rifle over her shoulder, paused to tighten her ponytail and turned towards her group.

'Here's how this goes down ...'

* * *

Quinn emerged from the command module with two men in tow and made immediately for the fences. The shooters in the platform were snapping off rounds indiscriminately. The fences were lining up with survivors with an array of improvised weaponry; he couldn't see what was coming around the crowd but his combat senses told him it was going to be a hell of a fight.

They had done a decent job of keeping the snow from piling up against the fences, but it could have been better. Hell, *everything* could have been better, but Quinn had limited resources and limited time.

A part of Quinn lamented the fact he hadn't worked them harder.

Perhaps he had been too soft; too accommodating.

He may have doomed them all.

The three rushed across the yard.

As those gathered saw Quinn arrive personally, it was evident their confidence swelled. They parted as if a troubled sea to allow him to survey the situation.

Quinn stopped in his tracks, but never lost his composure.

A throng of infected advanced down the hill; there had to be at least forty more.

'We're getting low!' the platform called down.

Quinn had about twelve survivors at the wall, including himself and his retinue from the module, and probably two up on the shooting platform. The only firearms among them were on the platform and in his company, and obviously only what ammunition they carried with them.

Quinn grabbed a civilian by the shoulder – a woman, mid-thirties, clad in a faded red coat and ineptly brandishing a heavy wrench – and spun her to face him.

'Find out what rounds the platform needs and get them.'

Terrified, she responded on instinct and ran to the base of the platform.

The dead advanced steadily, almost in unison.

One of his men ran up to the fence and opened fire into the wretched crowd. At this distance, his aim was unreliable. Some of the lead ghouls showed sign of impact to the torso or limbs, but few went down.

They scarcely slowed.

'*Cease fire!*' Quinn barked, 'Let them get closer. *Do not fire* at a target more than ten meters out; you're pissing away rounds we don't have.'

Quinn paced the makeshift line.

He knew immediately they had no hope of stopping the advance before it made their walls. They wouldn't have a shooter in the central nest before the wave hit, nor would the platform have their resupply; best he could hope for was the platform could make their last few shots count.

Under the combined weight of the mass of necrotic flesh, he needed to trust the wall would hold. If they could keep the wall from collapsing long enough to get some firing options, they could alleviate a substantial amount of pressure quickly. As the wave of dead hit the chain link they would pick as many more as possible with what weapons they had.

Their entire campaign would hinge on how long they could keep the wall standing.

Since the night the line broke, the fences had been tested against smaller packs – a half dozen or so at a time – but never against a group this size.

Quinn cursed the spotter in the civilian nest. His inattention meant Quinn needed to redeploy his assets, meant they needed to respond with guns to the threat he had allowed to congregate under his nose and on their doorstep.

As he watched the tireless army advance toward his gates, an unreasonable fury began to well up in Quinn; his blood began to boil.

He will pay.

Chapter 12

THE DEAD WERE UPON THEM.

The wave of ghouls was mere steps away from their walls. They were so close now that as Quinn scanned their disfigured faces he would pick out features in each that seemed vaguely familiar. They scraped onwards in a dysfunctional gait, clumsy gray limbs outstretched beneath tatters of ragged fabric.

Fevered.

Covetous.

The seconds began to drag.

The clap of rifle fire split the air from somewhere to Quinn's left; he scarcely noticed.

Quinn considered the faces of the nearest infected.

He wanted to feel contempt for them.

Instead, he felt nothing.

Their determined, unfeeling stares were met by his in equal measure.

The pieces around him rearranged, but Quinn stood only vaguely aware of their movements.

Pistol fire erupted from somewhere nearby.

Splashes of flesh and gore, sinew and bone burst throughout Quinn's sights, though he heard not a sound to accompany the display. Bits of death flared all around him, each precipitated by peripheral flashes.

Only a dull drone filled his ears.

He stood so enthralled by the morbid fireworks, Quinn didn't process the integrity of the fence was compromised.

The frostbitten dead piled against the chain link, jaws agape with supernatural tension. Their black hands heaved against the wall, frozen fingers twisted between the links. Several of the survivors resigned to throw their bodies against the fence as it bowed in surrender.

It was half comical.

As the fence yielded and its moorings began to buckle, the lifeless eyes flared. The mouths gnashed the fence itself as their sleepless patience gave way to lust.

The fence dipped and bowed, bent inwards and came down like the opening of a great and sinister drawbridge. Quinn stretched an empty hand to where the fence collapsed before him, as if to offer it in caress as it inched and lowered to greet him personally.

Quinn stared in unblinking admiration.

Their determination was impressive.

Like a mad tide, furious and erosive.

Those first in line were pressed against the fence as those behind clambered and trampled those in front, a tangled mass of limb intent to rend and devour.

Suddenly Quinn could see nothing else.

His world melted away, oblivious to all but the fence splayed out before him.

Instinctively, Quinn raised his M&P and steadied his aim with his already extended hand.

His thoughts focused unnaturally fast, so fast Quinn grew frustrated as his hands couldn't respond to his mental targeting adjustments. Each casing expelled from the breech hesitated midair as the muzzle flared in slow motion. Though Quinn could feel the recoil as the 9mm kicked into his hands, its customary staccato jolt was usurped by the crawl of delayed sensation.

As quickly as the dead could climb, he would cut them down.

Like pestilent weeds, the dead kept coming.

The depressed trigger answered with the mocking *click click click* of the hammer unable to find a mate. As Quinn exhausted the first clip, the world caught up to him in paroxysms of urgency.

Quinn dropped his spent mag to the snow and slammed his second one in.

The dead had only the section of downed fence as an entry point, and this limited their numbers to some extent. As his faculties returned to him, Quinn could once again make out the movements of the survivors around him. The more recently succumbed to infection were more nimble, more vigorous than their longer-dead counterparts; their movements were that much more agile and deliberate. The dead trapped behind their trampled cohort began to climb and spill over the sides of the downed fence, finding cruel solution to the bottleneck.

All were forced into an inglorious melee. The dead lunged at the exhausted survivors as each flailed with their ramshackle implements. They wrestled with the decayed throughout the yard and struggled to stem the tide of carrion.

Several of the defenders had fallen, savaged under the gluttonous mass, swallowed whole by the crowd of advancing dead. Splashes of bright crimson mixed with the detritus of the shattered corpses. The two shooters stationed on the platform jumped down to reinforce Quinn's line, each using their empty rifles to bludgeon whatever was in range.

The world sped up around him, but it did not diminish his aim. Quinn never moved from where he stood. He chose his targets with care. They fought in close quarters now; Quinn needed to cycle between those mired in the fence and those that grappled with his band. Frequently Quinn would drop a ghoul in the instant before its teeth found their mark only to refocus his fire at the fence a second later.

Gone were conscious thought and strategy.

He existed in an automated state.

Mechanical.

Quinn knew they were outmatched.

The dead spewed from the torn fence and spilled over the top. Though he and his defenders had inflicted terrible damage to the crowd, their sheer number would crush their resistance.

Quinn didn't bother to look back for support.

His runners had failed.

He dropped another ghoul as it was about to drag down one of his uniformed retinue. The shot drilled through its temple and drove it sideways.

Satisfied, Quinn turned his attention back to the torn gates.

Click, the M&P laughed.

Quinn turned the weapon over slightly in his hand and considered the profile of his sidearm.

Shouts and cries, crunched bones and wet thuds pounded around him and assaulted his senses. Quinn could hear the roar of the battle, but saw only red.

Resigned to the rage that boiled within, Quinn strode forward, wading headlong into the chaos.

* * *

Cox and her team advanced hard down the hill.

From this distance they could tell a section of fence had collapsed, but they had little indication of how many of the dead were inside their walls. The realization that their compound could be moments away from subjugation hastened their pace. She didn't need to urge anyone on; each fully understood the implications of what unfolded before them.

So fiendishly intent on the prey inside the walls, the ravenous horde of dead remained oblivious to their approach. Though unable to fire into the crowd for fear of a stray bullet, Cox and her column hacked and stabbed the back of the siege.

The rank had thinned fast, the element of surprise well utilized for full advantage. They made good progress against the dead outside the walls as those inside the courtyard continued to battle the ghouls within. The bottleneck and the incessant pressure from the back of the crowd to move forward limited their mobility, already significantly hindered in undeath.

Isaac stuck to the fringes and worked his knife into the base of skulls turned away from him, probed and severed the brain stem. Cox and Sullivan worked in unison; they alternated hauling corpses down and butt ending the brains as they lay on the snow.

As the crowd thinned out, it became evident that multiple survivors inside the courtyard had fallen in the attack. Several ghouls huddled around snow splashed in red, ignoring all but their ghastly meals. Only a handful of the faceless crowd hadn't yet been cut down, and one amongst them meandered towards Quinn.

It had been a woman. She would have been attractive at a time. Her blonde hair still retained some semblance of curl as it framed her slender face. The previously delicate features were severe now; high cheek bones threatened to tear the skin pulled impossibly tight about them. Her lips were cracked and parched, the corners of her mouth split. She wore simple clothes, an off white tank top that would have been well-fitting hung, limp and torn, sadly draped over protruded ribs and the evidence of her infection. She remained shapely, more curve than angle, though it was waning fast.

Quinn's vision had returned to him. In his periphery he took note of the fallen, half consumed survivors in the courtyard. Their limbs twitched as the dead gnawed the flesh from their bones.

Quinn glanced over her exposed shoulders to regard the fence, bent asunder, and the mound of corpses piled at their doorstep.

Their compound; their bloodstained home.

He visibly seethed as he approached the dead thing.

Her hands remained at her side and she stumbled forward.

Pitilessly, Quinn stomped on her knee. The force of the strike shattered her tibia with the snap of long dried wood and the bone poked out from the bloodless wound. With only vestigial motor control, she crumpled sideways to the ground.

He smashed the creature's head repeatedly with the handle of his M&P.

It was clearly terminated after the first strike, but Quinn continued to pound the skull with a fury so visceral that only a mangled pulp remained; each retracted strike dripped a viscous trail of gore in the snow. The weight of the savagery turned her body flat on its back.

The silence of those gathered was deafening; only the wet, slapping thuds were audible as Quinn continued to maul the woman. Each strike battered through the remnants of her face, only stopping as it came out the other side to meet the snow and ice beneath.

Sullivan searched the faces of his companions for a similar disgust. Quinn's persistent fury struck an uneasy chord; he couldn't help but feel uncomfortable at the display.

Isaac met his gaze, but didn't return his concern. He calmly wiped the gore from his blade against his sleeve.

Cox watched, wholly indifferent.

The other gunner turned his gaze to the snow and hugged his rifle.

Sleet began to fall from the skies. It pattered against the various artificial fabrics of their jackets and against the sheet metal roof of the shooting platform adjacent.

Quinn continued to batter the corpse.

No one spoke.

At last, with nothing left to bludgeon, Quinn slowly rose. His chest heaved and his eyes were wild with animosity. The corner of his mouth curled upwards into a vicious grin and he subtly swayed as his weight shifted between his feet. His face was peppered and streaked with splatters of blood and sleet, which appeared all the more pronounced against a face reddened with exertion.

Quinn's unblinking eyes never faltered.

* * *

It was long past midnight, but no stars were visible. The mixture of snow and sleet continued well into the night as the dense clouds lingered and prevented any light from shining through.

Jacob sat, knees bent, propped against a wall in the corner of the room.

He found no sleep tonight.

He stared at a bottle of water on the floor between his feet. He had enjoyed some success earlier in the day, and knew they had a few days' worth of water, but still he resisted his body's ache to hydrate.

He could wait a little longer.

He lifted the corner of a heavy woolen blanket they had nailed over the room's solitary window and peered outside.

The darkness was complete as the sleet continued to rap against the aged flat roof above him and the vintage glass window to his left. As the night deepened, the corners of the window had started to ice over. The condensation from his breath fogged the glass as he stared into the cold abyss.

A single pillar candle sputtered in the center of the room. Despite the sparse furnishings, it cast far stranger shadows than he expected.

Jacob dropped the corner of the blanket so it once again covered the entire window; the heavy woven fabric muffled the sleet as it beat against the glass. He produced a cigarette from his coat and pulled an engraved Zippo lighter from his pocket and lit up.

He drew a long, slow drag, and allowed the acrid smoke to fill his lungs and warm his insides. Jacob hated the taste of cigarettes, but it helped assuage his hunger.

They were on the ragged edge.

Two figures slept restlessly on the floor in a makeshift bed; a collection of stained couch cushions and piecemeal blankets.

Jacob drew another long haul off the cigarette, closed his eyes and exhaled slowly through his nose. The warmth of the smoke licked his skin and clung to his face.

They had found their hermitage by chance.

The barracks safe zone collapsed around them and those left alive were abandoned to the wasteland of the central peninsula. In the chaos, Jacob and a small band found themselves together in their midnight exile – they ran blindly from their failed refuge into the deep darkness of the cityscape.

Only three survived that night.

Jacob rested the hand which held the cigarette on his knee and leaned his head back against the wall. He turned his gaze downward and watched the smoke curl in the candlelight.

They needed refuge; somewhere to hunker down and catch their breath. Exhaustion had set in. They hadn't the strength to fight.

He led them into a two storey building with a single entrance; he knew it would be easier to defend. The entry hallway led to a staircase with the ground floor unit off the main corridor. On the second floor they found a three bedroom apartment that made little attempt to hide its age; it was dingy and unkempt, sparsely furnished, full of cheap period fixtures and nicotine-stained wallpaper. The windows were ancient and drafty, but Jacob paid no attention to the chill.

The previous occupants were long gone. They must have been in the process of moving out when the outbreak hit, abandoning this place for the final time.

Jacob selected the smallest bedroom of the three as their camp. A single entrance, a single window that overlooked the street, and a tiny closet with a folding door that hung limp, embarrassed that it had fallen off its track.

A plain desk sat against the wall opposite with a few empty cardboard boxes adjacent. The three had pillaged the unit and brought the limited trappings of comfort to their little hovel.

Each morning at first light, Jacob would leave the others to scavenge. He didn't know them before the night they shared in exile; had never seen either during life at the barracks or at the harbour safe zone previous to that.

It didn't change the fact he felt responsible for them now.

Jacob took another drag of his cigarette and glanced over to the nest where the two slept, truly unsure if they'd ever open their eyes again.

Emily never seemed to wake from her nightmare.

Madison seemed capable, at least.

Jacob trusted he could leave Emily with her as he canvassed the surrounding buildings for the supplies to keep them going. Madison would carefully arrange their provisions on the surface of the shabby desk; Jacob thought her compulsion for organization comical in the midst of the insanity outside. Whether it was out of a desire for a sense of normalcy, or to stave off a deeply ingrained sense of boredom was irrelevant.

The compulsion was kind of cute.

Endearing, even.

A few bottles of water, assorted packaged snack foods, a few cans, miscellaneous tools, a roll of adhesive tape, and a mostly-empty first aid kit were all they had amassed in their efforts to get beyond scraping by day-to-day.

The shadows flickered in the candlelight, grew tall and shrunk with the ebb of flame as it danced towards its ultimate end.

* * *

The fence had been partially repaired, but additional material would be required to properly reset their defenses. Quinn had ordered additional civilian overnight shifts along the walls and in the nests. Aside from the sentries posted in the staircases and on each floor, everyone housed within the civilian quarters was long asleep.

No one heard the several pairs of hard soled combat boots as they methodically climbed the staircases. As they approached each checkpoint, occasionally the civilian guards would chance to meet their gaze – though each could tell that this grim procession was not one they were meant to interrupt.

The soldiers snaked wordlessly through the empty, slender corridors as they advanced towards their quarry, their footfalls faintly resounding off the cold concrete walls.

When they arrived at their intended destination, the group splintered apart and flitted between the bunks until they came to the one they wanted. One of the soldiers subtly snapped his fingers and the others converged upon him.

The occupant snored peacefully, curled up in a patchwork blanket on a nondescript cot, blissfully unaware.

One of the soldiers silently unfurled a length of cloth and passed one end of it to the soldier standing opposite him. Together, they pulled the length taut. Without a sound, the pair wrested the fabric over the mouth and nose of the sleeping man as another grabbed his feet and pinned them down.

The man hadn't yet managed to shake the sleep from his eyes when he could process his true predicament. He thrashed helplessly under the weight of his attackers and choked out a pitiful cry through the heavy fabric that muzzled him.

Anders managed to regain his faculties just long enough to register several shapes about him as a heavy blow from the butt end of a shotgun crashed down into his cheekbone.

And back to sleep he went.

Chapter 13

THE ENTIRE COMPOUND WAS ON EDGE.

Near every post pulled double shifts.

The soldiers kept to themselves; they stalked the corridors and the grounds but interacted little with the civilian presence.

A mutual distrust simmered beneath the superficial pleasantries.

Rumours about the leadership permeated the civilian quarters.

Quinn became reclusive; he spent long hours in isolation.

Fanned by his absence, the tension mounted over the coming days.

Additional guards were posted outside the supply shed as food and water rations were halved. Meals became fewer and further between.

Whispers of Quinn's deepening madness began to take root. They became foundational, part of the fabric of the compound.

The civilians became uneasy, distrustful.

Quinn worked them harder.

Scuffles with the guard were more frequent, more violent.

The officials increasingly relied on intimidation and shows of force to keep order.

The civilians began to openly dispute command.

Quinn's grip was loosening.

His authority could no longer be questioned.

Martial law.

* * *

Daniel pondered over the patient's chart and woefully considered the infirmary's meager resources. While he was a promising student pre-outbreak, and as clever and capable as any among the compound's medical staff, his practical medical training had always been served in well-stocked hospitals. Though he could suggest a multitude of ideas on how to treat the swelling ranks of those needing care, without the inventory available – it simply wasn't feasible. Neither his theoretical nor his practical training had ever emphasized situations remotely reminiscent to this. The salvage team hadn't managed to bring back much of the list they had been tasked with, and the commotion at the wall only threw this reality into sharp relief.

He could mostly tolerate the presence of armed guards, accepted their necessity in a world where the dead infected would rise and hunger for flesh. He could even understand the callous disregard for the reanimated his fellow survivors felt. Even though most considered the living dead's existence an abomination, Daniel still thought of them as people afflicted by an incurable malady.

Though he had no illusions about treatment.

Nor did he question the generally prescribed way to deal with the infected.

Shit, we've all seen movies.

During life at the compound, Daniel had even grown accustomed to sporadic gunfire – almost to the point of an oblivious comfort.

Through it all, though, he had yet to grow accustomed to losing a patient. Each life lost – irrespective of the cause – weighed heavily upon him. Even the end of the known fucking world wasn't an adequate excuse.

Daniel mostly contained those frustrations – he didn't have much choice.

Through cataloguing the infirmary's inventory, it became obvious to Daniel that they'd soon be forced into some difficult cost/benefit analysis – the outcome of which would likely be grim. He didn't want to burden Keeley with the notion, nor Isaac with the consequence of their penniless return … but without successful resupply soon, the infirmary would be hard pressed to justify the expenditure of medical resources on many under their care.

Daniel watched across the room as Keeley sat with Isaac. Though Isaac was afforded a place of some comfort and given a chance to rest in a cot while most others were relegated to the floor, he had given it up to another patient and sat on a window ledge instead.

Isaac had either cracked or broken a few ribs; the area bruising was significant. Prescription-quality painkillers were in short supply – Isaac accepted some generic, over-the-counter ibuprofen when he was admitted, but otherwise made no request nor offered complaint.

He'd be fine in a few more days, but he wouldn't be comfortable.

Keeley didn't ask about the run.

It was clear it hadn't gone as planned.

She gave Isaac a quick kiss on the forehead and pressed her hand to his chest before replacing her particulate mask and resuming her rounds.

As Isaac sat and watched the infirmary staff, he quietly lamented their failure.

The beds were full, and the space seemed to overflow with casualties.

Though Keeley teetered on the brink of collapse, she worked every waking hour to ease the suffering of those patients.

Isaac watched helplessly as she moved about the infirmary.

* * *

Only dimly aware of his surroundings, Anders hadn't opened his eyes in a long time.

His hands were outstretched and wrists bound on either side.

Everything was dark, but he thought he could feel the heat of a fluorescent lamp above him.

He was hooded; the fabric clung to his skin in a claustrophobic mess, damp and muggy with some morbid combination of his sweat, tears and blood.

His tongue was swollen and thick with the taste of rust. As it moved about his mouth it came to rest in over a space previously occupied by several molars.

He sputtered awake, coughed hoarsely into the shroud.

Anders felt a stab of pain in his jaw; it didn't close quite right. The hinge was off.

His head swam from the pain and lolled forward.

Anders tried to bring a hand to his dislocated jaw but found them to be tightly secured to a metal frame with what felt like electrical wire.

'Wakey, wakey...,' chided a voice Anders struggled to recognize.

The words dripped, venomous with insult and ill intent.

Anders coughed again; spat some of his stale blood into the hood.

He moved to speak, but the terrible stab in his jaw stole the words.

A pitiful whimper was all he could manage.

Anders couldn't be sure, but he thought he heard more than one set of laughter.

'No, no...,' cooed the same voice, 'you're not done yet.'

There was a brief pause to let the implications settle in.

'You've still got a bill to pay.'

* * *

As he surveyed the compound from the central nest, Sullivan sipped on a cup of boiled water. The civilians had taken to supplementing their water intake by melting any patches of snow in the compound that looked clean enough to consume.

Sully scratched at his beard, felt the tangle of his red-blond whiskers as he watched the steam curl from his mug.

He found himself paired with the other SKS gunner from the hospital run with increasing frequency. The official's faith in them meant that even under the edict of martial law they were trusted alone and with weaponry. They were far from friends, but Sullivan trusted his mettle.

Erik had been working as a part time barista when the world went to shit, just happened to have the good fortune of working Uptown. He was a lot younger than he looked – Sullivan would have given him at least another ten years – but in reality he was just a child, a couple years out of high school.

Every time he looked at the kid there was a sting of lament.

Another reminder of the countless lives cut short.

What kind of world is this to grow into?

He should be worried about meeting girls and paying rent, not where his next meal would come from, or whether or not he'd be eaten alive by some infected ghoul today.

Sullivan shook such thoughts from his head.

'So… *martial law*,' Erik breathed as he produced a cigarette from the folds of his jacket.

Sullivan disregarded the comment, not interested in taking the bait.

Erik rested the cigarette between his lips as he dug for a lighter.

'Fuck, if people only knew,' he mumbled as he lit up.

Sullivan cocked his head to regard his partner more directly.

Erik replied with a wary look, as if unable to decide whether or not he could trust in his partner's discretion.

Sullivan stared at him expectantly.

Erik took another drag on his cigarette and peered out over the compound.

'Listen kid, spare me the fucking intrigue. I'm tired, I'm hungry. Spit it out.'

Erik glanced sideways at Sullivan and plucked the cigarette from his lips.

'Just a hunch, I guess.'

Sullivan scoffed.

'Don't waste my time with conjecture.'

Erik looked offended; it didn't escape Sully's notice.

He searched Erik's face for clues.

'We've got nothing but time to waste,' Erik retorted.

Sullivan turned back to face the wasteland.

Undeterred, Erik began.

'I've been watching the shed for days.'

Sullivan knew where this was going.

'No one ever goes in or out,' Erik continued. 'Never during daylight hours and they never open the gate without a wide perimeter, guards stationed everywhere.'

Sullivan shifted slightly in his seat, unblinking.

'Don't you find that strange?' Erik chided.

He paused for emphasis, waited for an apologetic look from Sullivan for the earlier slight.

When none was forthcoming, he continued.

'It's empty. Shelves upon shelves of nothing but dust.'

Sullivan weighed the reasoning. In truth, he had come to the same conclusion several days past, at least since the last round of ration cuts, but had hoped to convince himself otherwise.

Resigned to the debate, Sully asked plainly –

'So, why do you think they'd want to keep that quiet?'

Erik took a thoughtful drag on his cigarette.

'Wouldn't accomplish anything, just stir the place up,' he offered.

'That's right,' Sullivan stated, punctuating the statement with a piercing glance. 'We're at the boiling point already.'

As he turned back to the compound, Sullivan finished their conversation.

'Keep that to yourself.'

* * *

As a show of good faith, Quinn agreed to set aside time – by appointment – to personally hear and consider the concerns of the various civilian administrators. He had hoped this token gesture would help to calm the constituents, but their incessant whining tested his patience.

He could scarcely command now; his calendar brimmed with the concerns of lesser men, each of which demanded their few minutes to bathe in his spotlight. Each self-important gnat itched to be heard.

Despite the seemingly unending flow of representatives that filtered into his office, there was one above all whom Quinn despised.

William.

Quinn eyed him cautiously.

He looked far more disheveled of late.

William was spouting some diatribe about Quinn's 'failure' to provide for the community, his 'unjust' and 'illegal' decrees, and how the constituents William represented 'demanded' Quinn's resignation amidst an evident inability to lead. William even tabled the motion that Quinn should 'submit' himself to a vote of no confidence; a referendum on accepting the 'yoke' of his command.

The audacity of this entitled prick.

The type of corporate fat cat that would have lobbied for war because the economic spinoff would have been great for his portfolio.

Quinn wondered how many of his pre-outbreak comrades would still be alive today were it not for men like William. Men who wielded influence from the smoky backrooms, who'd never even seen the front lines he and his mates were so often shipped off to.

Quinn considered his adversary.

He could stir a crowd; whip them into frenzy through his choice of words and their intonation. He was a gifted public speaker and commanded the respect of his peers.

No doubt he had been among them, sowing discord amongst the people he claimed to represent, agitating them. In fact, he likely planted those seeds with such subterfuge that those listening probably thought they had formulated his ideas on their own.

If Quinn could bend this dog to heel, he'd prove a formidable ally.

No, Quinn thought to himself.

No, I don't think so.

* * *

After the lawyer was shown out, Quinn sent for one of his inner circle.

Andrew tried to look busy as he casually spied the slender corporal with the jet black hair as she reported to him a short while later.

She stood at attention and Quinn welcomed her, albeit curtly, and they commandeered the radio room. Andrew was once again relegated to the main module. He stood immediately outside the door in his trademark awkward slant, limp and lax, trying hard to appear as if he belonged amongst the officials despite being so contemptibly ill at ease.

Nevertheless, Andrew puffed out his sniveling chest.

Andrew strained his ears, hoping to eavesdrop on the hushed discussion. He wasn't sure what they were talking about, but he couldn't shake the sensation that – whatever it was – knowledge of it could prove useful.

He couldn't make out what they were saying, but thought he could hear Quinn whispering sharply to the woman; both their sentences were hurried.

They seemed to come to a long pause.

Andrew tensed himself and desperately tried to hear them, anything to ascertain the true nature of their conversation without betraying his motives.

The seconds dragged on.

Andrew shifted his feet and turned his head slightly in order to press his ear against the door as inconspicuously as possible.

'... alright, Quinn,' she finally sighed. 'You can count on me.'

'Don't disappoint me.'

Sensing he'd missed the valuable parts, Andrew slid away from the door and waited to be ushered back in to his post at the radio.

Chapter 14

SULLIVAN LEANED HIS BACK AGAINST THE exposed brick of the loading area wall and absently ran a finger over his shotgun's trigger guard.

He wasn't surprised by news of the assignment; the compound had been tense the last few days.

Tense, and hungry.

What did surprise him, however, was the supporting cast.

It didn't escape his notice that the assembly today was much smaller than their last sortie. The scant few bodies present and their relative spacing about the room made the usually tight quarters seem cavernous by comparison.

He didn't speak a word as he considered those gathered.

Isaac was being briefed and assigned his loadout by the armory staff. He had been pretty beat up their last time out, but so far seemed to be moving about just fine. Sully couldn't hear their discussion but could guess at the general detail.

Cox was seated at a table with a cleaning kit and ran a bore snake through the barrel of her C7, so concentrated in the motion she scarcely seemed conscious of anything else. After each pass, she would take a moment to glance over a map of the Uptown splayed out in front of her.

A few guardsmen stood watch by the armory entrance and chattered indistinctly between themselves.

Everyone seemed right at home, exactly as they belonged.

And then there was the new guy.

An older man sat opposite Sullivan, slumped against the wall and staring straight ahead. Sullivan let his eyes rest on the stranger.

He appeared disheveled; unkempt and ill-at-ease.

Glassy-eyed and distant, it readily betrayed his brimming anxiety.

He reeked of it.

Sullivan hadn't noticed how long he had allowed his gaze to linger when his focus was interrupted by a caustic chuckle.

Isaac strode over and hopped up onto a table next to Sully, sliding his rifle onto the same. Sullivan frowned as he noticed the slight wince and shallow breath as Isaac lifted his weight. The brass casings coldly sang, clinking against one another as Isaac picked through the handful of rounds he had been issued.

'If we get in deep... what am I supposed to do with this?' Isaac mused as he counted the half dozen or so rifle rounds he had been provided.

'Bullets are scarce,' Sullivan shrugged.

'*Everything's* scarce,' Isaac dryly reminded him. 'That's why they send us out.'

Sullivan thought of his last conversation with Erik and cleared his throat.

'How are the ribs?'

Isaac paused, surprised by the seeming sincerity of the question.

'They hurt,' he grinned halfheartedly as he moved to load the rifle.

Sullivan studied the subtle labor to Isaac's movements.

'Couldn't find anybody else?'

Though Sully meant no offence, Isaac couldn't help but feel slighted.

It was his turn to shrug.

'Guess not.'

Something about the response didn't sit well with Sullivan; something in the body language.

Isaac felt the need to save face. Daniel had protested his being pulled for this assignment, and Keeley wasn't particularly keen on him returning to the wastes until he had ample time to heal. While the monotony and the impotence of his last few days relegated to the infirmary wore on him, Isaac also understood the implications of walking wounded outside the compound walls.

Their arguments fell on deaf ears; Quinn's orders were specific.

Eager to shift the attention from his physical infirmity, Isaac motioned to the stranger slumped against the wall.

'Who's the new guy?'

'*That,*' Cox interrupted as she inserted the bore snake through the breech a final time, 'is William, our esteemed civilian administrator.'

Her tongue dripped sarcasm and venom in equal measure.

'And today is the day he finally gets his hands dirty.'

* * *

The plan was simple. The team would pick their way through the streets and make for a nearby high rise – at least insofar as Saint John was concerned – a short distance further down the waterfront. The building had been subsidized housing once, with a lean towards assisted living. In theory, there should be a variety of drugs and miscellany throughout the building and its dwellings.

Since the mall was abandoned, preference for scavenging had always been given to smaller structures, but the infirmary was in dire straits now. Painkillers, antibiotics, bedding, bandages and disinfectant were all in short supply. They were taxed to the limit. With the failure of St. Joseph's still fresh in mind and the Regional Hospital well outside their reach, necessity meant it was time to improvise.

Sully took up the rear and studied William's movements as they made their way towards the tenement building.

He was jumpy; clearly untested outside the walls. Every step was tentative and each breath ragged, as if he balanced on some great precipice and even the slightest breeze would send him tumbling over.

He had no place among them.

Why is he here?

The question gnawed at him.

As the team approached the entrance of the apartment complex, Isaac and Cox sped a few paces ahead and forced the doors.

The beams of their flashlights thrust into the long dark of the tenement foyer and perforated its brooding gloom. Like obscene fingers vainly probing a deep gash, the group flitted in, single file.

Several dark stains, long since dried, marred the marbled tile of the lobby floor.

But nothing stirred.

Lobby furniture and baggage were strewn about the floor and radiated outwards from the main entry. It appeared as though the previous residents had sought to barricade themselves in.

Before hastily trying to tear it back down.

The team fanned outwards and advanced cautiously into the room.

Chairs and collapsible tables were stacked haphazardly and blocked all but one hallway leading from the chamber. It wasn't immediately obvious whether the makeshift barricades were built from this side or not.

William threw himself against the wall and held his breath.

Isaac and Sullivan exchanged knowing glances.

Cox crept soundlessly to William's position and delivered an insistent nudge with the butt of her C7. He shook it off, brought his flashlight to bear and peered around the corner into the treacherous dark beyond.

The hungry light feasted on shadow, but nothing else.

Isaac leapt to the wall opposite and raised his rifle. Cox motioned for Sullivan to move ahead.

Sully rounded the corner and took patient strides forward. He stretched his fingers and adjusted his grip on the oversized pump. Careful not to disturb Isaac's line of sight, he advanced.

Sweat beaded on William's forehead. The circulation of his blood thundered in his ears and nausea ebbed within amid the slow tension.

Not a damn sound otherwise.

The accessible portion of the ground floor proved little more than halls and communal rooms bereft of a community. Each room was scrutinized for signs of the infected, but no time afforded for their canvassing. Their true prize would be found somewhere on the floors above, in the musty medicine cabinets of private dwellings or – if they were fortunate – as yet unpillaged storage lockers.

The team slipped by a row of defunct elevators and found the emergency stairs. The hinges begged for lubricant as the metallic door pressed open, its unapologetic wail echoed throughout the stairwell.

The four froze and waited for a response.

Still, none came.

The air in the stairwell was thick and suffocating, clearly undisturbed for some time. As the group rounded the stairs their flashlights danced chaotically between its catwalk treads.

Sully stopped at the entrance to the next floor and scanned his companions. Cox looked as she always did – fierce and unrepentant. William trembled and looked as though he would be sick at any moment. Isaac struggled slightly for breath as he crested the landing.

Why send a wounded man…

Sullivan shook the paranoia from his head and centered himself.

With no appetite to test their luck a second time, Cox gingerly slid the stairwell door open just wide enough for Isaac to inch out in the hallway. His flashlight pierced the dark and illuminated a row of apartment doors that lined either side of the corridor. The floor was carpeted with a tacky, patterned mess of polyester, any pride of its eighties heyday décor long since faded. While it was an affront to the senses, it offered some advantage for the scavengers as it meant their footfalls would be padded.

Isaac leaned back in for orders.

'Sully, you and Isaac. William, you're with me,' Cox breathed. 'Don't venture too far; this is our exit.'

Everyone squeezed from out the landing and set to work.

The air was significantly lighter in the hall, noticeably easier to breathe than the oppressive stagnancy of the stairwell. As he emerged from the landing, William realized he had forgotten how refreshing it felt to walk on carpeted floors – a much warmer sensation than the aged tile that dominated the Coast Guard site – and he didn't fail to appreciate how it muffled his uneasy steps. He wiped a layer of sweat from his brow and swallowed hard in an effort to calm his racing heartbeat.

Cox swatted at William's shoulder and pointed to one of the doors. Taking her meaning, they set off. Sully continued to light the hallway as Isaac pressed his ear against the door. As he tried the knob, Isaac found it to be unlocked.

Isaac and Sully slipped into the squat, square room and methodically bathed its features with their flashlights. It was sparsely furnished; simple and unassuming. They moved in slowly, deliberately and swept its contents. Satisfied it was empty, Isaac set about the kitchen cabinetry while Sullivan rummaged through the bathroom.

Cox and William also found their apartment to be unlocked. William was first through the door; his inexperience in such affairs was painfully evident. His flashlight jumped about erratically with little semblance of design behind its movements. Cox fell in behind William and let him fumble ahead of her.

The dwelling reeked of death and nicotine.

As William stepped into the bedroom, his flashlight's gaze fell to the figure of a woman. She was curled up, prostrate and fetal on a quilted duvet cover. A simple night table was moved away from the wall, adorned by a heavy glass ashtray that overflowed with cigarette butts.

The woman obviously would have been tiny and frail in life; her dehydrated corpse now couldn't have weighed more than forty kilos. Her gray hair fell limp about her sunken face, the remnants of blackened skin pulled as if vacuum sealed about her lips and eyes. Instinctively, William raised his hand to cover his mouth and nose. He recoiled from the scene and inched backwards until he collided with Cox.

William spun about and found Cox's glare burrowing into him.

'Check it out,' Cox cooed.

'Wh… what?' was all he could stammer in response.

'She didn't die from the cigarettes.'

'What's it matter? She's dead.'

'I don't care about how she died,' Cox's impatience was already at its limit. 'I want you to check that room.'

William's features scrunched up as he considered some form of protest.

'Get your hands dirty, William,' she chided. 'Welcome to the wastes.'

Being afforded no other option, William stepped into the room and surveyed it thoroughly with his flashlight. He kept one hand over his mouth as he vainly tried to prevent the inhalation of her decay. The woman offered no response to the beam of light as it danced about her. There were a few bottles of wine and a handful of prescription bottles strewn about her, and the duvet was stained immediately next to her face.

There was little doubt what had claimed her life.

Several multicoloured pills were bunched together on the night stand and on the blankets. Unsure of which were which, William gathered all the pills and bottles, hoping one of the infirmary techs could sort them out.

As he collected the pills, William felt a strange sensation from this woman. Almost as if she watched him plunder her final belongings. He picked up a bottle of wine and checked its vintage; swill compared to his usual brand.

How long had it been since he had enjoyed a quality wine?

William let the bottle fall unceremoniously from his grasp to the duvet. At the impact, he took note of the telltale rattle of a pill bottle somewhere on the bed. He swam the flashlight beam over the covers but revealed nothing; it had to be buried somewhere in the blankets or under her clothing.

As he leaned in, he let the light of his flashlight idle over her features.

Poor girl.

William wouldn't admit it to himself, but he could sense a familiarity in her. As he patted the blankets down he could isolate the faint sounds of the shifting pills from underneath the crook of her arms.

He needed to move her, shift her weight, but couldn't bring himself to disturb her sleep. Gingerly, William wrapped his fingers about her tiny wrist – the cold rigidity of the slender limb stole the warmth from his own hand.

William had never touched a corpse before.

Even when his second wife had died some years ago, he struggled to even look at her as she rest in her ornate casket. With no children of his own, and without the love of her two children, William had thrown himself back into his practice. He had always been severe, and though he legitimately tried, he couldn't forge a meaningful connection with either stepchild.

Once she had passed, they walked from his life forever.

Staring at the lifeless figure of this poor woman, William felt wounded.

He manipulated her body and revealed a small vial of pills obscured by her nightgown. As he reached to collect them, he thought he caught a flicker of movement from her face out of the corner of his eye. William indelicately dropped the arm and once again held her intent in the beam of his flashlight.

No sign of movement; no reaction to the light.

William cursed his nerves and turned to rejoin Cox, who met his return with a condescending smirk. She outstretched her hand and William surrendered the dead woman's bounty before they stepped back into the corridor with Sully and Isaac.

'How'd you do?' Cox whispered, as if in greeting.

'Not as well as you'd expect,' Sully replied, defeated. 'Wasn't much worth taking; figured this place would be a gold mine. No food but stale crackers, no medicine… just dust. You do any better?'

'Some pills,' Cox paused, not bothering to mention the suicide; in her capitulation, she deserved no further mention or laurel. Cox hadn't the time for her. William was unsettled, but rationalized this is how Cox needed to be; part of what had kept her safe outside the compound walls.

'They must have amassed their supplies somewhere central, picked the apartments clean and dug in,' William offered.

'Strength in numbers and such,' Isaac agreed and pointed his flashlight further down the corridor.

William's eyes nervously followed the beam. He added his own flashlight to its strength.

Cox subtly nodded.

'Clear another unit; we'll scout ahead.'

They set out and crept through the corridors. Isaac and Sully checked several doors as the group advanced, but found most to be locked. With no desire to risk the noise of forcing a door, they finally arrived at an unlocked dwelling. By this time, Cox and William were well ahead of them.

Cox came to a door that was unlike the rest; a double push door with a glass pane. Whatever it was, it clearly wasn't the entrance to a private dwelling. She signaled for William to fall in behind her as she peered into the small window.

William pressed up against the wall and studied Cox's movements. As much as he couldn't stand her, she was more than capable navigating the wastes.

A specialist in this environment; a professional.

He would learn from her.

* * *

Sully leaned against the wall and his eyes followed Cox's progress further down the hall as Isaac once again pressed his ear against a wooden door.

Even at their present distance, Sullivan could tell Cox had come upon something. The two distant flashlights dipped and illuminated the ground at their feet rather than reach into the continuing dark beyond.

Content the unit was unoccupied, Isaac glanced at Sullivan to find his attentions spent elsewhere. He gave Sully a tap to call him back to the task at hand.

Sully stepped out from the wall and shouldered his shotgun, but continued to glance further up the corridor to where Cox and William had stopped.

Something about this moment made him uneasy.

Exasperated, Isaac gave Sully another punch.

'*Focus*,' he chastised. 'You're going to get me killed; eyes in front.'

Sully refocused on the door they were about to breach, and leaned into his sights… but he couldn't shake the suspicious feeling.

* * *

'Alright, it's clear,' Cox whispered. She never took her eyes from the pane of glass and the abyss beyond as she dragged William to position in front of the entry.

William raised his flashlight and tried to get a glimpse inside the room, but couldn't see past the glare on the glass as it reflected off smears of grime.

He stood at the push bar on the door and rested his hands upon it as he considered the best approach to the room once he was inside. He replayed in his mind how Cox and the others entered a room, how they moved their flashlights and picked through a space.

Wait… he thought.

The glare…

Those smudges…

They looked like handprints…

William's head cocked quizzically and his posture stiffened.

Before he could turn his head, he was struck hard in the back and driven forward heavily into the doors, which burst open with a dreadful clamour. He sprawled headlong into the room and landed awkwardly on the cold floor. His flashlight spiraled out, its beam interrupted intermittently as it skipped away.

A crushing loneliness filled him as the door behind slammed shut.

William scrambled to his hands and knees.

He had almost climbed to his feet when a tide of hands and teeth swept him away.

* * *

Out of the corner of his eye, a sudden chaotic flash of distant torchlight pulled Sully's attention away from their door. He whipped his head around and broke rank from Isaac, instinctively taking a few steps towards the noise.

Isaac turned from his door and illuminated the corridor.

As their eyes adjusted to the rapid shift in distance and light, neither could be sure of what they had seen. Cox stood, feet shoulder width apart, back arched as she heaved the door closed with both hands pulling on the push bar.

Sully began to sprint down the corridor towards her as Isaac stood incredulous.

The anguished cries continued for only a few short moments.

Cox let go of the bar and thundered back down the corridor.

'*Fucking go, go!*' she commanded in a strange half-whisper, half-yell.

Sully stopped dead in his tracks as he registered the gravelly cries of the infected, their fists pounding against the walls further down the corridor. He stared into the vast emptiness of it even as Cox flew past him and the beam of Isaac's flashlight turned to follow suit.

'*Come on!*' Isaac roared from somewhere behind him.

Hesitantly, Sully turned from the darkness.

* * *

Sullivan emptied the unspent shells from his shotgun and handed them to the armory comptroller before he brusquely deposited the weapon on the desk in front of him.

Isaac had already turned over his weapon and ammunition and had made his way out of the room.

Cox never bothered to stop.

As Sully turned over the remaining items on his person, he studied the reactions of everyone gathered. All were official personnel, either guardsman or those who controlled the loadouts for the salvage teams.

No one seemed to mourn the absent returnee.

In fact, Sully thought to himself, *no one even seems surprised.*

Chapter 15

DANIEL WAS HALFWAY INTO HIS ROUNDS WHEN word had reached him. Again, the salvage team would come home virtually empty handed. Though they managed to bring back a mixed bag of medications, only a handful of the pills gathered were of any practical use.

Keeley knelt next to a patient on the floor. He was malnourished, exhausted and had run a fever out of the stress. He had no visible scratches or bite marks so the risk of infection was minimal. His body, like so many others gathered here, was simply giving out for the strain.

She removed a simple strip of cloth from the man's forehead and checked his pallor. He had been without colour for several hours. They had hoped to keep his core temperature down, but without proper medication he would be left to his fate.

She placed the fabric into a Tupperware container filled with melted snow she had gathered from the compound courtyard. Once thoroughly soaked, she squeezed a few drops of water onto the man's cracked lips. Her heart sank as his thirst didn't react to the sensation of the cool drops and she reached to check the man's pulse.

Still alive in there, she thought as she replaced the damp fabric to the man's forehead and pushed some of his hair away from his face. *Good…*

Keep fighting.

Keeley managed a weak smile for the man, and he seemed to shake his catatonia in acknowledgement of her touch.

Daniel rubbed his forehead and struggled to think of what else they could do improve the prospects for any of the patients. Dehydration and malnourishment only compounded their misery – Quinn expressly forbade 'extraordinary measures' for any who weren't more than worth their weight, and the posted guard kept close vigil on the medical staff and the disbursement of their inventory.

With supplies so thin, the infirmary needed to 'prioritize.'

Daniel was out of time, and he knew it – even as the procession of Quinn's soldiers came into the infirmary, he still had hope for a solution.

None of his efforts would matter.

One of the large garage bay doors at the face of the infirmary was opened as the soldier that led the column conferred with the head physician. Keeley rose and wandered over to where Daniel stood.

'What's going on?' she whispered in a hushed, desperate tone, such that it was audible to Daniel's ears alone.

The attending physician sat down in his chair, outstretched an arm towards the makeshift beds, and slumped forward in surrender.

The soldiers set about the room.

'Oh, my god…,' Keeley started in disbelief.

Fury swelled inside Daniel. The soldiers began to lift several of the patients from their beds, gripped by the shoulders and the feet, and carried them to the bay doors where they were discarded to the snow and slush outside. Any patients unable to resist sufficiently were added to the heap.

Daniel's hands clenched to fists at his side as Keeley put her head on his shoulder. Tears streaked her face as she quietly sobbed.

He couldn't take it.

In that moment, Daniel snapped.

With a guttural growl, he broke from Keeley and rushed the guard nearest. He tackled the soldier but landed awkwardly; Daniel landed a couple decent shots as they grappled, but he was quickly pulled off. Struck and subdued, Daniel found himself face down on the floor, pinned by a knee on his neck and several hands on his extremities.

'You can't do this!' he pleaded beneath the weight of his captors. 'These people aren't infected … they can be saved!'

'Please, don't hurt him!' Keeley cried as she raised her hands to cover her mouth.

Daniel continued to struggle under their combined weight.

'Come on, man, please, don't do this …' Daniel continued, words somehow retaining a strong and determined quality despite being thoroughly overwhelmed. 'You can't do this … they're people …'

Daniel was struck in the back around his kidneys.

The attending physician was on his feet, but his protests were silenced before they ever began. With a single look, the soldier who led the column ensured it was obvious any argument would fall on deaf ears.

'*Is that necessary*?' Keeley stammered between sobs.

The lead soldier strode over and knelt beside Daniel's face.

'Please … they just need food, medicine,' Daniel begged, undeterred. 'We can still help them …'

His last pleas were interrupted by the sound of a Beretta, its muzzle being pressed into the floor.

Under the soldier's weight, Daniel's face was fastened to the tile. His eyes fixated on the black metal finish of the 92FS.

He never said a word; just stared at Daniel as he fought for breath.

As the soldier slowly stood, he slid the muzzle a few inches across the floor, allowing its menacing scrape to reinforce its message.

Their course was set.

Their orders were absolute.

Daniel's eyes closed tightly as his spirit broke.

He stopped struggling.

As they relaxed their hold on him, Keeley rushed to Daniel. The soldier who had pressed his knee against Daniel's neck stood and intercepted her path. He set his shoulders – seemingly broader now that he stood upright – and stared at her in provocation, daring her to challenge them.

Adrenaline raged within her, and it swept aside all semblance of caution.

Keeley hauled back and slapped the soldier – a delicious, satisfying *smack* that left the imprints of her fingers embossed in the brightest of reds upon his cheek.

Now it was Keeley's turn to dare the soldier on.

His anger sweltered; his eyes widened and nostrils flared.

The two stood and locked glares with one another.

Both seethed, and neither yielded an inch.

'*Miss…*,' chided a voice behind, coming into frame as Keeley's tunnel vision dissolved and periphery returned.

As she peered around the shape of the man that barred her path, she noted the Beretta pointed squarely at Daniel's head.

Keeley shook with anger, but his aim never wavered.

As the adrenaline subsided and she could center herself again, her attention turned to the several sick and dying that were discarded outside.

She could hear their whimpers as they dared to crawl away.

None among them had the strength to stand and run.

The chill of the outside air filled the infirmary; the mocking wind lapped at her tear-stained cheeks.

As the soldiers broke from this standoff and jumped down from the concrete ledge to the heap outside, they didn't bother to close the bay doors.

This time, all would watch the cull.

Some of the soldiers secured a small perimeter as the others systematically put rounds into the heads of those piled in the snow.

* * *

Sullivan stared distantly at the ceiling from his cot.

It was late in the day and he continued to replay the events of the run, as if by the sheer force of his will alone he could transport himself back into the tenements.

What did he actually see…?

The scene was chaotic; the distance, the lighting, the stress… all factors that caused Sully to question the accuracy of his memory.

Could she really have…?

She had claimed that William was grabbed as soon as he entered the room; they were caught completely by surprise. He was snatched almost instantly. It was everything she had to close the doors behind him so they could escape.

What was William doing out with them today?

He wasn't fit for their kind of work.

It was possible Quinn needed to dig deep into his roster to staff the run; manpower was harder to come by.

Sully knew it wasn't exactly uncommon for new recruits to be called up suddenly, but typically they would be sent with a large force of veteran scavengers... at least until the rookie had a few notches on their belt.

Okay, assume this was his training day... why Isaac?

Sullivan scratched at his memory, ran through those final moments again and again.

It didn't feel right.

Isaac and Sully had been paired together. When Sully tried to keep an eye on Cox and William as they plumbed the further depths, Isaac interrupted him.

Jesus... had Isaac meant to divert his attention?

His thoughts returned to their conversation in the armory.

'Couldn't find anyone better?'

'Guess not.'

Mounting suspicions swirled.

He knew that Isaac was one of the early refugees to the Coast Guard site.

Apparently, he was one of the lucky few; even made it here with his wife.

Sully was treated well at the compound. Proficient in the wastes, he was respected amongst the civilians and officials alike. Not to say Sully didn't find Isaac useful outside the walls – he knew the Uptown and he had proven capable of taking care of himself – but somehow Isaac had garnered more 'position' with the officials, if such a thing existed beyond military rank.

Sullivan puzzled over what arrangement they may have struck for Isaac to secure and maintain such high standing with Quinn, wondered if they knew limits.

But his thoughts were unable to reach their conclusion.

The report of gunfire broke Sully's concentration; several shots split the air from deep within the compound.

He sat up and tuned his senses to the sound.

Pistol fire; 9mm mostly. Irregular intervals.

Something about the shots seemed deliberate, unhurried.

Even if a few infected had found a way into the compound, there were too many shots to take down a few stragglers. They originated from back towards the command module.

Mutiny?

Unlikely. The soldiers were loyal to Quinn. The civilians would be foolhardy to challenge their obvious superior strength.

Still, hunger can cloud judgment… and desperate people can do desperate things.

His insides knotted and something grew heavy in the pit of his stomach.

He rose from his cot and made his way outside.

* * *

A crowd had formed in the courtyard.

Quinn stood in its center, arms crossed, flanked by several uniformed men.

Each among his retinue armed for combat.

Sully found himself at the back of the line. He nervously scanned the courtyard and noted additional armed guards blocked any passage between the civilian quarters and the command building.

Sully studied Quinn's features between the shifting crowd.

He was hardened, unblinking.

A pillar of cold-forged steel.

Despite the clear show of force, it was his complete calm that was the most imposing.

Sully looked to the command nest and the shooting platform – their weapons trained at the gathering crowd.

Several of the civilians huddled together for warmth.

All eyes were upon Quinn.

'We are on the edge,' he solemnly began. 'We stand at the very precipice of extinction.'

His voice was eerily soothing. Only as loud as needed to ensure his words carried.

'We have been asked to endure the unimaginable, the impossible,' Quinn paused as if in reverence, 'and endure we will.'

'For all we know, we are all that remains; the last bastion of humanity. What we do here could determine the fate of the human race – we have no choice but to operate under those parameters.'

The crowd shifted uneasily. Several among them chattered in hushed disbelief.

Quinn paid them no heed.

'We will be tested. Our resolve will be tested. Our determination, our conviction, our willingness to do *whatever* it takes, to pay *whatever* price…,' Quinn allowed the words to hang over those gathered, '*must* be unwavering.'

'Difficult decisions have been made, and many more lay ahead. We have suffered, have been stretched thin… we all have. But in the end, our strength lies with one another, with our ability to make the hard decisions, the tough calls, for the good of us all.'

'To that end, let us be clear. Failure is not an option. Anything that makes us weaker, that exposes us to calamity will be dealt with – definitively.'

Tiny hairs stood on the back of Sullivan's neck.

The connotations were far more sinister than the winter cold.

'This compound has been – and remains – under edict of Martial Law; an unpopular decision, I know,' he continued. 'Depleted provisions have forced competing priorities, both for daily rations and for the limits of medical treatment. Our circumstances *necessitate* such realities.'

Aside from periodic emphasis, neither the tone nor tempo of Quinn's voice varied.

Its serenity was unnerving.

'Our last several salvage missions have failed; we are critical in even the most basic of supplies… miseries that are further compounded by those not wholly devoted to the cause.'

As if on cue, two soldiers appeared from around the corner of the command building. They carried with them a hooded figure, hands bound with a black zip tie in front. He was gripped under the arms, feet dragging limp through the snow behind him. His head lolled as if his neck couldn't bear its weight.

Several gasps issued from the crowd; the soldiers didn't bat an eye.

'This man was entrusted to the nests, trusted to watch over you, to detect early threats. He was charged with keeping you safe. But instead, this man lost focus. This man ignored his duty, his responsibility. Because of this man's negligence, our walls were compromised; lives were lost.'

The soldiers stopped immediately adjacent to Quinn, their quarry limp between them.

'Furthermore, as he answered for those crimes, it was discovered he stole provisions from the mess, provisions for his personal consumption...'

A deep breath.

'This cannot be condoned.'

Quinn stepped over and tore off the captive's hood.

Anders was scarcely recognizable. His jaw hung oddly; it had clearly been broken and remained unset. His right eye was swollen shut, rimmed with the brackish purple that indicated a shattered orbital bone. His lips were fat and caked with blood.

He wasn't conscious.

'*This* is the price of treachery,' Quinn began. '*This* is the price of placing individual *wants* before the *needs* of our community.'

Quinn thrust Anders to the ground, face down and unresponsive in the slush.

In unison, the crowd's breath was stolen.

Quinn surveyed the faces of those before him.

'See to him, but let it be known... any transgression that undermines the stability of this community will be met with,' Quinn turned from the gathering, but afforded himself one final passing look. Thick with derision, his gaze lingered over the broken man as he finished the thought.

'*Harshly.*'

The officials walked from the courtyard and returned to their posts, leaving the stunned congregation to flirt with the void between fury and sorrow.

'Is he fucking crazy…?' someone whispered.

'My god, does he really think we're all that's left?'

Sully didn't answer; he realized the truth underlying it all.

In here, they were alone.

* * *

She had finally cried herself to sleep.

Keeley and Isaac had retreated to the corner of their quarters, curled up in a piecemeal nest they built with some stray jackets. She slept soundly against his chest with one arm draped around her.

She refused to sleep in their cot tonight, would refuse any kindness from Quinn and the officials after the day's events.

Keeley had shared her story from the infirmary with Isaac while he sat in silence and processed the details.

'He's a monster…,' she whispered as she finally succumbed to exhaustion and slipped into slumber.

Isaac spun his wedding ring about his finger, the glint of the black titanium barely visible in the meager moonlight.

He would find no rest tonight.

Isaac's mind raced between the tenements and the infirmary.

Why was William with them today?

Isaac had recognized the man in the armory, but didn't know who he was; not exactly. Isaac only knew him to be an administrator.

Someone who could stir the pot.

But Isaac was focused on the door; he didn't see what happened.

He only heard the sounds.

But it was enough to raise suspicion.

Cox was more than capable – the likelihood of her being caught totally flatfooted was remote.

So, why send me?

Isaac wrestled with the possible reasons Quinn may have had to send him out.

As much as he tried to hide from it or convince himself otherwise, it was inevitable – there was but a single explanation.

Quinn knew Isaac could be trusted to do what was necessary.

Like the night the line broke.

Isaac couldn't force the scene from his mind, couldn't prevent the dreadful movie from playing anew.

He had been stationed in the nest.

The central terminals were overwhelmed and the crowd rushed their walls.

The speed, the ferocity…

In the deep darkness of the frigid night, it was impossible to separate the infected from those that were not. There were no clearly defined targets; only a wild mass that threatened to bring the fence down.

When the order came, Isaac didn't hesitate.

He opened fire into the crowd.

Indiscriminately, he cut them down as they pleaded for salvation.

Isaac snapped back to the present, recognized again the four walls around him and the stinging familiarity of the civilian quarters.

His eyes could no longer focus on his ring; he realized his hand shook violently.

He clenched his fist to chase away the tremor.

If Quinn sent William out to die…

Was Sullivan aware, party to it?

Isaac weighed the possibilities.

It was unlikely; he didn't think the Irishman would have the taste for murder.

What if Sullivan had caught on, fought back?

Isaac's eyes widened.

…was he sent to protect Cox?

Chapter 16

IT HAD GROWN LATE IN THE DAY. NOT YET LATE enough to worry that Jacob hadn't returned, but late enough she recognized the daylight would quickly fail.

Madison ran her fingers through her tangled auburn curls and massaged her scalp.

They had been cooped up for over two weeks in this tiny apartment.

In her restlessness, her legs ached with sympathy.

She knew she was going a bit stir crazy; she couldn't remember the last time she had been indoors for so long.

Madison was the quintessential 'small town' girl. She came from a small community in the neighbouring province of Nova Scotia, had grown up surrounded by fields and farmland. Countless trails wove between heirloom acreages, the type whose boundaries were decided generations past by handshake alone.

And she knew them all.

If time wandering these trails were measured in hours, she'd spent months amongst them. She grew up with horses and helped put their miles in, but above all there was one she cherished – an Arabian quarter horse half &

half, a rugged chestnut mare with stark white socks and an equally pronounced blaze. Her name was *Surprise,* and she was as stubborn and independent as Madison herself. When *Surprise* tired of the confines of the barn she would grow restless; if she remained well behaved, Madison would saddle her for a ride through the neighbouring trails as a reward.

Both of them were more at home in the outdoors, in the wild green spaces.

Nevertheless, a life lived to its conclusion in Kentville meant a life of predictable circumstance; a well trod path.

Wanderlust inevitably won over.

She needed to leave.

Madison was a horticulturist by trade and worked in Parks and Recreation department in the bedroom community of Quispamsis. She spent the vast majority of her time outside tending gardens or overseeing the town's greenhouses.

Plants had always proved therapeutic.

She meant to return home someday, after she'd saved enough money to buy a small farm for herself, live out her days in the quiet familiarity of country life.

Madison replaced the woolen blanket over the solitary window.

Such thoughts were foolish now.

Madison was small, but solid. Years of landscaping meant she was deceptively strong for her size, wits sharpened from often being the only woman at a given job site. Her round face was ringed with faint freckles, conspicuously absent from her cheeks. Despite the ceaseless hours worked outside, her skin stubbornly refused to tan and she was perpetually pale.

Madison's parents had separated when she was young, too young to fully understand why it left her to simultaneously find and project a sense of normalcy for herself and her younger sister. Each day as Jacob left to scavenge, she would channel that piece of her past and tidy their quarters, organize their supplies, straighten their affairs as best she could in a vain attempt to resist the crushing boredom of their present day-to-day.

She stood in stark contrast to Emily.

Emily wallowed in her malcontent. For the first several days she seldom spoke, preferring to sob silently with her arms wrapped around her knees in the corner of the cold room. Madison made every effort to comfort her and raise her spirits, but Emily was inconsolable. She was a few years older than Madison, but seemingly none the wiser for it – Emily's family was exceedingly wealthy, old money, and for several generations they had owned and operated a regional franchise of funeral homes. Aside from the exposure to the realities of death and grieving at a young age, Emily had mainly known carefree comfort throughout her life – not entirely spoiled, but certainly never wanting.

Her coddled upbringing left her ill equipped for their new realities; Madison knew it, as did Jacob. Though Madison would have been a tremendous asset to Jacob scavenging, neither could trust Emily alone. Thus, the daily burdens of her care fell to Madison.

Madison bore no ill will toward Emily, but couldn't help the resentment she felt each time Emily broke down and succumbed to self pity. Nevertheless, Madison played the dutiful friend – made sure Emily drank her water and ate her rations, kept her strength up... even went so far as to run a brush through her long, straight blonde hair whenever she thought it would help calm her nerves. Even the rare times Emily was lucid enough to carry a conversation, the banality would grate at Madison's nerves.

Maybe it was for the best she mostly kept quiet.

Madison knew that their days in the little hovel were numbered – she was partially surprised they had holed up there this long – but she knew the road and exposure would be unforgiving. Despite its shortcomings, their shelter had proved useful – without it, they surely wouldn't have survived until now. Though she and Jacob hadn't yet discussed their next moves, she had to think it likely they'd aim to leave town.

Jacob was reliable, and she could identify most types of edible plants and knew how to forage. Once the weather improved and the roads were passable, and once they had some basics assembled beyond their day-to-day needs, it seemed logical to head for the road.

Only the dead or dying would call this city home, now.

* * *

Jacob crossed his arms and assessed his surroundings.

His daily ventures were taking him further and further from their shelter. Though the days were lengthening, effective time management was still critical for their wellbeing.

He'd picked clean the buildings in their immediate vicinity, at least of all the day to day goods to keep the three of them going this far. With so many of the surrounding buildings burnt out from the fires, necessity dictated that his active radius continued to expand.

This section of the peninsula was dominated by Victorian-esque manor homes, renovated over several generations to multi-family dwellings. As the average family size shrunk over the years, many of these homes proved too large to accommodate all but the wealthiest single families – partitions were added and the manors became subdivided into rentable units. Many in the older quarters of the city retained their classic character and were deemed historically significant.

This building was no exception.

The snow must have drifted high against the cedar façade. Layers of paint fluttered and peeled from the shingles as if tatters of dead skin, hopelessly clinging to the lifeless body underneath. Several of the windows were blown out in the ground floor and he had climbed through one of them to gain access to the interior of the building. As Jacob studied the scene, the shattered glass cracked underfoot as it bit into the inlaid hardwood floors and crusty snow that had infiltrated the room.

He stood in the parlor.

It could have been in a magazine, once.

Cathedral ceilings, exposed wooden beams, richly stained wainscoting; an ornate marble mantle and fireplace dominated the room, its chimney of custom masonry and stacked fieldstone. Modern sconce light fixtures adorned the walls but weren't out of place in a seamless blend of the contemporary and the classic. Antique, solid wood furniture ringed the room.

Everything about it spoke of pomp, circumstance.

Though Jacob had plundered at least two dozen units since their exile, something about this one troubled him.

The air was sour. Though only barely discernible, the space retained the faint smell of long trapped moisture.

It was ransacked, but that was hardly uncommon – in the early days of the outbreak, looting was widespread. Desk and curio drawers were upturned, their mundane contents strewn all around. Majestic bookshelves leered over piles of jettisoned books.

The floors bore clear evidence of exposure to the elements. The stains emanated out from the window into the parlor and beyond.

Jacob studied the undersides of the overturned drawers. They appeared largely unspoiled, and yet retained the vibrancy of the natural wood grain and the subtle fragrance of the varnish.

The books were generally in good condition; he could find no evidence of their consumption by silverfish or mice.

Jacob continued to stare at the scene, silently taking the details in.

Something was amiss.

Absent were the familiar trappings of dust.

Something about the blemishes on the floor felt wrong.

The scent of mildew persisted, even with the obvious ventilation.

Those windows couldn't have been busted out for long.

Someone had been here.

Recently.

* * *

Lynn could hear raised voices.

Quinn had convened a meeting with several of the more senior staff and had commandeered the module for its purpose. She and the other administrators were relegated to a small offshoot of the central structure, and they sat together in relative silence. Lynn was the outcast, and the others held little desire to engage her in conversation.

Lynn's not-so-subtle advances had left her a pariah. She could feel their eyes upon her but she couldn't be bothered.

She peered out a grimy window at the back of the structure and again found some comfort in the sight of the storage facility. The guards were standing there, as always, though this time she felt they didn't look quite so regal.

Somehow not as comfortable as usual.

She chalked it up to the stresses of the job; it had to wear on everybody. But there was something about them that caused her anxiety to swell.

Lynn looked down to her hands and feet. Her nail polish had long since worn away and her designer boots were scuffed and showing their wear.

She was running out of time. The infirmary had proven that.

As the officials exited, Lynn caught something out of the corner of her wandering eyes – a nod, a signal to those gathered.

It was unmistakable.

From where she was standing she could see the intended direction was the communications room.

The office where that squirrely little man tinkered with the radio.

Lynn's attention piqued and her eyes no longer darted about; they fixated on the door to the comms.

One of the guardsmen pushed open the door to Andrew's chamber, and he spun about in his chair. His mouth hung agape in stunned silence as he fumbled to remove his headphones.

Lynn caught sight of her possible salvation. It never occurred to Lynn that her meal ticket maybe need not have been a soldier after all.

This one was obviously important to Quinn.

Though she would have much preferred to give herself to one of the strong, muscular soldiers, it had proved too hard to sway.

Even if they were brutes, they were trained for fighting.

For survival.

And, worst case – at least they'd know how to properly fuck.

The thought of his pathetic, clumsy hands pawing over her body, the labored wheezes as he climbed atop her turned her stomach, but she was out of time.

She couldn't be picky now.

* * *

Erik couldn't find his appetite.

He sat alone in the mess, mindlessly pushing his ration of stale rice about his plate.

He scanned the room. Only a handful of other civilians were gathered here, scattered about as if solitary islands battered by troubled seas. The mess used to be central to the community here; between shifts the civilian survivors would congregate, regale each other with tales of the day or fond memories of better times. A place where those gathered could forget about the grim realities outside, somewhere they could try to build a life worth living together.

As the compound's numbers thinned and the shifts increased, the mess became little more than a cold space where the weary were afforded a brief rest and some scant calories.

With dramatically reduced use, it was near spotless. The cleanliness bordered on the clinical, but rather than offering comfort, Erik found it cheerless and disquieting.

His fork scraped against the stainless steel plate.

He could almost count the sands of his youth as they slipped away.

Despite a genuine lack of interest, Erik shoveled another mouthful of the brown rice into his mouth. It tasted like parchment, but it didn't matter; he needed the carbohydrates. Furthermore, he never knew when his next meal would come.

Or, if his suspicions proved true about the shed, which meal would be his last.

Tomorrow would be another grueling day.

* * *

Daniel stared over the broken form of Anders.

Keeley had packed a compress with some snow and ice, did her best to keep the swelling down on his battered face. Of particular worry was the significant damage to the orbital bone. If they couldn't contain it, it was possible he would lose the use of his right eye, if not lose the eye altogether. Moreover, they still needed to set his mangled jaw.

Mercifully, Anders endured only periodic bouts of consciousness.

Unbeknownst to the increased soldier presence stationed in the infirmary, the lead surgeon had managed to smuggle a few higher-end painkillers into Daniel's pocket.

His intent was well received.

Whereas the better part of their patients had been removed from further consideration, Daniel and Keeley could be afforded some additional time and resource with this one. In a perfect situation, Daniel's preference would have been to keep Anders completely sedated – but their limited inventory meant this was impossible.

In his delusions, Anders would groan and mumble unintelligibly. It was obvious this sleep was not restful, but rather a manifestation of his broken body's desire to shut down.

Daniel watched as Keeley checked the compress and the horrible bruising beneath. Keeley's usual buoyant demeanor had given way to cold stoicism. Though her touch remained soothing as she saw to Anders' relative comfort, underneath the surface, she clearly burned.

She might be willing to listen to him.

Daniel surveyed the guards posted about the room and pretended to work out Anders' treatment regimen. Satisfied he was not being watched, he inched closer to Keeley.

'We can't stay here,' he whispered.

The sudden statement caught her off guard.

'... *what?*' Keeley exclaimed, an octave higher than intended.

Daniel masterfully deflected the surprise, casually brushed it off so as not to further attract any unwanted attention.

'We *can't* stay here,' he reiterated in a severe whisper. 'It isn't safe.'

Keeley glanced up to meet Daniel's eyes. For the first time, she noticed the ebb of bruising as it spread under his ebony skin.

Undeterred, he continued.

'We could have saved most of these people.'

He surveyed the several recently vacated cots.

Despite its newfound emptiness, the infirmary felt exponentially smaller now.

'Daniel, they had just sent a team out ...'

'*Bullshit,*' he spat. 'Whatever they were sent out for, it wasn't for our benefit.'

Keeley turned her eyes back to Anders and she leaned in to adjust the compress.

The guards continued to pay them little attention.

Daniel continued.

'I bet the butchers had their orders long before the team made it back.'

Something in that statement struck a chord in Keeley; she searched her feelings and her recollection of the events.

Keeley's head swam as she struggled to puzzle the pieces together.

'Think about it,' Daniel urged as he feigned to review the chart with Keeley. 'Isaac wasn't in any shape to be out there. The last time the scavengers were sent for medical supply they went out in force and they barely made it back. Why send such a small team this round, when our situation is even more desperate?'

Daniel felt the gaze of one of the guards burrow into him from afar. Instinctively, he moved about the cot and appeared to busy himself. Keeley sensed his motivations and they paused their conversation until they once again felt assured in their anonymity.

After a long moment, Keeley crouched down to adjust the bedding. The angle afforded her some obscurity.

'Daniel… what, *exactly,* are you saying?'

'I'm saying Quinn knew they'd come back empty handed… and most likely a man short.'

Keeley was stunned by the bluntness of the accusation.

It was no secret that the man who didn't return from that run was not a regular fixture with the salvage teams. Nor was it a secret he had the reputation of being a bit of an agitator.

Daniel's sober eyes were unblinking as they locked stares.

'I'm saying Quinn had always planned to clear the infirmary out.'

Her mind opened to the possibility that Daniel may have been on to something.

'Martial law,' Daniel began anew, incredulous and disgusted. He subtly motioned to the unconscious form sprawled before them. 'Jesus, look at this guy; for what? He took some fucking *sugar*?'

As Keeley looked over the broken wreck of Anders, she couldn't help herself from arriving at the same ominous conclusion.

Daniel was right.

Maybe now was the time for urgency.

They couldn't stay here.

Chapter 17

THE PLAN WAS HATCHED THAT NIGHT.

Keeley brought Isaac into the civilian mess near midnight. The moonlight scarcely pierced the battered windows, but it was sufficient to reveal Daniel sitting pensively at the end of the one of the long tables that occupied the center of the room. A dented steel camping mug sat in front of him, steam pouring off the boiled water.

The three sat together as Daniel outlined his version of the events in the infirmary, life in the compound from his viewpoint.

Isaac listened, quiet and careful, and tried to reconcile their experiences with his own outside the walls. He was so fixated on Daniel's words he didn't notice the tears welling in the corners of Keeley's eyes.

After they laid out their case, the three sat in silence. Daniel warmed his hands against the mug as Keeley's gaze wandered the confines of the empty room, vainly searching for escape.

Or, in the very least, distraction.

Isaac weighed the details in his mind.

As unfortunate as the business was, Anders had to expect some repercussions. His failure in the nests had left the compound exposed; an entire section of fence was compromised. Shit, people died because of him. Furthermore, he had stolen provisions; meager though they may have been, it was the principle.

Isaac felt nothing but contempt for the man.

Even with the cull in the infirmary, Isaac could appreciate its cold logic. Whether it was too early – or too late, for that matter – was arbitrary. This was a siege, a war of attrition, and the compound was being starved out of everything.

The arithmetic may have been grim, but it was straightforward.

If he was being entirely truthful, Isaac wondered what decisions he would have made in similar circumstances.

What additional lengths would he be willing to go?

It chilled him a bit to realize he may yet have the chance to find out.

In principle, the three agreed. They would leave this place by cover of nightfall; try their luck and their will in the wasteland beyond.

'There's one more thing…,' Keeley began, punctuating the heavy silence surrounding them.

Both Daniel and Isaac turned to face her, each believing the matter already settled.

'We're taking Anders with us,' she stated flatly.

Isaac scoffed at the suggestion.

'You can't be serious…'

Keeley never faltered.

'He's suffered more than anyone.'

'*And rightly so*,' Isaac shot back. 'Besides, I saw how he looked. He's banged up. He'll be slow, and *out there* slow is dead.'

'His chances are better *out there* than they are in here,' Daniel replied, mimicking the emphasis.

Keeley noticeably warmed at the support.

'Maybe that's for a fucking reason, Daniel,' Isaac retorted, sharper than he needed. 'And in any event, that's not our fucking problem. He's going to be a liability.'

Isaac pushed himself from the table and sat back in his chair.

'Look at what Quinn's done in here,' Daniel whispered hoarsely, drawing closer. 'Look at the shit we're left with.'

Daniel motioned to the emptiness surrounding them.

'This place is a tomb.'

Isaac considered the words.

'*Heavy* is the head that wears the crown.'

Isaac's inference was obvious.

Daniel couldn't believe his ears.

'How can you defend that animal, those choices?'

Isaac shook his head dismissively.

'There's a point you need to cut your losses, Daniel.'

'*Fuck* that,' Daniel replied, the surge in emotion causing his normally repressed African accent to surface. 'She's right, he's coming.'

Isaac's glare lingered, but Daniel would not be swayed. He had failed his other patients – this one was going to make it past Quinn's influence.

As Isaac turned his eyes to Keeley, she solemnly nodded her affirmation.

'He's coming.'

* * *

They had agreed to give Anders a few days to come around, reasoning they'd find little opposition to their offer of self-imposed exile. It would afford them a bit of time to gather what provisions they could, but they had no illusions – inventory control was strict. They'd be hard pressed to pull together much in the way of meaningful supplies. They'd need to sweep as they went, try to tame the wicked balance of stealth with the bleak haste of smash-and-grab scavenging.

Isaac genuinely wondered if Daniel had the stomach for the wastes. Keeley wasn't built for them, that much he knew – he had hoped to spare her from the cruelties that lie in wait outside their walls.

In the end, he realized it didn't matter.

They'd all be party to it soon enough.

Isaac knew he couldn't keep the lot of them safe for long, not on his own. He may have been a seasoned veteran now, but he was only one man… and still wounded at that.

They needed muscle.

Isaac never allowed himself to get particularly close with the other scavengers. Longevity wasn't a characteristic associated with the work, and watching your friends getting torn apart was infinitely harder than some stranger.

Hence the need for some depth in their roster.

They would need someone they could trust.

Someone proven in the wasteland.

Someone that wasn't ultimately loyal to Quinn.

Isaac puzzled through his memories, settling on but one option:

Sullivan.

* * *

The next few days Quinn kept his retinue close and the scavengers inside. The weather had warmed and there was an increase in the amount of ghoul activity. Many of the salvagers walked perimeter and kept the dead from bunching up at their walls as they waited for an opportunity to get back out.

The armory wasn't issuing guns to anyone but the officials. The civilians walked the fences with knives and various implements, hacking and stabbing wherever the infected congregated. Several of those manning the fence required frequent rests. They dotted the snow as they dozed in the courtyard.

The rations were almost entirely cut; clearing the walls was taxing work. Malnourishment and exhaustion were as real a threat as the dead outside.

Each calorie burnt was dearly felt.

Sullivan tirelessly went about the grim detail. Even as those about him succumbed to exhaustion, he pushed on.

It was uneasy work. Sully only recognized a scant few of the survivors working the walls, and one among them only added to his sense of trepidation. For the last two shifts, Sully could feel Isaac's eyes bearing down on him, scrutinizing his every movement. Isaac shadowed his every step, was seemingly around every corner.

It was unnerving.

A group of infected was pressed up against the northern fence, a few dozen yards towards the waterfront and across from where the Boardwalk used to be. They beat their fists against the chain link, their fingers clumsily grasping at it as if there were some vague compulsion to climb but their minds couldn't fully process the notion.

Their voices rasped like the sound of churning gravel.

Sully glanced about the courtyard and saw only a handful of survivors were still upright. He had been working this lot in tandem with another survivor – a woman he didn't know – but Sully judged by the forcefulness in her thrust she still had sufficient gas in the tank to handle those that remained in this grouping. He would start work on the northern section alone, and he plodded over to meet their threat.

Sullivan was about to take one down when he noticed Isaac approaching from the corner of his eye.

Frustrated, Sully turned back to the fence and rammed the business end of his crowbar into the eye socket of a ghoul as it feebly pawed at the fence.

'You've been dogging my steps,' Sullivan warned as Isaac entered earshot, 'I want it to stop.'

Only a thin veil concealed the intended threat.

Isaac froze in embarrassment his attempts had been so obvious, but had little time to dwell on it.

'Trying to catch you alone,' he conceded. 'Trust me, man; I would have loved the discretion, but time is a factor, here.'

Sullivan studied Isaac.

He *wanted* to trust him; they'd inevitably be out on a run together again. If Sully questioned his loyalties in the wasteland, they'd both be as good as dead.

Nevertheless, he had survived this long because his guard was both keen and intact – no sense abandoning that philosophy just yet.

Sullivan wiped the gore from his crowbar with a gloved hand, flicking the blood and spatter into the snow.

'I'm listening.'

Isaac stepped to the fence and buried his blade into the forehead of a ghoul, the remnants of a lanky man that yet retained a shock of red hair.

'We're leaving here,' Isaac whispered as he pulled the blade out and let the corpse slip to the ground, 'soon.'

Sullivan stood rigid and cocked his head to the side as Isaac lined up the next ghoul at the fence

'*Who* are *we*?' Sully asked.

Isaac stopped and peered over his shoulder before he took another ghoul down.

'A few of us,' Isaac replied cryptically, examining his knife to ensure he hadn't nicked the blade. 'Is that really important?'

Isaac adjusted his position to line up another infected.

Sullivan clearly didn't appreciate the secrecy; it hadn't instilled much in the way of newfound trust.

When he didn't reply, Isaac turned to face him.

Sully's stare burrowed into Isaac as the dead continued to clamour against the fences.

'I'm going to ask you a question,' Sully began.

Isaac nodded and turned back to the fences. He was about to thrust his knife into another skull when he was brusquely spun about.

'You're going to look me in the eyes when you answer me,' Sully stated flatly.

He would gauge the truth for himself.

'Fair enough,' Isaac replied and met his gaze.

'Did you know William was sent to die?'

Isaac's features contorted a bit and his eyes narrowed.

'How would I? Shit, how do you even know that's what went down?'

'I know what I fucking saw,' Sully's eyes flared. 'And so do you.'

Isaac shook his head.

'I was looking at a fucking door.'

Sully scoffed and resumed his gruesome work.

'Listen man, I'm not asking you for me,' Isaac pleaded over the noise of their labours, his tone growing noticeably more desperate. 'I'm asking you for them. I can't take them out there alone, we wouldn't last a week.'

Sully hated to admit it, but both the message and its delivery were convincing.

He paused his work and faced Isaac again.

'You need to tell me who is in on this.'

It was obvious that Isaac struggled with revealing the identities of his co-conspirators, but Sullivan had the upper hand. If Isaac wanted his help, he'd need to open up.

Isaac resigned himself to showing his hand.

'Me and Keeley, one of the nurses from the infirmary,' Isaac blurted, averting his gaze at his betrayal. 'The Nigerian guy, Daniel's his name.'

Isaac drew a deep breath.

'And Anders, buddy who had his face smashed in.'

Sullivan considered the answer.

'Quite an eclectic group,' he replied.

Isaac managed a sarcastic smile.

Sully didn't trust Isaac, not completely. He knew without question or debate what he had seen with Cox and William; moreover, Sully felt it in his bones. The fact Isaac wouldn't admit to the same gnawed at his faith. It was possible Isaac didn't have the same vantage, but surely he would have to agree the circumstantial evidence was damning enough.

Sully was convinced Cox was a coldblooded killer; wasn't sure how long he could restrain his distrust for her.

How long before he was in her sights?

Was Isaac trying to set him up?

If that was the case, Sully had to think it would take some serious work for Quinn or Cox to have convinced Isaac to commit Keeley to the deception. Sully didn't know her well, but her demeanor and the way she carried herself seemed to discount that possibility. Far more likely Isaac would have concocted a scheme unbeknownst to her rather than her being a willing player in his execution.

When it came to Anders, it's possible he'd be looking for an angle to reestablish his loyalty to Quinn, but much more likely he would want to put as many miles between him and this place as possible.

The guy from the infirmary was a wildcard, but it wasn't farfetched to think someone who worked at saving all those people only to watch them get put down like lame animals could be looking for an exit strategy.

The skepticism lingered, however.

Maybe this is how Isaac earned his station in the compound.

Lining up dissidents.

In any event, Sully was confident that if Isaac betrayed him in the wastes that he would get the better of any exchange. So long as he wasn't caught off guard, he would be the one to walk away.

He would do what he needed.

Conversely, if Isaac was good to his word… this might be the best chance any of them would get.

Sully weighed his options as he dealt with another few corpses at the fence.

Isaac waited patiently for a response, no longer noticing the dead.

Sullivan stood silent for a long while and subtly nodded his head.

'Alright pal,' he began. 'I'm in.'

They'd be brothers at arms.

…at least for now.

Chapter 18

TONIGHT WOULD BE THE NIGHT.

Sullivan allowed his eyes to wander aimlessly between the rows of buildings visible from the familiar trappings of the central nest.

They didn't know what they'd be in for, and yet Sullivan felt completely calm with their decision to leave. No performance anxiety, no friction.

It reinforced his belief that this was the right decision for them all.

The winds had picked up over the last few days, but there was no sign of precipitation over the harbour – the surf was rough, but the weather otherwise tame beneath the overcast ceiling.

The scavengers hadn't been allowed out of the compound for days. The only sorties were official and the civilians – even the experienced among them – were relegated to watch duty.

With the combined pressures of the recent increase in ghoul activity and the subsurface tension between the civilian and soldier presence, Quinn controlled the deployment of man and material with hawkish scrutiny.

Isaac and Sullivan had hoped to be sent on one final run before their escape, had hoped for an opportunity to squirrel away something useful – a weapon, some ammunition, food or water – but it wasn't to be. Even here in the nest, Sullivan had his familiar SKS propped up in the corner of the space and a handful of cartridges.

So tantalizingly close…

But Sully knew every round would be meticulously counted.

He'd never be able to bluff the armory attendants.

This time tomorrow, the lot of them would be over the walls. No shelter, scouring the wastes to scratch whatever living they could find.

Assuming they survived the night.

As Sullivan swept the streets for activity with his binoculars, Erik slept soundlessly beside him. He was slumped against the nest wall, long since succumbed to either hunger or exhaustion.

Sullivan lowered the aperture from his eyes and glanced over at his slumbering colleague.

He had wanted to share the plan with Erik, but had always managed to stop himself before he gave them away.

He wasn't sure of the reason why.

Maybe he was concerned how he would handle the news.

Maybe he was concerned the kid would actually want to come with them.

Sullivan rubbed his chin with a gloved hand, satisfying the itch of a tangled beard cultivated over several weeks.

Erik didn't have any trouble with it.

Shit, the kid can't even grow a beard yet.

Erik has a chance here; probably even better than ours.

Something gnawed at him, a dread feeling that he'd one day regret this silence between them.

Sullivan subdued the notion and raised the binoculars.

* * *

About damn time…

After several days of turning over apartments with minimal return, Jacob finally had some luck. Several canned fruits, soups and pasta sauces satisfyingly stuffed his pack.

He could almost smell the vitamins.

This was the heaviest Jacob's pack had ever felt; the distance he'd need to cart the stuff home would be well worth the effort, even on an empty stomach. Reinvigorated by the prospects of a decent meal, he slung the pack over his shoulders.

Jacob was taking stock of anything remaining in the unit when his ears perked up.

Something caught his attention, something he hadn't heard in days. Something so woefully unfamiliar it scarcely registered.

Laughter.

Not jovial, not innocent.

Raucous, braying laughter. Like a hyena.

Jacob threw himself against the wall and peered through the curtains. His eyes darted about the streets below.

He held his breath as he studied their movements, hoping to divine some semblance of their intent.

Two men in tandem strode confidently down the center of the road, each brandishing an improvised weapon. One wore elbow pads and a chest protector for ice hockey, the other seemed to wear a few layers of improperly sized leather jackets. Jacob strained his ears, but from this high vantage couldn't make out any of the words they were saying. Periodically the men would stop and motion at the various buildings lining the street; Jacob could only guess at their meaning.

Though there was nothing immediate to suggest they would have any ill intention towards him, Jacob couldn't shake the feeling it'd be in his best interests to avoid being discovered. Benevolent or not, he didn't like being at the disadvantage.

A deep pit grew in his stomach.

As the men continued their indistinct chatter, Jacob was about to turn from the scene when new movement caught the corner of his eye, further up the street from where the two men came.

A third figure kept pace behind them, albeit a little slower.

Jacob couldn't risk disturbing the curtains for fear it would draw their attention, instead opting to freeze in place and wait for the last figure to come into frame.

The straggler must have called out to the other two. They stopped in their tracks directly outside and turned about to face him.

As the third figure approached, Jacob's pulse quickened.

The man raised a black rifle and pointed it skywards, resting the barrel against his shoulder.

It was clearly semiautomatic.

His finger never came off the trigger.

Shit, shit, shit…

He had to move.

He needed options.

Jacob was on the third floor; the front door was obviously out of the question. Surely there was a back way out

– a fire escape, deck or balcony – and if not, he needed to find somewhere to hide.

Jacob removed his hatchet from the hip support and wrung his fingers about the grip, finding some reassurance in its familiar weight.

'*Come on… come on…*,' he breathed nervously to himself as he lingered at the window, anxious for the group outside to settle on their course. Though his gut screamed at him to turn tail and haul ass, his head overruled instinct – he needed to know where they were heading and if they would split up.

The three men milled about in the street below, seemingly without urgency.

Their complacency was unnerving. They seemed far too comfortable.

Perspiration beaded on Jacob's brow.

The men seemed to come to some agreement between them and they separated. The two brandishing the improvised weapons headed to a building across the street, and the man with the rifle made his way towards the entrance to the building Jacob now found himself in.

'*Fuck…*,' Jacob muttered beneath his breath.

He turned to leave the apartment, caring little for the noise as he careened for the exit. He had a fleeting opportunity and meant to seize every ounce of it. As Jacob exited the unit, he heard the wooden door splinter off its hinges, bowled over by the heavy boot of the man downstairs.

As Jacob slipped toward the back of the building, he prayed the remaining units were empty.

No time to clear them now.

Jacob struggled to hear anything from the floors beneath him; some sign the man had entered an apartment, was climbing the stairs… anything.

He could hear nothing over the dull pounding of his circulation.

Ignoring the doors with numbers awkwardly tacked to them, he hurried to the shabby exit at the end of the hallway. Believing it to be his salvation, he leaned into it.

But it wouldn't budge.

Frozen shut.

Jacob had little time to consider his options; go through, or go back.

Hanging the hatchet off his belt, he dropped his shoulder and threw himself into the door.

It didn't move.

The pain was tremendous – the impact rattled his teeth and reverberated down his spine.

Jacob still couldn't hear anything from the floors below him.

He took a few steps back and slammed his body into the door again.

The frost shattered from the gaps between the jambs and yielded a few inches. The crusty snow amassed on the fire escape and resisted further.

Little doubt anyone in the building heard it that time.

The opening wasn't wide enough for Jacob to slip through, especially with his burdened pack. He needed a few more inches. He grabbed the handle and slammed the door shut, hoping the force from another charge would give him the space he needed.

Caring nothing for the throbbing in his shoulder, Jacob plowed into the door. He threw himself with such weight that he couldn't properly compensate for his momentum on the slippery surface and spilled headlong on the sleet covered landing. He helplessly tumbled down the ice-covered stairs, vainly searching for a hand or foothold as the weighted pack shifted contemptibly as he fell.

Battered, bruised and bloodied, Jacob finally came to a rest.

He was closer to the ground; that much he knew.

As he tried to haul himself up his breath sputtered into a vicious cough. There was little doubt he had damaged his ribs, but he had no idea to what extent. His hands still retained feeling but ached with the cold and feverish attempts to grab onto something. The back of his head was wet with a warm liquid, sufficient enough for his shirt collar to cling to his skin.

Instinctively, his hand fell to his hatchet, and he was relieved to find it hadn't abandoned him.

Through sheer determination, Jacob willed himself to his feet. He scrambled down the remaining steps, doubled over the railing. He had precious little time and needed to create some distance between him and the three strangers.

He hobbled through the snow, propped himself up on the buildings in the alley and stumbled along. He could hear muffled shouts and pounding behind him.

Jacob swooned from the combined pain and effort, but doggedly kept his footing.

He should be unconscious.

Though his eyes grew heavy, they continued to feed images to his brain.

And his brain stubbornly continued to process them.

* * *

Andrew lowered the microphone and rested his weary eyes in the crook of his arm upon the desk. His other hand absently removed the headphones from his head, finally absolved from the enduring drone of static.

He felt an abnormal sense of patriotism after the events of the day.

The implications of their true predicament were very real to Andrew now; maybe for the first time since he had weaseled his way into the communications room.

As if on cue, the door to the radio room clicked open. Andrew thought nothing of it, half surprised one of the guards hadn't come to check on him earlier. Overtime was hardly something he was known for.

Maybe he had finally gained some measure of respect around here.

A moment later, Andrew still hadn't heard a word or a footfall.

Barely awake, he lazily lifted his head and turned toward the door.

And there she was.

Lynn eyed Andrew like a meal.

She stood before him, lithe and taut, hair pulled back tight into a bun.

Andrew had never seen her dressed like this before.

Andrew had never really seen *anyone* dressed like this before.

She wore a tight, black, spaghetti strapped tank top which openly exposed her collar bone and emphasized the contour of her breasts, and a tartan miniskirt with a long slit up the right thigh.

Andrew spun the chair around far too sudden to have lent himself any degree of finesse; the momentum carried him a few clumsy inches to the side.

Lynn strode confidently towards him.

Andrew shrunk and shifted in his chair, visibly unsure of what to do.

She stopped directly in front of him, dropped to her knees and set her hands to work at Andrew's belt.

* * *

Daniel nervously tapped his fingers against the tabletop, absently arranging and rearranging the cutlery in a vain attempt to pass the time.

He had finished his last shift in the infirmary and managed to stuff a few spools of gauze and some assorted medications in his pockets. It'd be morning before their absence was noticed, and by morning he'd be long gone from this terrible place.

And if not, he'd have far more serious crimes to answer for than simple theft.

Finding no relaxation elsewhere, he'd made his way to the mess well before the appointed hour. He sat and watched the erratic flow of survivors as they filtered in and out.

Despite their varied backgrounds, they all shared the same pale, long expressions. The same drawn out, spread-too-thin weariness that personified the compound.

This place was dead; it just didn't know it.

Sheets of cold but gentle rain fell against the grimy windows and an overcast sky all but shrouded the moonlight. They'd have some cover, at least, but if the temperature dipped overnight, exhaustion and the elements would prove a danger. None of them had tasted fruit or vegetable in weeks; they subsisted on water and stale rice and the occasional bit of something tinned, with the rare addition of an expired multivitamin.

Daniel hated Quinn; it was carved in his very bones. He despised the man, but as he anxiously shifted in his seat and surveyed the mothballed kitchen, he bitterly conceded there may have been some wisdom to Isaac's assessment.

So engrossed in thought, Daniel hadn't noticed he was no longer alone.

Isaac pushed open one of the faded double doors at the far end of the mess, allowing Keeley to slip into the room. She was wrapped in a stained woolen blanket, lint covered and pilled. As she entered the room he fell in behind her and the two strode over to join Daniel. The three sat without speaking. Daniel's fingers continued to tap the table and Keeley nervously scanned the empty room leering over them.

Just as the awkward silence was about to boil over, the double doors slowly opened again with the long drawl of a hinge begging for lubricant.

The Irishman sauntered over to the counters where the rations were previously lined up. He didn't perceptibly acknowledge the others; Isaac's eyes followed his movements. Sully leaned against a wall and crossed his arms over his chest. He met Isaac's gaze for a moment and subtly nodded before turning his gaze to his boots.

The irregular drum of the rain quickened.

Daniel studied Sully. They had never met, not formally at least, but Daniel knew of his reputation. He was tough – had been in the wastes as often as anyone – and he'd always made it home. His expression was serious, deadpan; a grizzled professional, the image complete with the short yet inexplicably wild beard. While Daniel trusted Isaac, Isaac was built more like a financier than a fighter.

This brick shithouse was obviously built for this kind of work.

Keeley pulled the blanket tight about her shoulders, trying to chase away the looming promise of a damp night spent running through the wasteland outside. Though fear smoldered just behind her eyes, she sat steadfast. Isaac placed his hand upon her shoulder and attempted a comforting smile.

The moments dragged on, the tense silence punctuated only by the occasional flaring of the rain and Daniel's nervous tapping. Everyone gathered seemed to hold their breath, as if the slightest sound shared between them would betray their every intention.

Finally, the double doors creaked open, just wide enough for a slender figure to slip into the room. The form shuffled towards them in silence, scarcely lit by the dim moonlight filtering through the dirty windows. The limp was uncharacteristic, but unmistakable.

Anders felt the weight of their many stares.

Isaac studied Anders as he slid out a chair to join them. His face still retained the distinct evidence of a brutal beating. The swelling may have abated over the majority of his face, but his jaw hung unevenly. He looked weathered. Gone was the fair haired and happy-go-lucky Finn; before them sat a battered man.

Isaac had to wonder about his state of mind.

One of Keeley's slender hands emerged from beneath the blanket and tucked some stray hairs behind her ear.

Daniel's incessant tapping reached a crescendo; he struck the table in finality and cleared his throat. The vast emptiness of the mess responded with a pitiful echo.

Isaac glanced at Sully, who wordlessly confirmed they were free from prying eyes and ears. He shifted his feet and stepped away from the wall.

'Alright,' Daniel began, drawing a shallow breath. 'This is it…'

Chapter 19

IT'S LATE.

He's not back yet.

Madison paced the room, unable to shake the feeling it had shrunk since that morning.

Emily blissfully slept in the corner. She slept more than she was awake.

The night was as deep and thick as any ink; a sinister dark that belied the calmness. The skies were clouded over and rain was falling in sheets. Visibility was minimal but she needed something to occupy her restless mind.

It was long past the latest Jacob had ever been out scavenging.

Madison's stomach let out a low growl as she approached the window for another peek. They still had food stashed away, but she hadn't touched any of it for fear it would prove the last Jacob would ever return with.

Careful to position herself between the flickering candles and the window, she lifted the heavy blanket and scanned the wastes below.

The rain feasted on the snow that still clung to the streets and trees, though it would be some time before the layers of it fully washed away. Pools of melt water collected in divots carved throughout the streets. Her eyes struggled to adjust from the dim candlelight to the encroaching black outside, but there was little in the way of movement.

She had noticed during the long forays of Jacob's absence that the infected tended to be more active in warmer temperatures. From her little vantage, the few visible streets may as well have been the whole world to Madison.

She ran her fingers through her hair as she considered the prospects of leading Emily into the ruined landscape beyond.

Hey dark eyes grew worried.

* * *

As they emerged from the mess, the band was greeted by the lash of cold rain. Though the air was warm, it was scarcely sufficient to prevent the rain from freezing before it fell to the earth. In the distance, the surf lapped against the pier, its frigid waters tirelessly announcing their escape.

The compound was kept dark throughout the night both to avoid attracting unwanted attention and to preserve the limited fuel; only the infirmary and the command module were lit, and only sparsely at that. Sullivan was confident they faced little risk of being caught by searchlight.

The only real risk of discovery was the perimeter patrol.

They moved quickly to the southern fences, those that ran the border of the Coast Guard site and the adjacent cruise terminals. It offered them the most cover from the rest of the compound, but took them directly against the soldier's quarters.

Sullivan took point and darted between buildings, peering around corners before signaling the rest to advance along the fences. The rainfall interfered with his senses, but it would also serve to muffle the sound of their movements.

An even trade.

As they rounded the second-to-last corner, they were making excellent time and faced no resistance. Now between the civilian and soldier quarters, they had complete defilade from the sniper's nests and the shooting platform opposite.

As Sullivan leaned around the final corner, his back went flat against the wall.

Damn it, he thought to himself and signaled the rest to hold tight.

'What's wrong?' Daniel whispered from behind.

Isaac turned to face the others and silently mouthed the word 'company.'

Keeley became very aware of the sound the rain made as it beat against the synthetic fabrics of their clothes. In her anxiety, each patter of rain was amplified to deafening proportions.

Sullivan glanced around the corner again.

A single silhouette.

He guessed a man standing in the rain and staring out into the blackness beyond.

He wasn't dressed for patrol; no visible kit.

The shadowy figure took a long drag off a cigarette, the faint orange from the flaring cherry throwing his shape into relief against the gloom. He didn't seem to be talking with anyone.

He looked alone.

Sullivan leaned back and whispered, 'I think it's just one.'

'Why can't we go over the fence here?' Daniel asked, eager to find a solution. Getting caught like this would have serious repercussions – there'd be no believable deception they could spin.

Isaac shook his head.

'We'd have no cover here,' he began. 'We'd need to change our route... and all the nests would have a line on us.'

'It's dark,' Daniel offered plaintively. 'They might not see us, let alone have time to shoot?'

'Doesn't matter, he'd hear us,' Keeley stated flatly, 'raise the alarm.'

Sullivan considered their options. If they jumped the fence where they stood, they'd have a moderate distance to cross until cover, but face a heightened risk of discovery. If they scaled the southern fence, they'd need to cross a greater distance, but only the civilian nest would have a bead on them.

'No, we stick with the plan,' Sully affirmed.

Anders didn't speak. Isaac solemnly nodded his head in agreement. Keeley shrunk against the wall and buried herself in the folds of the blanket. Daniel took a deep breath and turned his eyes skywards, welcoming the rain.

Sullivan needed to close the distance with the figure. He'd be spotted long before he ever got close from here. Sully kept his vigil around the corner while the others waited.

After several moments that seemingly stretched into eternity, the tension peaked. It became apparent they would need to force the issue.

Sullivan extended his arm and tightly gripped his fingers between the links, giving the fence a slight tug so it gently rattled. It was desperate ploy; Sully couldn't risk another look around the corner. He'd need to trust the soldier would be drawn to investigate the sound.

Mere seconds later, the dull beam of a flashlight probed the adjacent darkness. The light was weakened by obviously failing batteries, but it had sufficient strength to reflect an eerie glow in the raindrops that sped through its focus.

Isaac unsheathed his knife and offered the hilt to Sully, who only shook his head in response.

Sully once again fell flat against the wall, careful to ensure no part of him was exposed about the corner of the structure. He wouldn't be able to hear the figure's footfalls as he approached, but he strained his ears for the sound of the rain against his clothing.

The beam of the flashlight darted about, but graciously revealed only emptiness beyond.

Keeley and Anders kept a close watch beyond the fence – they didn't want to attract unwanted attention. The longer the flashlight was lit, the greater their chances of discovery… and the greater the chances a group of passing corpses would be drawn to it.

Sullivan took a final deep breath and tuned his ears around the corner, doing his best to shrug off the muddling sounds.

The flashlight continued its mad sweep. The beam seemed to narrow and intensify, leading Sullivan to the conclusion the figure had taken the bait.

Sully came off the wall a few inches and changed his stance. Speed would be the essence here.

Speed… and ferocity.

With a brutal right hand, Sullivan stunned the soldier. He fell backward into the chain link, but kept his footing; the fence cried out as it responded to the crashing weight.

The flashlight spun wildly, its beam throwing a dizzying display into the night air as it fell to the snow. On instinct, the soldier rebounded and clinched with the Irishman, but his dazed faculties were no match for the coming onslaught. As the two grappled, Sullivan won the better of the exchange, landing a few short shots until he had the soldier's back pressed against the wall. One final, savage elbow crumpled the soldier, sending his head snapping back against the brick and into the depths of unconsciousness.

Sullivan veered around the corner and was relieved to find the soldier had been alone. Isaac immediately set about turning over his pockets as Daniel grabbed the flashlight and clicked it off.

'*Let's go, let's go*,' Sullivan signaled back to the group and Keeley and Anders rushed up to join him. Anders and Sully boosted her up and she threw the tattered blanket over the razor wire, pausing a moment to carefully arrange it. A serious gash going over the fence would slow them considerably, if it didn't mean leaving someone behind altogether.

Isaac was frustrated the only items the man carried were the flashlight, some wet cigarettes and an engraved lighter. Knowing his absence would soon be noticed, the group closed ranks at the fence and set about their escape.

Daniel and Sullivan did the lifting as Keeley, Isaac and Anders were sprung from the compound. Sully then boosted Daniel to crest the fence, where he paused to offer a hand and haul the Irishman up behind them.

The blanket would be left behind, bearing final witness to their desertion.

The first leg of their journey would take them to the ruins of the cruise terminals.

Privately, it seemed poetic to Isaac he would now be crossing the very earth where he had shot – and likely killed – desperate survivors as they fled for the supposed safety of the Coast Guard site. Despite his every attempt to deny them, the memories of that night forced their way into the forefront of his mind. Pools of rainwater dotted the yard in pits of uneven snow, and in the deep gloom of the night they appeared to him as if gathering pools of blood. Isaac shook the disgraceful mirage from his head and focused on moving his feet.

There was little benefit to any feelings of remorse, now.

There was yet several dozen meters left to cross when the first shot split the air. Though muffled by the rain, it was unmistakable. It sailed overhead and buried in the snow beyond.

'They're shooting at us!?' Anders exclaimed between panting breaths, disbelieving the words even as he spoke them.

'Don't stop moving,' Sully called back – not that it needed to be said.

The group sprinted with abandon.

Several rounds thudded about them, causing bits of snow and sleet to erupt from the ground.

Daniel was the first to make the structure and dove in through the space where a great window had once been. Wet from the rain, he slid across the stained tile and scrambled on his hands and knees out of the line of fire.

Immediately he noted the vulgar stench of decomposition.

The rest fell in behind him, the chorus of sporadic gunfire chasing behind.

The group was split in two, huddled behind the stone walls on either side of the window frame. Hearts pounding, their breath was hurried and erratic, disrupting the relative tranquility.

No more shots pursued them.

'We need to keep going,' Isaac pleaded, pushing them on. 'We can't stop here.'

'Will they follow us?' Keeley asked, wiping the rain from her face.

Anders shot her a plaintive look.

'Doesn't matter, he's right,' Sully affirmed, motioning to Isaac as he moved about the building. 'Our best chance of escape is distance. We need to cover more ground.'

'There might be some stuff here we can use,' Daniel offered, clicking the flashlight on and surveying the interior.

Rows of corpses, mostly consumed, sprawled out before them. The spray of old blood and small arms fire painted the walls. Furniture was overturned and spilled about. Shards of shattered glass littered the floor throughout.

'Salvage has already picked through this place,' Isaac replied.

'After they cleared the bodies from the yard,' Keeley remembered, though she wished she couldn't. The morning after the line broke, she stood at the fences and watched as a group from the compound stacked the bodies from the yard. They burned some before the rest were dumped unceremoniously in the harbour.

'Yeah,' Isaac muttered dismissively.

'So why is this place still full of corpses?' Daniel pondered.

'We got tired of moving bodies,' Sully responded heavy-handedly.

Anders leaned out to survey the yard as another round struck the brick a few inches from his head. The shot caused the frame to splinter with an audible *crack* that echoed off the vaulted ceilings, sending a chunk of brick skittering across the floor. Anders fell backwards away from the window; a thin streak of red lit his cheek from where a splinter of the shattered rock had cut him.

'*Naida,*' he cursed aloud as his hand instinctively rose to the gash.

'Look, we'll pick through it fast, catch our breath for a minute,' Daniel reiterated. 'Surely you could have missed something.'

Neither Sullivan nor Isaac appreciated the remark. They always made a point to be thorough. The road can be challenging, neither were sure if Daniel truly appreciated the loosely organized chaos of scavenging in the wasteland. Still, they had to admit it was entirely plausible to have overlooked something valuable, especially considering they now found themselves essentially destitute and without provisions.

In any event, time was a luxury they couldn't afford.

'We don't have time to catch our breath,' Sully continued as he produced a flashlight from his jacket.

It looked vaguely familiar; Isaac grinned wryly.

'Kept that one, did you?'

'Thought it might come in handy someday,' Sully replied with a shrug as he ran the flashlight between the jagged rows of dead, 'besides, I didn't think Quinn would miss it.'

Daniel's face grew hot at the mention of Quinn's name.

Anders rubbed the blood from his cheek between his fingers.

'The shots will draw them,' Anders remarked, shivering slightly.

Sully nodded and turned his torch to the far end of the terminal, the meager light scarcely able to illuminate the distance.

'That's our path,' he began. 'Gives us cover from the compound, they won't be able to see where we head from there.'

Sullivan turned to the others as a signal it was time to get moving.

'Turn your lights off,' Isaac ordered, 'no need to paint them a target.'

'Stay close to the walls. Keep in cover and don't venture into the middle of the room,' Sullivan added.

Daniel clambered to his feet and both flashlights clicked off. The group momentarily allowed their eyes to readjust in the crushing darkness.

With only the faint natural light bleeding through the skylights and blown out windows, the rows of bodies on the floor were mere shapes; lumps and heaps haphazardly arranged, eerily reflecting the anarchy of their deaths. Most wore tatters of civilian clothing and nearly all were gnawed away, just the ghastly leftovers from some cruel feast.

The terminal was gallows silent, its depths disturbed only by the elements and their own footfalls as they stepped over the dead.

As Keeley negotiated the space between what she thought may have been a man in a suit and half a woman in the remnants of a uniform, her ears seemed to be playing tricks on her. She froze in place and held her breath, hoping to divine the source.

A gentle rustling; something stirred.

Daniel and Sullivan were ahead of her, Anders and Isaac behind. Panicked, her eyes scanned the floors for any indication of movement. In the bleak mausoleum of the terminal, nothing was apparent. Keeley backed up until she was flat against the terminal wall.

'*Hey*,' she whispered harshly, loud enough for all to hear, '*something's moving*.'

Their progression came to halt. They were spread out, staggered amongst the columns of dead. Everyone froze.

For a moment, there was nothing.

The rain continued to tap against the skylights.

The wind continued to gust through the broken windows.

Their pulses quickened.

'I don't hear anything,' Daniel whispered from somewhere ahead.

'There's nothing here,' Sullivan agreed.

'I'm telling you,' Keeley continued, the second burst of adrenaline hurrying her speech, 'something's here.'

Isaac bounded ahead a few quick steps and fell in beside Keeley.

'C'mon love,' he whispered into her ear, 'we need to go.'

'I'm *telling* you ...,' she pleaded.

'I'm not arguing,' he began with a reassuring look, 'all the more reason to move.'

Keeley nodded nervously and placed a hand on Isaac's shoulder to steady herself. Isaac turned and peered ahead, vainly attempting to penetrate the shadow.

Somewhere beyond them in the darkness Sullivan and Daniel began to trudge ahead.

Suddenly very unconfident his position at the rear, Anders picked up his pace and closed ranks with Isaac and Keeley.

Daniel's eyes were taking much longer to adjust to the darkness than he liked; he cursed himself for staring into the beam of his flashlight as long as he did. The floor was uneven with bits and pieces of people and debris throughout. More than once his footing was tested.

Tiptoeing through a graveyard, he thought to himself.

Another few unsure steps and a much more audible rasp greeted his passing.

Maybe even a minefield.

Daniel's boot came down on a creature's arm. As his heel slipped off the rancid flesh, he tumbled to the floor. He lost the grip on the flashlight on the way down and watched helplessly as it launched into the pile of dead somewhere beyond his sight.

As Daniel came up to his elbows, something coiled around his ankle.

In the absolute dark, he couldn't see what it was, but he could guess.

Fingers wrapped around his leg.

Panicked, Daniel cried out in alarm and kicked with his boots. Though unseen by the others, the scuffle was unmistakable.

Being the first to detect the movement in the terminal, Keeley was the fastest to react. She leapt ahead and grabbed Daniel by his jacket and tried to haul him away from the ghoul's fumbling grasp. Sullivan came pounding back and stomped repeatedly on the wrist and elbow of the creature, the dried bones crunching beneath the weight of each strike.

A low growl emanated from the ghoul as it tried to pull itself onto Daniel.

Daniel's boot must have connected with whatever remained of the thing's face; he thought he could feel the ghoul's nose and front teeth buckle under the weight of his heel.

Its grip remained firm as it continued to paw for him.

The commotion spawned more stirrings.

Anders scanned the jumble ahead of him and moved towards the source of the sounds. Isaac did his best to pick the same path as Keeley amongst the ruined bodies and grabbed the creature by the collar. Its stubborn grip on Daniel's ankle did not yield until Sullivan delivered a climactic blow that separated the rotten limb from its torso. With the sudden drop in resistance, Keeley and Daniel both tumbled backwards and Isaac tossed the thing aside. Anders finished it with several fierce stomps.

Daniel's adrenaline dumped and he struggled to find his breath. Still gripped by the arms of Keeley, he thanked her between gasps.

As Keeley and Daniel came to their feet, the group became sensitive to the restless dead sprinkled throughout the terminal.

'*Fuuuuuck*,' Sullivan droned as he scanned the darkness.

There was sporadic rustling all around. Against the backdrop it seemed to come from all directions. The vast majority of the corpses were merely corpses; only a few seemed reanimated, but their numbers and their position couldn't properly be assessed.

Their exit was still a fair distance away. They had barely crossed half of the floor.

'We need light,' Anders begged, 'I can't see shit.'

Keeley gripped Isaac's arm tightly.

'I dropped my flashlight,' Daniel conceded as he surveyed the darkened floors, 'help me find it …'

'Leave it,' Isaac interjected.

Sullivan clicked his flashlight on.

Any relief the group felt to not be in the bitter dark of the terminal was short lived. Several ghouls at various distances now reacted to the disturbance and reached for them. Their dead voices groaned and some began to rise.

A moment after the beam was lit, the faint report of rifle fire echoed from behind them. A burst of rotten flesh and bone exploded from the back of one of the misfortunate souls who lay unmoving on the tile.

'Fuck sakes,' Sully spat, as he turned the light away from the middle of the room.

There was no time. Sullivan led them on a wild run, alternating illuminating the floor at their feet, the monsters stirring throughout the room, and the path before them. The beam of the flashlight pierced the long darkness, but offered precious little comfort in their frantic dash.

Knowing he carried the only light, Sully tried to ensure the others behind him could match his pace and have a fair read on the obstacle-laden floor. He spent far more time lighting the path behind and checking the distance of the ghouls than the obstacles before him.

It was only a matter of time before he tripped.

He sprawled to the floor but maintained his grip on the flashlight. Those that followed behind didn't hear the fall but had little trouble in deciphering it as the beam from the flashlight now jutted into the darkness awkwardly at floor level. They took particular note to how it revealed a ghoul as it dove into the source of the beam.

The creature's pestilent jaws snapped at his flesh. Sullivan was able to frame himself against the attacker, inserting his knee between its pelvis and his torso and an arm against its clavicle. The ghoul's fingers dug at his clothing but found no hold as he struggled against it.

Anders rushed the corpse and recklessly tackled it headlong, hitting it flush with his shoulder and brutally spilling it sideways. Still wet from the rain outside, Anders slid a short distance before he thudded against an overturned set of bunk beds.

Keeley gave her hand to help Sullivan regain his footing as Isaac stood guard over them. As the tackled ghoul began to rise, Daniel sped past them and viciously struck the thing in the head with such savagery its neck snapped. Its head swiveled violently as the ghoul crumpled and lay still.

Anders was still trying to come to his hands and knees when he felt something gripping him. Unable to shake the fog from his senses, he resigned himself to his fate.

As he was lifted off the floor he scarcely recognized Daniel's beaming smile.

'You're a *madman*!' the Nigerian belted with a buoyant laugh, slapping him on the shoulder.

Several shapes yet shuffled towards them, a mournful chorus of hunger and torment.

With the group now together and organized anew, they hurried for the exit.

Thus began the mad dash into the night.

Chapter 20

THE PAIN WAS TREMENDOUS.

Jacob sat upright and held a makeshift compress against the back of his head. For fear of being concussed, he struggled against his body's ache for sleep.

The back of his shirt bore a significant stain and his collar was soaked through from the wound; it clung uncomfortably against his skin. Even if he couldn't see the gash, he had little doubt it needed to be stitched to properly close. With nothing but food in his pack, he resorted to fashioning a compress out of the cleanest fabric he could find in this apartment, which happened to be some patterned chocolate brown curtains that hung preposterously long for the windows they covered.

His path was erratic as he ran from his earlier encounter, but he picked his footfalls as best he could so as not to leave a track for any pursuers. Once the rain started to fall, he believed his course would have been sufficiently muddled that he could afford himself some rest. Regrettably, by then the twilight had deepened to the point that he had no choice but to find somewhere to hole up for the night.

He was blessed to have avoided detection. As his head swam from the pain of the compress, he realized now he likely wouldn't have had the strength to fight.

It was all a blur.

He would attempt to return to Madison and Emily in the morning; now came the enormous task of resisting the urge to succumb to exhaustion.

Jacob propped himself up on a stained forest green couch with some ratty throw pillows, struggling to stay awake. He initially tried to occupy his time by canvassing the apartment, but resigned himself to the sofa when his knees began to weaken. In any event, whoever had been here before him had tried to hold out until they exhausted their supplies – the food was all gone, there were no pills or bandages, the only potential weapon some cutlery and assorted kitchen implements. The bathroom had nothing but a bucket mostly full of waste.

Thinking he could in the very least change out of his bloodstained clothing, he rummaged through the drawers and closets, but to no avail.

Nothing here would fit his frame.

So he sat in an apartment that reeked of piss, in clothing half soaked with his own blood, body throbbing with cold and pain, unable to sleep it all away.

Knowing his battered body would need to refuel, he afforded himself a bottle of water and some tinned tuna.

He would save the canned fruit for the reunion.

With little to occupy his time, Jacob picked through the bookshelves for something to read. The combination of absent moonlight and the terrible pain in his head made reading a daunting task.

In any event, the books here were all shit.

Decent collection of movies, though.

Not that it mattered.

Jacob needed to find something to stave off the terrible quiet until dawn.

It was the quiet times that the ghosts could infiltrate your thoughts, those memories best left forgotten.

A cruel parade of faces danced before his eyes.

Faces from the world before.

The terminal.

The barracks.

All dead.

Jacob's eyelids grew heavy. He shut them momentarily and he drew a long, sullen breath.

Unable to chase them away, he started recounting their names.

Most fell easily from his lips, but there was one he still struggled to pronounce:

Samantha.

Jacob worked as a mail carrier pre-outbreak, and Samantha was a teacher's assistant in one of the neighbourhoods where Jacob delivered. When news of the quarantine broke over the radio, he rushed to get her from the school.

Jacob chuckled to himself, thinking how absurd it must have looked rolling into the shelter in his postal uniform with his fiancée and a load of people in the back of a mail truck.

At least it didn't go to waste; cube vans were a valuable commodity.

His days carrying mail meant he knew the streets better than most. He knew the demographic each area served and a significant number of the little hard-to-find shops sprinkled throughout the various subdivisions.

He used to think it a boring job, delivering bills and flyers for shit people didn't need.

He'd trade anything for that carefree monotony again.

He pressed firmly on the compress, driving it into his wound.

The shock caused his vision to swoon and redden.

Anything to chase those ghosts away.

* * *

They wound through the city streets, their passing announced only by the erratic thrashings of a single faint beam of flashlight. Their path was arbitrary – a few blocks south, a few blocks east, alternating at irregular intervals.

The temperature was falling as the night deepened around them. The heavy drops of rain were being replaced by sleet and ice pellets as it transitioned into flurries.

Daniel kept pace with Sullivan, but he grew worried.

Sweat clung to their bodies beneath their clothes, and the stinging rain lashed and coated their exposed skin. They were running a very real risk of hypothermia, and when coupled with the general state of exhaustion and malnourishment, he knew inevitably their strength would give out.

They'd be running on fumes soon.

As the group approached another intersection, they fell in and huddled alongside a corner lot building. Sully leaned out, shielded his eyes from the rain to peer ahead. In the sleet and darkness, visibility was shit – but surely that would impair the sight of the infected, as well.

Isaac scanned the faces of their cohort; exhaustion was obvious on all of them. Their breath was ragged and laboured. He knew Keeley would be too tough to be the first to ask for rest, and Daniel was focused on leaving that sinister place far behind. Neither would suggest they stop.

His thoughts turned to Anders' recent, but as yet incomplete, recovery.

Isaac could tell that Sully wanted them to push on. He understood, and had to agree to a point – the more ground they covered, the less likely they would be followed. Any pursuit would need to consider every building along their chaotic path as a possible hiding place. But in their weakened state, the group could only handle one or two ghouls at a time – if they were swarmed, they wouldn't have the strength to fend them off.

Just a little further...

Isaac hadn't counted how many blocks they had put behind them, but even through the blighted and burnt out landscape he had a sense they were making good time. He and Keeley had always lived along the outskirts of the Uptown area; they were somewhere deep in the core of it now. They'd probably walked these streets a hundred times, but none of the buildings seemed familiar.

Memories of a life, long since faded away.

With Sully's signal, the group emerged and slipped through another intersection.

Their path was blessed and they encountered little in the way of resistance. The occasional ghoul was spotted but easily evaded; one of the benefits of only having a general direction in mind in which to flee.

Maybe the shots from the compound had cleared a bit of a path for them, after all.

Nevertheless, their luck could run out. Believing the distance they'd put between themselves and the enclave to be sufficient, Sully began turning his attention to the buildings themselves. He used the flashlight to illuminate the doors and windows of the structures they passed until one caught his eye.

It was a squat building, cedar shingled and set back from the road a little ways. In conjunction with the recent rain, its position relative to the neighbouring structures meant its front door and windows weren't entirely iced over and looked reasonably accessible. It had a quaint little wrought iron fence which framed the front walkway and barely poked through the snow.

It almost appeared welcoming.

With weariness setting in, the group approached the entrance.

Sully ran the lone flashlight over the structure but saw no sign of movement. He clicked the flashlight off.

He gripped Isaac by the arm as he passed.

'Get everyone upstairs,' he began and scanned the window again. 'We'll settle in here for the night.'

* * *

Quinn was awoken by a knock at his chamber door.

Actually, 'awoken' was a bit of a misstatement; Quinn seldom slept of late.

Staring at the ceiling from his cot, Quinn had heard the muffled gunfire from the compound. He had divined its purpose long before his sentries brought the news of it.

He listened to the hurried speech of his underling as he recounted the defection.

Quinn stared into the soldier, watched intently at how his mouth formed the words and syllables of the report.

It all drowned out under the subtle drone of Quinn's cold arithmetic.

He wasn't pleased his snipers had opened fire into the night. Ammunition was a precious commodity; a few errant rounds could easily conjure a stack of infected at their doorstep.

Quinn was – at least partially – grateful for having fewer mouths to feed. But the news he had lost two trained infirmary staff, coupled with two experienced scavengers, was not received so kindly.

Nor was a physical attack on one of his soldiers something he could abide.

Despite the ancillary benefit of a lesser strain on the compound's inventory, Quinn needed to weigh the implications of its reflection upon his command. His hold over the compound was tenuous. If he allowed their desertion, he could be perceived as weak – seen to be losing control of the situation.

And perception is reality.

Though he had stopped listening to the report several moments past, Quinn remained silent until his sentry finished the briefing.

Quinn smiled and thanked the soldier.

'Advise the nests they are to hold fire; I want them to spot only. Double the presence at the fences overnight and find another patrol to walk the perimeter.'

The soldier saluted; Quinn offered a solemn nod in response.

As the young man turned to leave, Quinn gestured to him.

'And soldier,' he began.

The sentry froze midstride and spun on his heels to face his commander.

'Please wake the corporal; send her in.'

* * *

Jacob's head swam.

His eyelids were heavy as they fluttered open.

His mouth was parched and tasted of stale cotton.

The room was wholly unfamiliar.

Christ, how long was I out?

As Jacob tried to straighten his posture and sit up, a splitting pain seethed at the back of his head. He swooned from the effort and slumped back into the couch. Instinctively, his hand probed the source of the pain and fumbled over the wound still struggling to properly scab over.

A faint ringing persisted in his ears, something signaling alarm.

Slowly, Jacob sat forward and tried to steady himself.

A dull ache emanated behind his eyes.

He fought vainly to peel back the layers of fog in his head.

The room was immersed in a watchful darkness; rain gently rapped against the roof above him. It remained pitch black outside – he hadn't slept the night away.

Jacob cursed himself for falling asleep, but simultaneously counted his blessings.

There could have been any number of reasons for not waking.

Images from the day slowly began to filter into his mind, though it seemed a confusing movie. He remembered fleeing the strangers and his efforts to evade pursuit. He saw the faces of Emily and Madison and their little hermitage.

As he recalled his earlier successes foraging, a thin grin pierced the pain.

Recognizing he remained feverishly thirsty, Jacob slowly attempted to sit up anew and reached for the straps of his pack. He loosened the drawstrings on the main compartment and fished inside for water.

Something caught his ear.

Something beneath him.

The crack of a door breaking free from the shackles of frost that bound it.

Footsteps.

Panicked, Jacob reached for his hatchet. His fingers groped the plastic loops on the hip supports of his pack, but found them empty.

Jacob turned his head sharply and his vision faded from the effort. It returned slowly as his hands pawed at the couch cushions, searching for a familiar handle.

The footsteps below were muddled; he could make no sense of their number or intent. Their trespass echoed all around him.

Realizing how valuable the treasures in his pack would be, he nearly toppled over as he forced himself to his feet.

Jacob fell sideways back into the couch and shifted the furniture several inches on the floor before he managed to catch himself between the arm rest and the coffee table.

His vision darkened and his stomach knotted.

Refusing to succumb to unconsciousness, Jacob clenched his teeth and fought to set his legs beneath him as the apartment door swung open.

Chapter 21

THE ROOM SPUN IN A HAZE OF PAIN AND shadow.

Goddammit..., Jacob cursed himself.

How could I forget to lock the fucking door?

Jacob's heart raced as several shapes filtered into the room. The palpitations caused the back of his head to throb and stung the space deep behind his eyes as they struggled to adjust in the darkness.

Daniel was the first to recognize they weren't alone; his steps stuttered and he squared himself to the figure opposite. He raised his hands, palms outstretched before him.

'*Jesus Christ,*' he stammered, flatfooted and unsure how to react. Daniel stood rigid with Keeley right behind; she was quickly supplanted by Isaac who brandished his knife menacingly.

Jacob's knees felt weak and his vision clouded.

In the darkness, it was difficult to pick out the source of the voice; Daniel's ebony skin cast him as little more than a silhouette against the gloom.

Jacob's head swiveled as his brain fought to process the images before him. Instinctively, he backed up, stumbling slightly as he bumped into the coffee table.

'*Woah, pal,*' Daniel continued, voice finding a more level tone. 'Take it easy, man; we didn't know this was occupied.'

As Sullivan entered the room he picked up on Isaac's positioning. The two circled out from the entrance on either side of the couch. They slowly flanked the silent stranger, angling themselves out as a fifth person froze in the doorway. Sullivan turned the flashlight over in his hands but didn't light it.

Jacob immediately understood the significance of their movements. If they were to come at him, he would need to divide his attentions. The assailants meant to establish a wide angle, something he couldn't contain.

Their movements were practiced, deliberate.

They'd done this before; quick and wordless, it was automatic for them.

The problem he now faced was whether they had developed that comfort on ghouls – or people.

Jacob frantically scanned the floor and couch cushions for his hatchet.

Aside from the glint of the knife, the intruders looked unarmed.

Nevertheless, he didn't like his odds.

Isaac and Sullivan continued to circle out.

'You better start fucking talking,' Isaac stated grimly.

Jacob inched away from the blade as he noticed the other shape was almost beside him.

The noose was tightening.

Recognizing that Isaac and Sully were fully focused on the task at hand, Daniel continued.

'Look man, we don't want any trouble…'

Jacob remained silent and used his leg to push the coffee table away, employing the newfound space to adjust his own positioning in the room.

'Nobody needs to get hurt here.'

Daniel's voice was calm, steady.

Sullivan cracked his knuckles audibly and Anders stepped in to stand beside Daniel and in front of Keeley.

Jacob's eyes bounced from figure to figure, fighting hard to process the scene. He held his breath as he struggled for words.

'You look a bit busted up,' Sullivan snipped.

The number of voices in the dark was dizzying.

'Are… are you hurt?'

Jacob froze.

He hadn't expected a woman's voice.

Daniel noted the slight change in the stranger's energy.

'Please, maybe we can help,' Keeley started, tone pleading. 'Are you alright?'

Isaac glared sideways at Keeley before refocusing on their quarry.

Jacob considered his options.

Her delivery was convincing, but the two kept circling.

Jacob shot another searching glance and caught sight of the hatchet. It must have slipped off the cushions as he slept and lay partially concealed under the couch.

If he could just get to it, his chances would improve dramatically.

Jacob's hands rose slightly to show he was unarmed.

Anders watched nervously as the dance continued.

Daniel was becoming frustrated the stranger remained mute; his continued silence did little to defuse the tension.

Jacob considered his adversaries. Their clothes looked nothing like the trio he had encountered earlier in the day. Plain clothed and simple, they looked like refugees.

Nevertheless, he was well aware that desperate people are capable of terrible things.

He was prepared to fight for his life.

His pulse quickened and his head swooned; Jacob stumbled slightly but caught himself.

The two men circling him didn't use his slip as their opportunity to pounce, but neither did they relinquish their angle.

'Look, I was studying to be an RN – if you're hurt, I might be able to help,' Daniel began. 'We were looking for a place for the night, get off the streets.'

It was believable, but it was difficult to trust.

Jacob finally broke his silence. His tone and words were pointed.

'I have food, and some water. I can give you *a bit*,' he paused for emphasis, 'but you need to leave.'

Daniel's heart sank. He vainly searched for the words to prolong their dialogue, hoping to negotiate.

'You're not in a position to make that kind of statement,' Isaac chided.

Now it was Keeley who shot Isaac a glare. The escalation was poorly timed.

'What, are you going to steal it from me?' Jacob shot back, squaring his shoulders. 'Going to kill me for a meal?'

Jacob's glare burrowed into Isaac, who returned it evenly.

'People die for less.'

The gravity of the statement wasn't lost on Sully.

'No one is fucking dying,' Anders interjected.

Jacob's eyes burned with an equal threat for Isaac.

Keeley scrambled to salvage the situation. She stepped from behind Anders and took center stage.

'Isaac, *Christ*,' she started, her disdain for the posturing plainly evident as she turned her eyes to the stranger. 'Listen, we're good people. We can help each other here.'

Jacob listened and the words did ring true – he didn't doubt her sincerity. She sounded kind, if kindness yet existed.

Isaac's stance eased and the tip of his blade lowered.

The severity in the room seemed to lighten.

Daniel stepped ahead to join Keeley.

'Look, I'm a nurse – if you're hurt, tell me what happened, we'll go from there.'

Everyone's eyes had grown more accustomed to the darkness and each could see their features softened. Though Jacob wanted no further quarrel, he'd still feel much more comfortable with his axe in easy reach.

Boldly, Jacob advanced and sat on the couch. Daniel took it as a sign of confidence, an indication the stranger trusted them and would pursue no further confrontation. Unbeknownst to the rest, Jacob had chosen his seat carefully, sitting with the hatchet imperceptibly at his feet. He used the heel of his boot to obscure the small portion of the handle that poked out from the sofa.

Daniel and Keeley could immediately see the wound at the base of his skull and the dark stain on his collar. They shared the realization that wounded animals fear being cornered.

'I fell,' Jacob explained. 'Got pretty banged up.'

'Yes, you did,' Daniel replied as he assessed the damage, 'that must have been one hell of a fall.'

Isaac sheathed his knife and Sully found somewhere to plunk down.

'Let me see the flashlight,' Daniel called over to Sully, who passed it over.

Daniel clicked the beam on. Jacob's eyes blurred with the sudden burst of light, faint as it was; he closed his eyes for a long moment before reopening them in a thin squint. His shadow was cast long and large against the floor.

'I don't think there's a crack in the skull; looks like it was just a nasty impact cut.'

Jacob winced as Daniel's fingers probed around the wound.

'You'll need that stitched; otherwise you'll keep aggravating it and risk infection. Keeley, can you look around, find me a sewing kit or something?'

Keeley nodded and immediately set to work canvassing drawers and cabinets with Anders following right behind. She smiled to herself; Anders always had a reputation for being helpful. She was glad his ordeal at the compound hadn't robbed him of that quality.

'Do you feel dizzy?' Daniel continued.

Jacob groaned but offered no further complaint as Daniel continued to work around the cut.

'Comes and goes.'

'How's your vision, hearing?'

'Not great,' Jacob admitted. 'Sudden movements make it worse.'

Daniel nodded, 'Bad headache, obviously.'

Jacob chuckled as Daniel dug through his jacket pockets and pulled out a bit of gauze and some assorted pills.

Isaac watched Daniel rifle through what little supplies they had managed to pull together with some contempt. He cared little for any outside their band, and would not condone anything to jeopardize Keeley's safety – even if that made him abrasive, it was a trade he would make every time. Nevertheless, patching the stranger up was the decent thing to do, and what she would have wanted.

Daniel leaned over the couch and checked Jacob's pupils for their response to the direct light.

'You're probably concussed.'

Jacob acknowledged the statement with a slow nod.

Anders managed to come up with a golden tin stacked with mismatched buttons, a few needles and some shabby thread.

Daniel frowned as he looked over the makeshift sutures.

Hardly surgical grade.

'The wound doesn't look dirty, but we should clean it all the same,' Daniel turned the sewing kit over in his hands. 'Ideally we'd have something to sterilize this with, too.'

Jacob reached into his pocket and produced the engraved lighter, held it over his shoulder for Daniel without turning to face him.

'I have some water,' he mentioned, motioning to the pack on the floor. Keeley knelt down, tucking her dark hair behind her ears. As she rummaged through the pack, the unmistakable clink of several tinned items echoed faintly through the fabric. It had been days since any of them had enjoyed a proper meal; she couldn't help the ensuing growl from her stomach.

The others heard it, too.

In the newfound light, Jacob could see their pallor. Clearly they were exhausted, and clearly they had been hungry for several days.

Jacob could almost hear them salivating.

'Please,' he offered. 'Take something to eat.'

Despite the invitation, Keeley refused the kindness, in no small part due to Isaac's indiscretion.

'No,' she replied dismissively, defying her hunger. 'This is yours.'

Keeley pulled a bottle of water out and broke the seal. She poured a bit onto a strip of gauze and gently scrubbed at the wound, careful so as not to dislodge the scabbing.

Daniel removed a needle and some thread from the kit and flicked the lighter. The flame licked and blackened the tiny metal. As he leaned in to start the stitching, Anders interrupted.

'Please,' he began, 'show me how to do this.'

The simple request caught everyone off guard.

Isaac and Sullivan exchanged glances from across the room.

'You alright with … that?' Daniel asked, unsure how to delicately phrase the request.

Jacob paused in consideration. Though more than a bit uncomfortable with his wound becoming the center of attention, this could be a rare opportunity for someone to learn a valuable skill.

'Have at it,' he snickered.

Isaac stood with his arms crossed and surveyed the scene.

Daniel passed the flashlight to Anders before turning back to his patient.

'This is going to hurt.'

* * *

Daniel swatted Jacob encouragingly on the shoulder.

Jacob loosened his fist and stretched his fingers as he opened his eyes, each firmly clenched to endure the digging needle as the wound was sewn closed.

'Well done,' Daniel's tone mirrored the smile on his face. 'All set. But take it easy, don't go ripping my masterpiece.'

Jacob ran his fingers along the needlework. Though the skin about the wound was pulled taut and felt itchy, the relief was near immediate. As he turned to face Daniel to offer his thanks, he was greeted by an open hand holding two nondescript white pills.

'Wish we had something better for you,' Daniel lamented. 'This is all we've got.'

Touched by the stranger's sincerity, Jacob was rendered speechless.

Daniel poured some water over his hands and wiped them clean as Anders lingered over the stitch work with the flashlight, trying to commit the finer details to memory. Keeley crossed the floor to stand with Isaac, who put his arms around her as she placed her head upon his shoulder. Sully sat quietly in the darkness, resting his chin in his hand, and listened to the last traces of the rain as it beat against the roof above them.

As Jacob processed their movements, he arrived at an inescapable conclusion.

Maybe they were just simple people.

Isaac interrupted the quiet reflection, voice thick with interrogation.

'What are you doing out here, alone?'

Keeley raised her head and woefully turned her eyes to Isaac, as if pleading with him to not start this line of questioning.

'Doesn't look like this is home,' Sully agreed as he straightened in his seat, lowering his hand to the arm rest.

Jacob turned his eyes and scratched at his scalp.

'It's not,' he replied flatly.

'Is there such a thing?' Anders asked sarcastically.

'... are you alone?' Daniel asked as he found a seat on the couch next to Jacob.

Jacob glanced sideways at the tall African and leaned forward.

There'd be no going back, now.

'No. There's a few of us,' he started before drawing a solemn breath, 'the leftovers.'

Keeley shivered in Isaac's arms as she considered the connotations.

'How many?' Isaac immediately shot.

Jacob leaned back in his seat.

'Three, myself included.'

'Where?' Sully broke in, suddenly very engaged in the conversation.

'Why aren't you with them?' Keeley added inquisitively.

Jacob proceeded to relay the story of the day's events, of his encounter with the armed trio and his graceless escape, the two women he felt responsible for and his need to return to them. Each listened intently and allowed him to complete the retelling without interruption.

'So,' he added in climax. 'I didn't know who you were, or what your intentions might be.'

Keeley knew the wasteland would inevitably be rife with the parasites of mankind, but she had allowed herself to hope their adopted hometown would be more or less immune.

This was another element they now needed to contend with.

Believing he had earned the painkillers with the narrative, Jacob swallowed the pills with a swig of water. The thin plastic crackled in his hands as he lowered it from his lips.

Daniel nodded his accord slowly, now fully appreciating their earlier standoff.

He extended a hand to the stranger.

'I'm Daniel.'

'Jacob,' Jacob shook his hand and scanned the assembly as they became acquainted.

Remembering the low growl of Keeley's stomach, Jacob reached for his pack and produced several assorted tins and a couple bottles of water from its depths. He motioned to the coffee table and Sully pushed it over with his boot.

Jacob pulled the coverings from off the tins and placed them individually on the table. The faint beam of flashlight danced excitedly over the spoils – it had been weeks since any of the compound survivors had seen a spread like this.

Jacob bid them welcome.

All congregated about the meager feast; Isaac was the last to join.

He afforded them several moments' unbroken peace, savoured their expressions as they laughed and ate. Their gaunt faces, severe with hunger, seemed to brighten at the mere sight of food.

It reminded him of better times.

When the meal was near completion, Jacob renewed their conversation.

'So… what about you lot? What's your story?'

The group exchanged glances, visibly unsure how to properly respond.

Anders slowly chewed his last mouthful but made no eye contact with the rest.

Jacob could feel the change in the density of the air; an uncomfortable energy swirled thick about them.

'*Ours* is a long story,' Daniel broke the silence as he replaced a tin of flaked ham on the coffee table, 'and perhaps for another time.'

Jacob firmly believed his offerings had bought him the right to their story in turn, and cared little for the bitter taste of secrecy. In any event, he would allow it to pass – for the time being.

They sat together, each searching for their own personal reprieve in the restless peace. Keeley curled into Isaac's arms; Sully dozed away in his armchair. Anders and Daniel each sat and silently tried to come to terms with the events of their recent past.

Jacob also allowed himself time to rest and recharge, lowering his guard and sinking slightly into the cushions of the stained couch.

As the night waned, daylight began to creep in through the windows and the rain seemed to relent, yielding to the faint promise of a new dawn.

Isaac continued to eye Jacob with suspicion.

'You seem pretty comfortable,' Isaac leveled at last.

Sully lazily opened an eye and fixed it on Jacob.

'Wounded and resting in a room of strangers,' Isaac continued.

Jacob paused for a moment before his lips curled into a knowing grin. He reached down and produced his hatchet from beneath the couch, laid it across his lap in as non-threatening a manner as possible.

'Insurance,' he coolly replied.

Daniel's eyes widened and Isaac's face made little attempt to conceal his utter lack of amusement. Fully appreciating the deception, Sully roared with approving laughter and rose from his seat.

'I like this guy.'

Chapter 22

MADISON'S EYES BURNED WITH EXHAUSTION.

Jacob hadn't made it back last night.

She recoiled from the window, retreated from the first rays of the morning sun and replaced the tattered blanket covering.

She had considered this scenario before, though she never allowed herself to believe it would play out.

Jacob would be there, with them.

He would always make it back.

Her cheeks grew sunken and etched with worry.

Madison's sorrowful gaze washed over their meager provisions. They gleamed in defiant irony against the backdrop, but the time she spent busying herself with their arrangement now felt wasted.

Her sleep deprived thoughts mulled over their immediate future.

She ran her fingers through her tangled curls and scratched at her scalp, vainly seeking to delay the inevitable recognition of her true circumstance.

Madison held no illusions over the likely fate of Jacob.

Nor did she have any illusions over her chances with Emily.

She wasn't ready for this.

Still, Madison couldn't leave her.

The thought of abandonment was terrifying.

Madison's eyes lingered over Emily, huddled limp in the corner amidst a patchwork nest of self pity and soiled blankets. Swollen, wide eyed and tear stained, she wept soundlessly throughout the night's bitter watch.

She didn't feel the implications any less clearly than Madison.

* * *

The reveille sounded early that morning.

Erik surveyed the courtyard as he and a small contingent were led to the gates. A couple carried packs, but otherwise they travelled light.

He had awoken in the night to the sounds of rifle fire. Though he and the other civilians forming the column had been briefed on their purpose, as he surveyed those gathered with him he realized a few of the details may have been conveniently left out.

A few of the usual, veteran players were conspicuously absent.

The briefing was simple – a handful of survivors had deserted last night.

They had assaulted a soldier, stolen supplies.

Erik and the rest were told their mission was to retrieve the defectors. Ensure their continued safety by bringing them and the stolen provisions home.

The wastes weren't fit for a small group on their own.

As Erik approached the fences he noted the shooting last night had attracted some attention. A handful of soldiers cleared bodies from the wall, casually carrying the corpses away for disposal. With the rains, the well trodden snows of the courtyard were mired in thick, slurping slush.

This would be an uncomfortable march.

As the column passed, he watched as two of the soldiers heaved the remnants of a shattered woman onto a cart. Half of her skull was missing; she was only recognizable as a woman by the length of her hair and the clothes that yet clung to her.

Erik flexed his fingers about the grip of the baseball bat and slung it over his shoulders. He turned his eyes skyward and felt the warm breeze as it kissed the exposed skin on his face and neck.

He held no illusions over their true purpose today.

He knew those that fled wouldn't come back willingly.

One of the grim faced soldiers pulled back the bolt of his C7, allowing it to ferociously chamber a round as it snapped back.

The low moan of the breeze lamented their passing.

Erik was terrified at the prospects, but refusing the post would prove no better an alternative. He didn't want to kill anyone, but being alone in the city was a death sentence. Scanning the faces of the other civilians pressed into service today, he knew they felt it, too.

The morning sun crept ominously between the jagged buildings ahead.

* * *

Lynn sat on their cot and absently flipped through the pages of a *Better Homes* magazine for the hundredth time. Though she could recite most every word from the articles and knew even the minutest detail in every picture, it helped occupy her mind – even if this particular edition was from the late nineties.

It reminded her of better days.

Opposite her in the room, Andrew hunched over his desk and continued to drone his script over the radio. Despite his many attempts to prove his value to Lynn and illustrate his inflated importance, Lynn could only think of how the oversized headphones looked ridiculous on his head; they gave her the impression his ears were several sizes too large. She simply rolled her eyes at his obvious attempts to impress her.

She was ashamed he was the best she could manage, but at least it ensured she enjoyed some semblance of the 'kept' status she was accustomed to. Lynn had plied her trade well enough that Andrew pleaded with the officials to let her bunk with him in the communications module – it helped her feel safe, and left him feeling important.

All she had to endure was his clumsy hands.

She rationalized it as a kind of service she provided the compound.

Though Lynn's isolation deepened, the glares she received from the officials and other administrators alike were well worth it. She could afford to be transparent to everyone else, so long as her target was oblivious.

Willingly or not.

Quinn didn't care. In Andrew's attempts to cultivate her approval, he worked the radio twice as hard.

It was a win-win for everyone.

* * *

For a long while, Madison stared at the wall and weighed their limited options.

Stay a while longer, or cut and run.

She'd never have forgiven herself if she led Emily into the wasteland, only to have Jacob miraculously return to find an empty apartment.

Though she'd likely never have known the truth in this, the possibility alone unnerved her.

When she could finally sit no more, Madison crawled to her feet and paced the tiny confines of the room.

Emily scarcely acknowledged Madison's movements.

Exasperated, she returned to the window and lifted the blanket covering to reveal the world outside.

Madison's eyes widened.

A small group filtered its way through the streets.

Instinctively, she ducked away from the window, cursing her carelessness. She licked her lips and slowly shifted the covering to peer outside.

She counted a total of six figures, seemingly unarmed.

A familiar figure walked in the center, flanked closely by the rest.

Jacob!

She studied their movements.

She didn't recognize the others, but something in Jacob's stride wasn't right.

His steps fell uneven; he swayed as he walked. It was almost as if he needed to be supported to remain upright.

He looked hurt, roughed up.

Though he didn't appear captive – he wasn't bound or being prodded along – there was nothing that would lead her to dismiss that possibility.

Madison's thoughts went into overdrive.

They had rehearsed this scenario together a hundred times. In the deep and desperate hours of the night, they discussed the possibility of unwelcome guests.

Bandits and thieves were one thing, but there were far worse fates.

Madison leapt from the window and retrieved two long, menacing kitchen knives. The blades were dull and far flimsier than they appeared, but they were the best available.

Emily froze as she began to understand the cause for Madison's haste.

Madison crossed the room and knelt at Emily's side, holding out the hilts to her.

'Emily, sweetie,' Madison cooed as calmly as she could muster.

Emily shook her head and recoiled.

'Emily, you need to take one of these,' she continued, voice firm and authoritative. 'Jacob is outside, but he isn't alone.'

'No…,' Emily refused them again, 'no… I can't.'

Madison's face hardened.

She thrust the knives out again with renewed emphasis.

'Emily, this is serious,' her tone was blunt and matter-of-fact – there was no comfort to be found here. 'There's no time for this, now.'

Madison could hear the door to their building swing open, several pairs of boots on the wood floor.

Emily whimpered and her eyes welled with fright.

Madison gripped the blanket covering Emily's legs with her free hand and gave it a firm shake.

'Emily, I *need* you here,' she begged.

It was like negotiating with a child.

The footfalls came ever louder as they crested the stairs.

Madison glanced over her shoulders, tried to guess how many moments they had before the door to their refuge swung open.

'Take the *fucking* knife,' Madison ordered.

Emily's fingers slowly wrapped around one of the handles; she clutched it resentfully. She pushed some of her blond hair out of her face and struggled to strip the blanket and stand. Madison could tell she wanted to sob and wail, but Emily held it back. Madison wasn't sure if it was out of terror or self-control, but it was irrelevant in the end.

Madison turned to square herself to the door, positioned herself a step in front of Emily and tried her best to appear threatening.

There was no point in locking it; this confrontation would be inevitable.

The appearance of confidence was all they could muster now.

Hopefully it would be all they needed.

Madison trembled as adrenaline swam through her tired veins.

There was a slight knock as the door slowly swung open.

Jacob was the first to enter.

'Honey,' he began, voice as thin and weary as the smile on his lips.

Madison's stance softened and her knife lowered.

'I'm home.'

* * *

After the tearful reunion and evasive introductions, the group settled in.

Madison watched quietly as the interactions unfolded around her.

The African chuckled as he worked at cleaning the knuckles of one of their group. The ruddy haired Irishman, Sully as he was introduced, didn't bat an eye as Daniel mockingly chastised him for not mentioning the cuts sooner.

Emily seemed lifted by the new faces; she chatted indistinctly with someone who bore an accent she couldn't place and a woman with kind eyes.

Generally, everyone seemed upbeat.

Except one.

A thin man with glasses leaned against a wall, not so far away from the group as to be wholly separate, but sufficiently so to be clearly uninterested in the pleasantries. He rubbed his hands together as his eyes nervously searched the room.

As Daniel finished bandaging the hands, he slapped Sully's shoulder. The Irishman replied with an appreciative nod as he flexed his fingers beneath the wrapping.

'You,' Daniel began as he turned to Jacob, 'you need to rest. Anders, you too; take a load off.'

Jacob and Anders looked to each other.

'Doctor's orders,' chided the Nigerian from between a wide smile.

They each recognized the wisdom in the instruction. Jacob shot a grin to Madison and found a place to sit comfortably. Anders slumped down next to the nest of blankets and cushions.

Madison turned to Keeley.

'So... what's next for you?'

Keeley replied with a smile that reflected her warmth.

'We don't really know, I guess... thought we'd try to get to the barracks, see if anyone was home,' she replied. 'But we really haven't gotten that far.'

The energy in the room changed immediately.

Emily became rigid.

Jacob froze in position and stared at the floor between his boots.

Madison's eyes faltered as if a mirror cracking.

Anders wearily propped himself up.

The room felt wounded as all eyes turned upon the hosts.

Jacob struggled to clear his throat.

'I'm sorry,' he started, noticeably without lifting his gaze. 'That won't be an option.'

Madison watched helplessly as a wave of defeat rolled over the gathering.

Isaac sunk into the wall; this meant a prolonged crawl through the streets.

And they would likely be pursued… a detail not yet confided in their new friends.

Nothing more needed to be said.

A long moment passed between them.

Sully broke the silence.

'Right then… what next?'

Anders lowered his head into his hands as Keeley pawed at the floor with her foot.

'We've just been trying to get by,' Madison offered plaintively. 'Jacob's been working through the buildings nearby, keeping us going… while we figured that out.'

'We can't stay here,' Anders stated flatly.

Jacob couldn't place it, but he felt something in the statement was more than just an assessment on their modest surroundings.

'Is that all you've managed?' Sully broke in, motioning to the desk where their supplies were displayed.

Madison felt insulted and more than a little uncomfortable as prying eyes appraised their only possessions.

'That, and the pack from yesterday,' Jacob answered, finding no offence in the question.

'We've been planning on leaving,' Emily interjected, 'once we had enough to leave with, I mean.'

Jacob was surprised to hear Emily participate in the conversation. He honestly wasn't sure if she had ever been listening as he and Madison discussed their plans.

Perhaps she'd turned a corner.

'Right,' Daniel pushed the ball forward. 'What do we need?'

Jacob considered their provisions.

'We're doing half decent with food, so long as we're smart with it. Water is obvious. Weapons would be ideal, first aid ...'

Isaac nodded his agreement.

'That'd all be at the barracks,' Daniel pondered. 'There's got to be something left, place that big.'

Jacob shook his head and looked away.

'Trust me, that's not an option. You'd never make it inside.'

His tone reflected the intended finality.

'How did it happen?' Keeley dared to ask, though there was little doubt.

Emily slunk away from the conversation.

'Infection got in,' Jacob lamented.

'Too many people, too tight a space,' Madison whispered.

'It got desperate,' Jacob continued. 'To keep the fences up, the soldiers had to use guns; the noise drew more. The perimeter failed and they just kept coming. Once the infection was in the halls, it just got overrun.'

'People were jumping from the windows wherever they could find a gap in the crowd, hoping for a safe landing and enough time to beat the mob.'

Each imagined the scene unfold in their own way.

'Maybe they wandered off,' Anders hoped.

'Maybe the ones outside,' Jacob retorted.

'Doesn't matter; anywhere we plan on going we're going to need weapons,' Daniel chimed, 'so long as there's snow down we can hydrate. Maybe not the most appetizing, but it's an option.'

'Alright then,' Sully piped in as he rose to his feet, 'weapons, water, first aid.'

Isaac fell in beside him. Anders and Jacob each started to shamble to their feet before Daniel interrupted them.

'Not you,' he reiterated, 'you both need rest.'

The impotence pained them both, but neither could refute the statement.

Jacob produced his notepad and walked Isaac and Sullivan through some possible options. He described some buildings and some units he hadn't been able to thoroughly canvas and reiterated where he had come across the other group. As Sully and Isaac suited up, he emptied his pack and threw it to them.

Isaac nodded and adjusted the straps around his considerably smaller frame. Keeley rose to embrace him, and held his eyes in hers for a long moment.

'Make sure you come back,' she whispered.

'Don't worry, love,' Sully grinned, 'I've got him.'

Isaac rolled his eyes and kissed Keeley on the forehead.

Madison began to clamber to her feet as a surrogate.

Sullivan looked her over.

'Are you used to this kind of thing?'

She paused as she met his eyes; her hesitation was the only response he needed.

'Stay; your friends could use some looking after,' he offered and motioned to Isaac with his chin, 'we aren't new at this.'

Sully fought to find an uneasy trust with Isaac. He wasn't yet convinced whether or not Isaac was involved in

William's murder, but he could find little reason to question his companion's current motivations.

As they began to move towards the door, Jacob extended the handle of his hatchet to Madison. As she ferried it across the room, Sullivan nodded in appreciation.

'I'll get this back to you,' he promised over his shoulder as they exited.

Chapter 23

IT WAS A SLOW GRIND.

The war band picked its way through the streets, ever searching for their intended quarry. The sun's rays had some strength to them, but the air remained cold. The previous night's rain had obscured any hope of a trail; with temperatures straddling the freezing point, any depressions in the pockmarked snow filled and partially froze over.

Erik kept pace with the lead of the column, carrying his bat lengthwise across his shoulders so he could rest the back of his neck against it. He inhaled deeply through his nose and allowed the cool air to fill his lungs, savouring the luxury of its lightness relative to the stifling airs of the compound.

It was past midday now, and progress was sluggish. Though they had caught sight of a handful of ghouls in the streets, they had been too far to bother engaging. As each intersection was passed, the group grew more restless. Erik could sense the rest of the civilians – a ragtag bunch – had little experience outside the walls. Their nervous energy was contagious, arcing between them as they were relegated to boredom each time the soldiers discussed their course.

It was obvious to Erik they had little hope of tracking the deserters. Not that it was meant as a scathing criticism; the circumstances of their pursuit were simply far from ideal.

Barring a lucky break, this hunt would prove fruitless.

Maybe it was for the best.

Erik shuddered to think of how the confrontation would play out.

Quinn was a man who would do anything for the greater good, as he saw it.

The column came to a halt again near the crest of a hill. As the soldiers convened, several of the civilians took the moment to sit and soak in the sun's warmth.

After a few moments, the soldiers had everyone on their feet and heading down the hill to their left – a sudden change in course.

'What's down there?' one of the survivors innocently inquired. He was a middle aged man, rugged looking with a face roughly hewn with stubble. He looked like a tradesman to Erik, stacked together solid, obviously still strong despite the weeks of tight rationing.

One of the soldiers glowered at him in response. Erik imagined he had somehow taken the question as a slight.

Hunger put everyone on edge.

'There's a strip mall down there,' came a calmer voice, 'a grocery store. They may have holed up there looking for food or water.'

He had seen her around the compound before. She was pretty, even if a bit tomboyish, with lively red hair, a pleasant face with large, friendly green eyes. They would have been vibrant once, shining like emeralds, Erik thought – but now she looked tired.

Road worn and weary.

'We're going to check it out,' added the glowering soldier, balanced temperament restored. 'Day's getting long. Worst case maybe we can find something useful to bring back with us.'

Erik struggled to hide his smile. Maybe if they were able to find sufficient valuables, they'd turn back to the compound and abandon the hunt. He knew the place, though he'd never stepped foot inside – earlier scouts had reported the streets around this area were swarming with corpses and thus Quinn had focused his scavengers elsewhere. The strip mall also had a liquor store, but the entrances were separated by a long stretch of vacant commercial space. Barely old enough to buy a beer himself, Erik's appetite whet for something with some strength to it, something to chase away the cold nights and unwelcome dreams. Though very likely it was picked clean already – if they had time on the way out – maybe he'd pop in next door.

As the band made it to the base of the hill, they lined up tightly behind the soldiers as they surveyed the intended target. The streets on this side of the building appeared bare except for a few stragglers, scarcely visible several blocks up the street. The group sat patiently as the soldier scanned the area with the scope of the C7 before being waved forward. Led by the redhead, they filtered around the building and crossed the street towards the strip mall as their advance was covered.

They inched alongside the brick building, fully bathed in sunlight as they emerged from the denser canopy of the residential streets. The activity seemed to have removed the nervousness of inaction, and they advanced to the corner where they could survey the parking area.

An expanse dotted with a few vehicles, comically covered in several inches of ice from the cycle of snow and freezing rain. A few ghouls shambled by on the road at the far end of the lot, but otherwise nothing stirred. Opposite the entry to the strip mall stood a midrise apartment building – a mass of black glass and dark metal, jutting from the asphalt. A few of the windows were open, some with tattered drapes billowing listlessly in the breeze, others with makeshift signs and pleas for '*S.O.S.*' and '*Please Help*' scrawled onto whatever fabric could be found.

The building looked dead.

No sign of movement save the gentle flap of the signage.

Likely the occupants had succumbed to the outbreak weeks ago. It was a significant structure by the city's standards, likely boasting several dozen units. It could be teeming with dead.

The redhead waved her partner over and he fell in at the back of the line. Erik watched as they communicated through a series of abstract hand signals. They must have been content any threat was sufficiently far away to pay their advance little notice; the group slid out and made for the main entrance.

The entryway was sheltered and set well back from the parking lot; only a dusting of old snow yet clung to it. Several of the double doors were shattered, littering their tinted glass throughout cement walkway and inside the structure. As they crept inside, the breeze disappeared and the air became heavy and stagnant. Frigid shade replaced the warmth of the sun, and the deep misery of the place rooted within you.

The store was huge relative to such a small group.

Erik wrung his hands about his bat as he was waved in. His eyes greedily searched the dim corners, illuminated in a strange tapestry of light from the broken windows and tinted glass. Shafts of natural light pierced the gloom at irregular intervals, making depth and distance difficult to judge.

Some racks of clothing were overturned while others hung limp and off centre, dangling meekly from cheap hangers. The cashier's stations were smashed; their components and casings cluttered the narrow lanes between them. The little displays of candy bars and gum were picked clean.

At the other end of the store, however, it was evident some of the shelves yet had stock.

The gloom hung off Erik's skin as he pushed deeper into the eerie quiet. Pools formed beneath the refrigerated units, spreading sporadically throughout the otherwise grime-stained checkered tile. The smell of wet cardboard and spoiled microwave dinners permeated the air. Somewhere to his right, Erik could hear some indistinct but decidedly excited chatter; his companions were enjoying some luck. Some bottles faintly clinked as they were loaded into a pack. A flashlight clicked on behind him and Erik peered over his shoulder to see the pretty redhead flash him a smile before she slipped down another aisle.

Erik thanked the shadow as it obscured an involuntary blush. He rested his bat against an empty display and started sifting through the sparse inventory.

Someone laughed loudly elsewhere in the cavernous store; they must have found something particularly appetizing. Of course, given the last several days' worth of life at the compound, anything would have been good.

Erik allowed a wide grin to spread from ear to ear. Surely they'd have enough of a score to derail any further thoughts of pursuit. They could easily justify an immediate return to the compound, and Quinn would be hard pressed to call their run anything but a success.

All that, *and* he was feeling confident in approaching that redhead.

Erik grabbed a couple boxes of dehydrated mashed potatoes and whatever jars of salsas and jams he could handle. When he could stuff no more into his pockets, he collected his trusty bat and returned to the front of the store. He rejoined a couple of his companions as they struggled to contain their satisfaction.

After a few more moments, the entire group was ready to depart. Erik shot a playful look to the redhead, who pinched her mouth into a bashful smile.

Even as the group started towards the exit, chattering excitedly away, Erik couldn't hear a word of it. They bragged about their various treasures, the fun they would have that night.

They would be heroes to the beleaguered compound.

He was fixated on her, and though she tried to play it cool, he knew he was in. That recognition must have crept its way onto his face, as she rolled her eyes and motioned him to fall in with the column.

Erik moved to join them and turned his head to hide his smile from her. Once convinced he was concealed from her prying eyes, he even allowed himself a chance to laugh.

The lighthearted flirting was going well.

It reminded him of the days before, days pre-outbreak when he and his buddies would work their charms to meet girls wherever they could.

They were young, after all.

Consumed with thoughts of their imminent success and the inevitable excitement their return would bring the demoralized compound, he never stopped to question their luck until this perfect moment.

How could there be no dead here?

Erik's pace slowed half a step.

No corpses at all.

His laughter trailed off as he considered the scene.

Something he hadn't noticed on the way in.

Erik stopped in his tracks, turned his back to the group and faced the wall opposite the line of windows at the front of the store.

The drywall there was peppered with holes of varying sizes.

Erik's head cocked quizzically to the side.

What the hell… ?

A sudden split to the air – a thin sound, a muffled *crack*; Erik couldn't process it before it was replaced with a searing pain. The bullet tore through the left side of his neck with sufficient force to spin him around. His bat flung from his grasp and clattered across the floor. As he crashed to the tile, his hand instinctively went to the wound, but he found no strength in his fingers.

The world dimmed as he heard another shot. Blood spray burst overhead and coloured the air somewhere nearby. He thought he could hear the distant cries of his companions' alarm.

In an instant, the redhead was over him, steadying his head and applying pressure to his neck. He could see her lips moving, but couldn't hear her. He couldn't make out the words.

She's so lovely…

Tears, swollen with terror, drowned her emerald eyes.

With each beat of his heart, Erik could see a shock of his lifeblood pulse between her fingers as they vainly struggled to stem the bleeding. Her lips continued to move and plead, but Erik was lost in those flooded eyes.

Another *crack* and one of the heavy, tinted windows shattered at the front of the building. Erik could hear the splinters of glass faintly dance on the black and white tile, felt as if he could feel their reverberation through his back as he lie on the floor.

Time was getting hurried, now.

Another uniformed figure appeared, wrapped his arms about the redhead and tore her away.

She made every effort to keep her hands on his neck as long as possible.

He appreciated that.

Erik sputtered beneath the crushing tide.

* * *

Jacob's notes proved only somewhat useful.

He had taken the time to highlight a couple structures he thought looked to be in reasonable shape, buildings he had come across while scavenging but was unable to gain entry due to ghoul activity in the streets around them. Of course there was no way to know what was inside; only an indication that the buildings weren't completely derelict.

While the first unit they broke into had little of use, with all the telltale evidence of hasty packing, the second main floor apartment was occupied. A couple of ghouls – old, decrepit things – hadn't even managed to lift their battered forms from off the floor before being dispatched.

Sully had taken a liking to the hatchet.

Portraits and a thin layer of dust bore the only witness to the apocalypse from this vantage; likely the previous occupants were out of town when the world fell apart. Maybe they found shelter and yet survived somewhere along the road, maybe they died trying to make it back home.

Isaac cared little for the fate of those that lived here. His only interest was ensuring their survival for another day. Nevertheless, he couldn't make eye contact with the family photos leering down at him as he looted their belongings.

They hadn't made much progress. They collected a few hand tools – pliers, screwdrivers and the like – but no real weapons. A couple hard plastic water bottles, some batteries, some twine.

Hardly the successes they hoped for.

Well, such is the luck of things.

The unit with the elderly couple did have a small medical kit with dressings and assorted bandages, and a host of multicoloured medications. But judging from the appearance of the corpses, Sully and Isaac each suspected they'd be of little use. Not knowing any differently they collected the lot, figuring Daniel could sort through it.

Isaac was rifling through bottles of household cleaners beneath a sink when Sullivan emerged from a bedroom with a small black pouch in hand.

'Whatcha got there?' Isaac asked as he rocked back on his heels.

Sullivan turned the package over in his hands.

'Binoculars,' he chimed as he undid the Velcro clasp, 'not too powerful, but quality.'

They were small and simple – a folding set of Bushnell binoculars.

They might just prove to be the highlight of the day.

'Any luck on your end?' Sully asked.

Isaac turned back to face the rows of cleaning products and gently shut the cupboard doors.

'Might be something you can do with that stuff, but I'm no chemist,' Isaac replied as he rose to his feet and strode over to the refrigerator. 'It's just dead weight as far as I can tell.'

Sully nodded.

'No sense carrying anything we aren't sure to need,' he agreed as he folded the binoculars back into their case and tucked them into his jacket.

Isaac frowned at the mess of rotten food and opened the freezer door. He reached in and produced a thick glass bottle, squarish with a fondly familiar black label. As he pulled the bottle out, he flashed the *Jack Daniel's* to his companion.

'...would this be considered unnecessary?' he pondered aloud.

Sully shrugged.

'Doubles as disinfectant.'

The corner of Isaac's mouth curled into a grin as he slid the bottle into his pack.

'Now you're thinking.'

The two rhythmically turned over the remaining drawers and cupboards.

After he completed his section of the apartment, Isaac allowed himself to slump down on the couch. It was old and the springs were worn unevenly, but he didn't mind; it felt good to be off his feet for a moment. He pinched the bridge of his nose and rubbed his fingers over his eyes, allowing his head to drift back into the headrest of the battered sofa.

Sully crossed his arms and leaned against the living room wall.

'So,' he began, staring at Isaac expectantly, 'what do you think of them?'

Isaac's eyes flared open.

Ever the pragmatist, Isaac had been running the numbers since the moment he and Sully left. He had stood off to the side and allowed the introductions to unfold around him so as to gauge the strangers' worth.

Jacob seemed more than capable. He had kept the three of them safe and fed for a remarkable length of time considering how poorly equipped they were. But he was damaged; no telling how badly. Concussions have a funny way about them – latent symptoms, exhaustion, subtle tricks on your perception. Tomorrow the bruises would deepen and his muscles would be sore and tense. He would be slow, likely for several days, even if they spent what little medicine they had on his care.

One of the women looked broken, ready to shatter at the slightest touch. Emily had the perpetual glassy look of incompetency. She would be a liability.

Isaac was undecided about Madison. He had overheard her talk about work in the parks department, so he reasoned she'd likely be fit, not afraid to be outdoors. But she had been protected from the wastes due to Jacob's sacrifice; no telling how she would react in a tough situation. She would be a wildcard.

Isaac couldn't escape the conclusion that the math wasn't favourable.

Too many variables, and too few of them controllable.

Long term, Jacob's group stood to benefit more from any alliance.

But right now, they had food.

'I don't know yet,' Isaac bluntly evaded the question, leaning forward in his seat and running a hand through his matted brown hair.

Sullivan peered out the window.

'They seem like decent people.'

Isaac was thankful Sullivan couldn't see his face from where he stood.

Decent people, the words echoed in his head.

Decent people don't make it now.

'Yeah,' was the only response Isaac could muster as he rose to his feet.

Sullivan watched Isaac's movements and studied his body language.

Isaac was fast becoming uncomfortable with being the subject of Sully's attention.

'How much daylight do we have left?' he asked.

Sully could sense the deflection but let it pass.

'Couple hours, maybe; the days are getting longer.'

Thank god.

'Alright, let's get moving,' Isaac offered as he collected his pack, 'we can probably hit another building before we start to lose the light.'

Isaac ran his thumb under one of the shoulder straps and adjusted the weight on his back.

Sullivan didn't stray from his vantage at the window.

'I've got a different idea.'

Isaac stared at Sully quizzically.

Sully turned his head to face Isaac without coming off the wall, lazily lifting a finger and pointing in the distance.

'We're not far from the barracks – a couple blocks or so,' he unzipped a jacket pocket and produced the small black case, 'let's take a look.'

Isaac considered the suggestion. Their packs had some provisions in it, but if their haul today was any indication of what remained in this burnt out quarter of the city, they might need to make a bigger play. Jacob had come back with a respectable haul of food, and they had sufficient snow and ice they could melt for water if their bottles ran out.

A little recon might prove useful.

'What are you thinking?'

Sully resumed his vigil.

'Find somewhere with a decent line of sight, survey the grounds...,' Sully began, 'get a read on it, then head back.'

Isaac weighed the benefits against trying their luck for supplies in another unit. Given Jacob's description of the ruins, it would likely be higher risk than plundering a few apartments.

'If it looks doable, we make a plan,' Sully continued with a shrug, 'if it doesn't, at least we know.'

Isaac contemplated their limited success. He would have greatly preferred to return with their packs a little heavier, but the certain benefit of some intel on the barracks trumped the uncertain benefits of another canvassed building.

'Alright, let's do it.'

Sully replaced the binoculars in his jacket pocket.

'Your wife's going to hate me,' he grinned.

'She'd be right to,' Isaac flatly replied, 'you're a bad influence.'

Sully scratched at his beard as he turned from the window.

The attempts at humour felt strained between them.

Sullivan fought to keep memories of William from crowding his thoughts.

They wordlessly left the apartment and made their way to the streets below.

They pressed due south, towards the tip of the peninsula overlooking the cold waters of the harbour. It wasn't a straight shot to the grouping of buildings commonly known as the Barrack Green Armories. While ghoul presence was sporadic amidst the burnt out remnants of the old part of town, Sully and Isaac opted to avoid confrontation, quietly slipping between buildings as they crept closer.

As they emerged from between the narrow lots, they paused to catch their breath at the ruined corner of a mixed commercial and residential block.

The Barrack Green structures were ancient by most Canadian standards, some two hundred years old and among the last vestiges of the early fortress system for the Loyalist city. The buildings were imposing, formidable brick structures that jutted out from the southernmost tip of the peninsula. Though chronically understaffed, several reserve units had called the place home pre-outbreak.

As Sully and Isaac put their eyes on the structures for the first time since the outbreak, their hearts sank at the thought that even a reinforced facility such as this had fallen to the tide of dead that engulfed the city.

Neither could resist the feeling of dread that washed over them.

Sully interrupted the tension.

'Come on,' he urged, motioning onward. 'We'll get a better view from over there.'

Isaac shook the fear from his head and fell in behind Sullivan as they sprinted the distance. Their course took them beside the remnants of a municipal park.

It lingered in bright-coloured silence, a mournful witness to long departed laughter, undisturbed since the falling of the world.

Isaac had been here many times before. In the summer months, occasionally farmer's markets would grace the playground. Music, the many smells of ethnic cuisine and fresh produce, the sounds children playing and filling the air with gleeful celebrations.

Conceptually, Isaac could remember them now.

Not the *actual* sounds or smells; just their concept.

As they crossed the open expanse alongside the park, they noted a few scattered infected appeared to have picked up their movements. Several distant figures shambled towards them. Isaac kept a close eye to gauge their speed; these ghouls seemed from an early generation. Their approach was slow and labored. So long as he and Sully didn't linger unnecessarily, they could easily outrun them.

Sully leaned out around the building.

'We're going to have company,' Isaac asserted between breaths.

'We'll be quick,' Sully promised as he dug the binoculars out. Raising the aperture to his eyes, Sully drew deep breaths through his nose to calm his heart rate.

'*Fuck*,' he cursed, 'No good… gotta get closer.'

Isaac wasn't thrilled, but knew they'd likely not find themselves this close again. It was now or never; any advance would take them between a series of congested buildings and compromise their sight lines. They would lose the ability to gauge their berth from the advancing corpses.

Their shadows were cast long as the sun continued its slide towards the western horizon.

He took a quick scan about them. The infected drew closer but their distance was still relatively comfortable.

'Okay, okay… let's go.'

Sully grit his teeth. The complications mounted.

He led Isaac on.

The two rounded the corner and advanced up a side street.

With his line of sight disrupted, Isaac was beginning to feel claustrophobic. He unsheathed his knife and flexed his fingers around its handle.

Finally satisfied with their vantage, Sully raised the binoculars and took a thorough scan of the complex.

The fence was breached in multiple spots.

The grounds and the streets outside were littered with a combination of dead ghouls and half consumed bodies, some of which wore plainclothes while others were uniformed.

But the ghoul presence – outside at least – was minimal.

A few stragglers, unaware they were being watched, paced about mindlessly in the yard.

Several of the windows were shattered on every level.

An assortment of large military trucks and vehicles dotted the landscape.

Sully lowered the aperture and considered the scene.

Half the surface area was obscured to him by the building.

Nevertheless, they had multiple potential points of entry; might even be able to pick up something useful from the yard.

Isaac leaned over Sully's shoulder.

'What do you think?' Isaac whispered.

'Looks better than I thou…,' Sully trailed off.

Both froze as the sun's rays behind them were interrupted.

A cold shadow fell over them, lengthening across the snows beyond.

Believing a ghoul had closed the distance faster than expected, Sully reached for the hatchet as Isaac spun to intercept.

Isaac rocked back on his heels as he was greeted by a familiar face.

A figure coldly embossed against the failing sun.

A silhouette, lithe and sleek; like a serpent coiled.

At least like a serpent brandishing a .45.

'Hello, boys,' she chided.

Chapter 24

A SINISTER SMILE SPREAD OVER HER THIN LIPS.

'Good to see you again,' the voice continued from behind the iron sights.

Eyes burning with contempt, Sully's hand retreated from the hatchet.

'Now, now,' she scolded, menacingly waving the pistol, 'this is hardly the time to be smug.'

Isaac's stare leveled.

'If you pull the trigger, you'll bring them all down,' he rebutted, 'we'd all be dead.'

Cox smirked and derisively cocked her head to the side.

'Nah… I like my chances.'

Despite the convincing smile, her voice remained cheerless and grim.

Neither Isaac nor Sully doubted her.

'So, what, then? Why come find us?'

Cox turned to Isaac. The smile left her face.

'You're going to take me with you.'

'The hell we are,' Sully scoffed.

Isaac didn't like the prospects any more than Sullivan, but sensed now was perhaps the time to be diplomatic.

As Cox and Isaac continued their banter, Sully adjusted his footing, covertly shifting his weight beneath his sturdy frame.

He wanted to rush her, take her down and pound the life from her, but he'd never beat her speed with the gun. He resented himself in equal measure for both feelings – wanting to tear her apart, and his inability to do so.

Isaac considered the demand.

'Why?'

'Do you mean aside from the fact I have a gun in your face?'

Sully clenched his teeth. He was growing restless, crouched in the snow and ready to pounce.

'Yeah, I do.'

Cox's stare didn't waver.

'Quinn's lost it.'

Sully couldn't keep his eyes from rolling.

'Right, what else?'

Cox adjusted her grip on the pistol.

'That place is collapsing. He's losing the handle.'

Isaac continued to stare into her. He was more intent on her body language than the actual words, but he wanted to hear her out.

Sensing Isaac wanted her to continue, she obliged.

'You've thought this through; your chances are better out here,' she professed before pausing for emphasis, 'and they'd be better with someone like me.'

Isaac didn't move.

'I know you, Isaac,' she continued, 'you see the wisdom in what I'm saying.'

Thoughts swirled in Isaac's mind as he ran through the variables.

She was becoming impatient.

'You need to make up your mind,' she insisted, 'before I change mine.'

The threat was heavy.

'Give us a minute,' Isaac replied.

Cox chuckled mockingly.

'Take all the time you need.'

Isaac could have tripped over the sarcasm. He knew the dead continued to converge on them; between this cluster of buildings he couldn't tell how much longer they had.

Isaac turned to Sullivan, but his eyes darted nervously between structures.

He motioned to Sully to join him in conference a few steps away.

Resigning himself to his present inability to settle the score with Cox, Sully rose to look Isaac in the eye.

'We should consider this.'

'You can't be fucking serious,' Sully scoffed.

'I am.'

Sully's face clouded with dark imagery.

'She's a murderer,' he spat, making no effort to conceal the accusation.

In fact, if Sully was being entirely honest with himself, he wasn't yet wholly convinced Isaac didn't deserve the same title.

He didn't care for their seeming familiarity.

Isaac shrugged off the lack of tact.

'You don't know that.'

'*Yes*, I fucking do,' Sully growled, jabbing his finger into Isaac's chest, 'and *you* do, too.'

Under the weight of the assertion, Isaac broke eye contact with Sully. He glanced down to the snow before turning to face the corporal.

Cox stood, unflinching and unmoved, as if chiseled from the ice itself.

'*Shit* man, she's not even denying it,' Sully continued, gesturing incredulously, '... do you want that around Keeley, around everyone?'

The words stung Isaac.

He stepped into Sully and spoke in a hushed but sharp tone.

'What's the alternative? She shoots us like dogs in the street?'

Sully shook his head in disgust.

'Hear me out,' Isaac continued. 'Even if she doesn't kill us, assume she finds a remarkable sense of charity and lets us walk away from this; if she reports back to Quinn, we're all fucked. We would need to leave *tonight*, right now, and that's not plausible.'

Sully furrowed his brow and his nostrils flared.

Reestablishing eye contact with Sully, he added –

'We're not ready for that.'

Sully's lips curled into a snarl, but there was undeniable truth in the words.

'If she's serious, we stand to gain a huge asset. You've been on runs with her; who knows what we'll encounter on the road. If she's not, if she's playing us, at least we can dictate how quickly news of our whereabouts gets back to the compound.'

Sully considered the proposal.

He hated Cox; not because he bore any love for William, but because of what she represented. The thought of her proximity, of sharing her company was abhorrent, but Isaac was right. Distasteful though it may be, this way offered them the only control they could find in the situation.

Besides, if she were to try anything, in the tight confines of the apartment refuge they would have the advantage.

The prospects of settling their score was disconcertingly satisfying.

Begrudgingly, he nodded his acceptance.

Isaac couldn't prevent a wry smile from turning the corner of his mouth. He turned to address Cox.

'Right, let's go then.'

Sully scanned between the buildings and began tracing their route back.

'... not even going to ask for my gun?' she chided, thick with triumph.

Course set, Sully paid her no heed.

Isaac cast one last sideways glance in her direction.

'Would you have turned it over?'

A wicked smile curled her lips.

'Not a chance.'

* * *

Quinn didn't take the news well.

The knowledge that others in the city had survived the plague up until this point was unsurprising. He had suspected there'd be pockets of survivors spread throughout the ruins.

The fact one of these bands had the audacity to attack his patrol was infuriating.

The redheaded soldier completed her report and Quinn gave her leave to wash the blood from her skin and uniform.

As the door closed and she departed, the module fell silent for a moment.

Several of the administrators and soldiers gathered exchanged defeated glances.

Quinn sat in silence.

Smaller bands would be more agile in the field, and assuming they had been active outside since the outset of the First Wave, they would likely be home to experienced killers.

Lynn cringed at the pounding thuds and sounds of breaking glass.

* * *

Jacob couldn't resist the sensation of doubt as it steadily crept in.

Madison felt it, too.

Tonight should have been one of joy – a celebratory evening.

Instead the energy was unnerving, uncomfortable. It smothered the gathering and threatened to drown all those present.

The little refuge wasn't much, and it wasn't particularly happy. It was desperate, and though they struggled to ascend beyond scraping for their basic necessities, at least it was theirs.

Theirs – their little space, carved out and partially insulated from the end of days, now infiltrated with the encroaching dark of their newfound companions' troubled past.

Jacob and Madison huddled together in the corner of the room. They watched silently as the rest, who now seemed more like strangers than ever, debated amongst themselves.

The hour was growing late.

Several worn pillar candles danced in the shadows, occasionally disturbed by an exaggerated movement.

Jacob considered the room, trying to establish intent.

This soldier, this new one – she was a pariah.

The clear source of tension.

Daniel and Keeley kept a wide berth from her, and Isaac and Sully were perpetually stationed between her and the rest of their group. Even Anders, who was growing friendly and curled up with Emily, seldom took his eyes off the dark-haired woman for more than a few moments. Though Sully and Isaac never said as much, Jacob guessed she accompanied them now under threat of duress.

The highlight of the day's spoils was a bottle of whiskey. It was shared between them, each taking a stinging swig before passing it along.

Only Jacob refused it at each pass.

As the bottle rounded the congregation again it fell to Daniel. He swirled the remaining amber liquid inside the glass bottle and frowned slightly. He wandered over to where Jacob and Madison sat and plunked down beside them, extending the bottle to Jacob with a friendly smile.

'Have a sip, mate,' he grinned, his rich accent coming through thick like molasses. 'Today is a good day.'

Madison squeezed his leg encouragingly.

Jacob took the bottle and swallowed a burning mouthful.

'I get the feeling you've had some bad days,' Jacob leveled.

The smile left Daniel's face as he conceded the point.

'Who hasn't?'

Isaac shot a glance to Sully, confirmed his intent was understood before he crossed the floor to where Keeley stood. She backed into him and he wrapped his arms around her, resting his chin on her shoulder. Emily sat up from where she cuddled with Anders and turned to face Daniel and Jacob.

Anders stared at Cox.

Daniel held his hand out for the bottle, but Jacob retained his grip on its neck.

'You never did tell me your story,' Jacob continued, taking another small hit from the bottle. 'In fact, you've avoided it each time I've asked.'

The room fell suddenly quiet; only the occasional sputter from the candles punctuated the space between them.

The normally jovial lights in Daniel's eyes steeled and grew severe.

'It's a long story,' he plaintively began.

'Look around you,' Jacob insisted with a clear edge to his voice, 'we've got nothing but time.'

Daniel cast a glance to his companions as his ebony skin seemed to shrink into the shadows. He recounted their trials at the compound at length, at least from his own perspective – the beginning of the outbreak, life at the Coast Guard site.

The infirmary.

The cull.

Their escape.

Daniel never broke eye contact with Jacob throughout the retelling, and none interrupted. There were details each would have added, but Daniel's version was close enough.

Jacob listened intently, searching for any holes or contradictions; anything that would have led him to doubt their authenticity. As the story neared its close, Emily squirmed back into Anders, nuzzling her head against his chest and wrapping her arms around his body. Though Anders welcomed her affections, his attention was fixed squarely on Cox.

Unblinking, he stared at her as she reclined comfortably.

She smugly returned his gaze.

'So, these soldiers,' Jacob finally added, motioning to the corporal at the back of the room. 'She's one of them?'

Daniel was visibly wearied by the story, painfully relived in its sordid entirety. He merely nodded as he lied back and interwove his fingers behind his head, staring blankly at the ceiling as he hoped to crowd out the more sinister of his memories.

Jacob drew another mouthful from the bottle and rose to his feet.

Madison looked at him, silently pleading the line of questioning didn't advance where she knew it would.

'Why are you here?'

The corporal turned to assess her interrogator, but didn't speak.

'How did you find us?'

The faint tracings of a smile were her only reply.

Jacob stared expectantly.

'You need to start fucking talking.'

It was evident Cox was at least partially considering playing this out.

But maybe now was the time for diplomacy.

'I left,' was all she said.

Jacob placed the whiskey on the desk authoritatively.

Cox drew a deep breath and adjusted in her seat.

She clearly felt no need to explain her actions.

Jacob was containing his agitation, but his patience was being tried.

'Why?'

The corporal rolled her head back on her shoulders in a half circle.

'Orders,' she lazily proclaimed.

'*Orders?*' Jacob reiterated.

'At first,' she mused.

Growing tired of the stalled conversation, Anders sat up.

'Orders to find us and bring us back ... or orders to track us down and kill us?'

Cox grinned wickedly; someone was finally asking the right questions.

'The latter,' she mocked, allowing the admission to settle over the room.

Sully's bandaged hand curled into a fist.

In the dim orange flicker of the candlelight, Cox seemed thoroughly amused to be continuing her role as the antagonist.

'You can relax. If I wanted any of you dead, I would have done it by now.'

'So why are we here?' Jacob interjected, seeking to gain control of the room once more.

'Because I'm not the enemy now,' she chided. 'There are far worse people out there.'

The words struck Jacob.

'*Far worse people,*' he began.

Cox regarded him suspiciously.

'Let me tell you what I know of *people,*' he continued.

Jacob recounted the story of the night the line broke, when he and Samantha and countless others ran from the terminal to the supposed safety of the Coast Guard site – only to be greeted by gunfire.

Jacob's eyes welled with tears, but none fell.

His voice was constant.

Cox admired it.

Keeley held her breath and hung off Jacob's every word, weeping silently for his loss.

But there was something else.

It was subtle, but unmistakable.

Isaac's embrace grew cold in the retelling, as if all the warmth had been bled from him.

In her incomprehension, she turned her head to look at his face.

It was severe; uncompromising.

Fixated on the corporal.

Not yet fully understanding, she caught momentary eye contact with Cox. It was only for a second, faster than anyone else could have picked up on, but it was all she needed.

In that moment, she realized what he had done.

In her horror, she froze. Imprisoned by his alien embrace, her eyes vainly searched the floorboards for an escape to his vacuous gravity.

But none came.

'I'm sorry for your loss,' Daniel lamented from his post prostrate on the floor, 'truly.'

Jacob turned his head and managed a weak smile in acknowledgement.

Cox wisely held her tongue. Though she herself wasn't on the walls that night, she understood the order. She would have given it herself.

Some eggs get broken.

'All bullshit aside,' Sully interjected, 'how did you find us?'

Cox smirked.

'Without much difficulty. We never ventured this far south after the fires tore through the area; I figured you'd camp in the one section we didn't thoroughly canvas. And if I was wrong, I figured my chances of evading pursuit would be better here. Maybe I'd make for the barracks, see if anyone was home.'

'So why leave in the first place, abandon your post?' Jacob asked.

Cox didn't like the insinuation of dereliction of duty, but she let it slide.

'Quinn lost it.'

Anders sneered.

'That's an understatement.'

Daniel found no levity in their jabs.

Cox shrugged off the comment.

'It was a fool's errand; a poor use of resources.'

'You would have done it differently?' Sully piped in.

'Yes,' she leveled. 'He risks too much to save face. The assets he has looking for you would be better spent scavenging, guarding the walls.'

The confirmation they were being pursued was not missed by anyone – least of all Jacob and Madison, who now more completely realized what they were becoming tangled up with.

'How did you get away?'

'Recon,' she casually replied, mournfully removing her pistol from its holster, 'which is why I've only got a .45 as opposed to some more serious hardware. I was to find signs of your passing and narrow the search.'

Sully couldn't help but feel the response seemed rehearsed.

'What's coming for us?'

Cox's mischievous demeanor turned suddenly grim.

'You know what's coming.'

The room fell solemn as each considered the implications.

Madison surveyed their little hovel, recognizing the fact they would soon need to abandon its shelter.

'We can't stay here.'

None could deny the obvious logic.

The group debated their next steps deep into the night. If they were to leave the city, they would need significant provisions – more than they could likely scavenge on the move.

They would need a big play.

Most of the obvious targets would long have been pillaged, and they were a significant distance from the major retail and shopping district of the eastern parts of the city. They could place little hope in finding pharmacies, department, hardware or sporting goods stores that weren't picked clean already, or otherwise settled by less-than-friendly sorts.

No, they needed somewhere they could hit with a reasonable chance of finding most every vital supply.

Somewhere they were reasonably confident wasn't occupied by anything but the dead.

Somewhere nearby.

The barracks.

Chapter 25

SLEEP PROVED EVASIVE.

Unable to find rest, Madison and Emily occupied their time by sketching the layout to the barracks interior as best they could remember.

Despite the late hours of planning, the group was early to rise.

The plan was simple enough. Break into a building with a decent line of sight, clear it, and hole up. There they would split the group.

Madison, Emily, and Jacob would stay put and guard the vantage. Though they protested the assignment, Daniel's combination of charm and insistent '*doctor's orders*' were sufficient to silence their argument. Whereas most wouldn't be able to differentiate between medicines and other desirables in the medical supply department – should there be any – he would volunteer in their stead.

Though Jacob hated the feeling of being relegated to the sidelines, he understood he was certainly in the worst shape among them. His body ached, his breath was labored, and his head swam if he moved too quickly. He cursed himself for being so liberal with the whiskey the night before.

The rest would clear the yard to ensure safe access to the site, with Anders and Keeley sifting through the exterior for anything useful. Sully, Isaac and Cox were natural choices to breach the halls of the barracks. Each was experienced in their own right, and in any event no one trusted Cox alone. If they arrived and the courtyard looked insurmountable, or it became obvious they would be unable to get in or out safely, they'd simply move on and head east.

Hope for the best.

As the group packed their limited belongings and suited up, Madison offered a solemn farewell to their hermitage.

While her eyes rolled over its contents for what would prove the final time, she regarded its simplicity with a strange fondness. These simple trappings had provided shelter in the storm, a home for a time in what would prove a nomadic and brutal future.

As she stepped out and reverently clicked the door closed behind them, she forced such nonsense from her mind.

Isaac stood at the head of the staircase as the column filtered by.

Keeley didn't make eye contact as she stepped past.

She had withdrawn from him; recoiled from his touch and rebuked any attempt he made to speak with her. Mercifully, most of their group was too preoccupied to have noticed the behaviour.

Isaac hated to make a spectacle of their problems.

He was used to it. When she was like this, he couldn't control it. It may take a long while to wind her up, but once she was there – she was immovable.

Like stone.

Her stubborn determination was infuriating; frustrating to no end.

He took a long breath, staring straight ahead into the wall.

Everything he had done since the outbreak, he had done to ensure their safety.

She would see that someday.

As the last among them rounded the staircase, Isaac slowly followed behind them, twisting the black titanium ring about his finger.

* * *

The sun was already gathering strength despite the crisp air.

As the group crossed some of the larger open expanses they attracted the attention of the occasional wayward ghoul, but they remained focused on their path and made good speed to their destination. They worried little of the stragglers that caught their sight, believing they'd cover sufficient distance and find shelter before the threat would build to uncomfortable proportion.

They advanced in pairs – with Cox running point alone – almost parallel to the line that Sully and Isaac had run the day before until the barracks was almost in sight. As they neared the target, Cox veered them sharply to the east, towards the rail lines and the causeway, darting between several short and squat residential units.

The Armouries loomed ahead, its imposing mass of stone and steel muted the morning sun.

They settled on a two storey building, a combination of red brick and vinyl siding. It was positioned diagonally across the street that served as the third point in a triangle between the Armouries and the remnants of a church. The church would have been a significant parish once, probably the epicenter of the community in the early days of the city.

But as with all things, the faithful waned, and the building fell into disrepair.

Emily would never have identified herself as religious, though her time spent at the family's funeral home had exposed her to a wide variety of faiths and funerary customs. Looking at the church, something about its architecture was unsettling. As she considered the failing brick and pockmarked roof, she couldn't help but to question its complacency.

What kind of god would have sat idly by as the world descended into such horror?

Almost on cue, the possibility dawned on her that perhaps this wasn't the failure of inattentive hands, but rather a deliberate hammer stroke on a corrupted anvil.

So fixated on her thoughts and the church opposite her, Emily inadvertently stuttered in her steps, causing Anders to collide with her. Not understanding, but sensing her unease, he placed a reassuring hand on her shoulder and urged her on. Her face reddened as she graciously squeezed his hand, and they bounded along to rejoin their cohort, waiting for their next signal.

With her sidearm readied, Cox peered into the basement-level windows, trying to find an angle around the tattered blinds. Once satisfied the unit was clear, she rested her back against the building and waved everyone forward.

As they converged on her position, Cox kicked out the window, which shattered with surprisingly little complaint. A few shards clattered off the sill but the majority of the glass bounced across the carpeted floors within. Pushing the blinds aside and content there was no other movement, Cox lowered herself in.

For the first time in many weeks, fresh air filled the room. Cox kept her Colt 1911 at the ready and was already sweeping the second room as the rest of her party was getting inside. She knew there'd likely be nothing of value here – the immediate proximity to the barracks virtually guaranteed the place had been looted several times over – so she focused her attentions on identifying the signs of unfortunate refugees who may have succumbed to the infection after fleeing the Armouries.

They would need to clear each apartment individually to be sure.

The door to the unit was splintered, obviously having been kicked from its hinges by scavengers. Completing her sweep, Cox peered out into the hallway and determined every door had met with the same unceremonious end.

Obviously the salvagers saw no reason to be delicate.

Isaac, Sully and Anders fell in behind Cox and began sweeping the remaining apartments while the rest got settled. Daniel and Keeley took one last opportunity to check over Jacob's sutures and ensured he, Madison and Emily had everything they needed.

Satisfied they were alone, the group moved upstairs to a ground floor apartment. It had windows on two sides of the building, one facing the Armouries and the other overlooking the street with the church opposite. The apartment itself was bare – most all the furniture was missing, likely carted away by the barracks crews for makeshift bedding and comforts.

The group fidgeted as they settled in; no words were shared between them.

Keeley fumed and paid no attention to Isaac, who stood in one of the dark corners, rolling his knife back and forth in his hands.

Though the tension wasn't missed, most believed it to be immaterial; little attention was paid to their squabble.

Only Jacob questioned it.

He studied Isaac, mind turning with possibilities despite the fog that dulled his thoughts.

Sully parted the blinds, drew his binoculars and surveyed the yard.

From here, he could get eyes on the other side of the structure and complete the general layout of the site. He had a better line of the jagged rows of vehicles parked in the yard, and they seemed relatively unencumbered. The only real ghoul presence was at the far end, towards the rear of the structure. A few stragglers milled about, but they were scattered, oblivious – dead for some time.

It felt like more than yesterday, but the combination of their need to leave the city and his confidence that they were collectively due for some good fortune spurred him on.

Sully lowered the binoculars and glanced over his shoulder. The rest took his meaning.

Madison pursed her lips and watched anxiously as the scavengers slipped out the unit and crossed the street at full sprint.

The group fell in behind a large military transport truck with an open back, covered with a canvas fabric stretched over metal ribbing. The canvas was riddled with tears and holes and the sides of the truck were peppered with small arms fire. Anders and Keeley needed to move quickly; they would dart between vehicles, plunder anything useful while making every effort to not attract attention. If they were spotted, they would take the path of least resistance to their nearest allies – either into the Armouries or back to the apartment.

Cox held everyone back while she scanned the grounds, carefully assessing their odds of advancing without announcing their presence.

The appointed time would be fast upon them.

'Good luck,' Isaac whispered as he reached for Keeley's arm, 'stay safe.'

It killed him that she wouldn't stay in the vantage with the others, but she was adamant. He held out his knife out to her, handle first.

She met his eyes briefly before turning away.

'We'll be fine.'

Isaac nodded and buried the blade to the hilt in the snow beside her.

Cox waved them on; it was time to go.

Anders popped the door to the truck and started sifting through its contents while Keeley watched over him. Cox led them across the yard to a large, wooden door with brass rivets. She positioned herself to the side and held her sidearm to a low ready as Sully tried the handle, finding the door to be heavy but unlocked. Cox leaned in with her sidearm, angling off the opening as she slipped inside.

Keeley watched as the massive door closed behind the group, wondering if perhaps she had made a terrible mistake.

She pulled the knife from the snow.

* * *

The interior was a warzone.

Dozens of bodies littered the floor in a morbid tapestry of blood, bone and sinew. The sickly sweet perfume of slow decay filled their nostrils and choked their breath even with the shattered windows ventilating the place.

The corpses lining the floors seemed to be mostly the inedible bits and bones, what flesh remained spared only by synthetic fibers that presumably couldn't be gnawed through.

The enormity of this undertaking was now plain before them.

Daniel recoiled, having never witnessed death on this scale. Neither had the others – but their trials in the wastes had largely desensitized them to this level of violence.

The Nigerian recovered from the initial shock and shook it off.

The corridor opened to a gymnasium lined on either side with doors to old offices, hastily repurposed for the needs of the compound. Coloured banners representing the various units previously stationed here hung limply overhead. A balcony ran the circumference above, apparently also lined with rooms. The main chamber was cordoned off and partitioned, many of which were strewn across the floor, no doubt trampled during the commotion of the fighting. Those that yet stood were punctuated by bullet holes and the streaks of bloody handprints.

The group waited in revered silence as they surveyed the scene for signs of movement. Cox considered the layout. Though she was unfamiliar with the Armouries, instinctively she knew that the truly high value merchandise would be fortified; unlikely it would be within easy reach of the exits. In the event a threat managed to get inside, a defending force would want narrow corridors, bottlenecks, and a clear line to fall back to.

Satisfied there were no immediate threats aware of their intrusion, Cox motioned for Sully and Isaac to canvas the nearby offices and work their way up to the balcony while she and Daniel pressed on.

Sully was uncomfortable taking orders from the corporal; his skin crawled in her presence. Nevertheless, she was undeniably skilled in this environment, and she had successfully led mission after mission for Quinn. Out here, Isaac was right – her cold logic and sheer determination were significant assets.

Isaac and Sully kept their backs along the wall and slid up the left side, eyes carefully scanning the death that covered floor as Cox led Daniel right.

As they came to the first entry, Isaac leaned out and peered in. It was long and skinny; the mouth of the office had an overturned desk pressed up against it as a simple barrier. The skeletal remains of a plainly clothed man, torn open and consumed, lay on the floor just beyond. What bones were visible had clear bursts of trauma from bullet wounds. The far end of the office bent suddenly and was obscured around a corner. The wall was adorned with several portraits of ranking military officials, interrupted by a single large textured glass window.

Isaac climbed over the desk and lowered himself gingerly to the floor. Knowing he was without a weapon, his pulse quickened – the blood flow warmed his ears and his body tingled with anticipation. Hatchet in hand, Sully was just behind. They held their breath and crept slowly toward the end of the line. Soundlessly, they rounded the corner to reveal a corpse, prostrate and with the back of its head sprayed onto the wall, crouched over the body of a uniformed man.

As they broke the dim light cast through the textured glass, the uniformed thing stirred. Its dead eyes opened lazily as its chin rose awkwardly before Sully buried the hatchet into its head. He struck the thing with such fury that he needed to wrench the blade from the ghoul's skull, rocking the handle back and forth until the wound widened sufficiently for the axe to wriggle free.

Considering he could see clear into the skull of the prostrate ghoul, Isaac had no fear of its sudden animation and shoved it aside with his boot. As he crouched down to search the corpses, Isaac couldn't hide his disappointment that he didn't turn up with the sidearm that had clearly put this one down.

Nothing in here was of any use.

As Isaac prepared to rise he locked gazes with the lifeless eyes. Jaw agape, skin gray and tightening around the stubble on its face, deep divide from the hatchet wound in the crown of its forehead.

Isaac frowned and rejoined Sully in the main expanse, moving further along the wall towards the next office.

Cox and Daniel were now at the corner opposite where they had entered the room, peering between heavy set double doors and down a dark and windowless corridor. The doors were held open by a hinging mechanism that engaged when they were opened beyond a certain point in their arc.

Their wide angle was deceivingly inviting.

Cox shined her flashlight down the corridor, and found it to be largely empty. The flooring changed from the polished gymnasium to an embossed and rubberized white honeycomb. While the floors were boot scuffed and bloodstained, the fighting had obviously been heavier elsewhere in the complex. Exposed wires were tacked along the ceilings, likely linked to gas generators that had long since run dry.

As she and Daniel delved into the belly of the structure, the darkness deepened. Empty lockers ran along the wall beside them. Sidearm readied, Cox carefully worked each corner as they wound through the network of corridors until they arrived at the precipice of a black metallic stairwell.

Daniel choked back the feeling of sincere dread as he leaned over the railing, following the lone beam of the flashlight into the depths below. The stairwell was steel grating, similar to industrial catwalk. As the light pierced its gloom, the grating threw cage-like patterns over the landing to reveal the resting place of several gory husks. A dozen mice, disturbed by the lighting, hastily scurried from sight.

Cox considered their options. The way up at this juncture was free of corpses, but was barricaded with stacks of chairs and shelving. The bodies at the base of the stairwell indicated to her the soldiers who once occupied this place had fallen back to some point below.

Corridors continued in two directions.

Cox turned to Daniel, but he didn't need her instructions.

She led him down the staircase into the incredible black. She was significantly smaller and lighter on her feet than Daniel; even as he made every attempt to tread lightly, his footfalls resounded with a dull metallic echo as they crept down the stairs.

Cox kept her flashlight in continuous motion, sidearm poised as they descended. The walls here were stacked concrete block, nondescript and painted a clinical grayish white. Several exposed water pipes ran overhead, encased in aged sheathing. The line was compromised somewhere;

the faint sound of dripping water felt as if distant thunder in the silence of the basement dark.

Daniel kept close to the corporal, daring not to disrupt her focus as she inched forward.

They passed an opening in the wall without a door. Cox paused outside and flashed the light about the offset entry, determined it to be a washroom. The absence of a door troubled her, and they opted to clear the space before continuing. Several flies reacted to the flashlight and buzzed about the low ceiling as the flashlight reflected off the line of grimy mirrors. The sinks clearly showed their age, basins stained with rings of brown water. Bits of gore and ripped clothing dotted the floors. A row of lockers, several with doors ajar, lined the walls opposite the stalls.

Daniel stepped to the lockers and peered through their slats for anything useful as Cox kept the center of the floor. As he opened one of the lockers its hinge creaked loudly. Daniel cringed and turned to be greeted by the corporal, the beam of her flashlight focused disdainfully at his face. Wincing, he turned from the abrasive light and raised a hand to shield his eyes. To emphasize her contempt, she let the flashlight linger over him much longer than was necessary before squaring back to the entry.

Daniel rifled through the remaining lockers, delicately turning over their contents. Though it was nothing more than some toothpaste and assorted toiletries, he knew the value of personal hygiene both in terms of health and morale. As he packed the supplies, he became thoroughly aware of the staleness of the whiskey on his breath. Daniel stuffed the supplies into a canvas messenger bag and signaled his completion to Cox.

The two slipped back out from the washroom and continued along the hallway. At the far end, the floor became congested with bits of corpses and the signs of carnage increased in both frequency and severity. In the closeness of the basement, the stench of death hung heavy in the air and on the walls. Cox and Daniel progressed slowly, choosing their footfalls carefully. They passed several closed doors, pausing outside each to listen for the shuffling of feet or sounds of ragged movement from within. Though it would have been safer if they paused to clear every room, she was convinced they'd encounter opposition and jeopardize their stealth.

She wanted the big prize – the Alamo. They could canvas the smaller rooms on the way back, after they accomplished the mission. As they pressed on, the corpses noticeably became more and more official staff than civilian refugees.

Cox's intuition told her they were getting close.

At last, they arrived outside a set of bloodstained double doors, riddled with small arms fire. The floor immediately outside in the hallway was densely packed with corpses. Each of the doors held a pane of frosted glass; a corner of one was shot out and would allow Cox to peer within. She pressed her back flat against the wall outside and strained her ears.

Nothing.

Now or never, she raised the flashlight and allowed it to wash over the room.

* * *

Anders tapped Keeley on the shoulder.

She had been fixated on a crow as it feasted on the remnants of a partially buried corpse in the yard.

He needed her present.

Theirs was a slow and patient game, punctuated by sudden periods of intense speed. They darted from cover to cover, moving between vehicles in the yard, systematically picking through their consoles and glove boxes. They had found some success, a few MREs and a multi-tool, though it did little to alleviate her feeling of unease.

Keeley snapped back to the moment and he passed her some maps and a compass he had procured from a glove box in one of the military trucks.

Anders smiled at her as he clambered out of the cab.

'They're fine,' he reassured her with a wink.

She meekly returned his smile. She couldn't help but feel guilty about his jaw.

Nevertheless, his upbeat attitude was infectious, and she did find herself partially warmed by it.

Keeley gripped Isaac's blade tightly as she and Anders crouched down, watching and waiting for their next opportunity to advance.

* * *

Sully turned the weapon over in his hands as he stepped over the shattered bodies of two ghouls they had just dispatched.

This office had been particularly productive.

He dropped the box mag out of the Savage .308 and found it contained a single round. It was surprisingly light with a sleek black polymer stock and a silver weather coated barrel. Hardly military grade, but a fine rifle nonetheless – some civilian must have brought this in with them.

Probably one of the two he just sacked with the hatchet.

Isaac patted down the pockets of the now silenced corpses. He was working fast, more than a little apprehensive about the noise their scuffle may have dusted up, but he couldn't stifle a grin when the search turned up a few unspent cartridges.

Sully replenished the mag and chambered a round as quietly as he could. The bolt's action was smooth, but the throw was wider than most rifles he'd handled – the scope was mounted high and forward on spacers to compensate. It felt a little awkward to look through the aperture given its height, but he was confident he'd get comfortable with it.

He passed the hatchet to Isaac who took a moment to acclimate to the weapon, practicing some slow arcs in the air. Sully's eyebrows raised and he quietly snickered at the clumsy movements; Isaac looked ridiculous.

City boys.

They had kept to the offices, only venturing a few steps into the main expanse to silence a ghoul if it stirred. The majority of the bodies were completely consumed, but the occasional creature – impossibly clinging to unlife – would react to their movement. Though it was no threat to their passing, typically only being a portion of a man or woman attached to ragged stumps of limbs, they couldn't risk the noise attracting a more virile sibling.

Content they had found everything of use in the room, Sully shouldered the rifle and moved back toward the exit with Isaac close behind.

He allowed himself a wide, satisfied smile.

Things were going well.

Chapter 26

THE FLASHLIGHT GORGED ITSELF ON SHADOWS as it probed the chamber beyond.

Triage.

It was unmistakable. Cots and stainless steel tables filled the room, some upturned, their trappings spilled about the crimson stained floors. IV units maintained their silent vigil from perches about the corners of the room. Rows of shelves and cupboards lined the walls above a work table where a lone microscope waited.

The hairs on the back of the corporal's neck stood up as they responded to the synapses firing in her brain. She stood on her toes and peered at the floor immediately inside the room. Seeing only stained tile and bits of flesh, she reached for the handle.

As delicately as possible, she pushed the door open. As it swung, the rubber fins of the door sweep buffed the gore and produced a disturbing suction sound. With her sidearm raised high and the flashlight cross-gripped at the wrists, she squeezed her way into the room with Daniel close behind.

Two of the stainless operating tables had been overturned and were a few feet back from the doorway, angled outwards. They were likely stacked against the doors as a barricade before the doors were forced.

This was the most violent display Daniel had ever witnessed. The knot of consumed corpses was indistinguishable from one another but for any bits of uniform or skeletal structure that remained intact. He paused and leaned against a table, struggling to prevent himself from retching.

The corporal continued her sweep, patiently angling off the chamber and identifying how many rooms led from it. Though perspiration beaded on her forehead and her mouth felt impossibly dry, she remained unshaken.

She waited patiently at the entrance to the next room, listening attentively for any sounds within. She afforded Daniel a few moments to regain his composure.

Forcing the bile back down, he averted his eyes from the mess and stepped over to the cupboards. Though most shelves were bare, he was able to grab several spools of gauze, a box of bandages and a small bottle of rubbing alcohol.

Satisfied they had captured everything of value in the first room, they slipped into the second. Daniel kept pace just behind Cox as she methodically bathed the room in the flashlight, illuminating the corners and probing the dimensions of the space. This room was small and square, having no additional exits except for something that appeared to be a storage closet. The closet door had a vertical slat of a window that revealed only further blackness. A large slab table sat plumb in the center of the room and the wall opposite them was a single length of deep countertop with a sink, stretched over several sections of wide drawers.

The slab had several strips of leather bands wreathing it, no doubt used as restraints. Daniel could tell immediately this was the operating room, used to treat the most serious of the casualties. He could still detect the faint traces of antiseptic under the more pronounced perfumes of death, nicotine and cordite.

As they stepped into the room and towards the closet, something stirred on the floor beyond the slab table. A solitary ghoul, half of a man in what was once a white lab coat, clawed at the air as they passed. Scarcely able to lift his head from the floor, it issued a low hiss from desiccated lungs. It had but one arm and both its legs were missing, shorn off near the pelvic bowl which writhed into the tile. The searching hand was missing a couple fingers and what flesh yet clung to the creature was ragged and torn. Lacking the strength to move its body, it pitifully scratched the air, hoping its meal would wander into its perverted jaws.

Cox moved towards the thing to silence it, but Daniel stopped her.

He would deal with this one.

The creature's movements intensified as he approached and bent down beside it. A tray of medical implements was spilled on the floor next to a trampled set of prescription glasses. The ghoul's eyes widened with hunger as it gnashed the air with broken teeth.

Daniel collected a scalpel and buried it deep in the thing's ear canal.

The writhing stopped.

Daniel removed the implement and wiped the more viscous bits off on his jeans.

Cox snapped her fingers softly, and he bounded over to her.

'*Jackpot*,' she whispered, motioning into the closet.

Daniel peered through the glass slat as the flashlight bathed row upon row of bottles, compresses and serums.

A wave of relief rolled over Daniel. He couldn't contain his excitement as sincere tears of joy welled in his eyes.

Even Cox had to admit; it felt *good*.

She tried the door. Locked tight, it rattled in response, but it didn't matter – so uplifted were they by the contents of the closet, this was only a minor inconvenience.

Cox started working through the drawers as Daniel returned to the ghoul at the center of the room. With only one flashlight between them, Cox alternated illuminating both their fields of view periodically. As she slid the drawers out, their tracks groaned from dust and disuse. Within, steel surgical implements happily chimed off each other while plastic tubes and bottles rattled about.

The lab coat was stained to the colour of deep rust. Daniel turned out the pockets, patting down the outside to get a gauge as to what they might contain. Though it felt like grave robbing, he had little choice but to ignore his apprehension.

The Good Doctor was a smoker, it would seem. Daniel pulled out a pack of cigarettes with less than half a deck and a paper matchbook with eight or nine matches remaining. After exhausting the lab coat, Daniel flipped the corpse onto its side and checked the tattered pants pockets.

Cox was about to open her fourth drawer when the telltale clinking of a key ring caused her spirits to soar. She wheeled about and flashed the beam onto Daniel's face without thinking, causing him to shield his eyes again.

The two shared a private laugh.

Daniel sprung to his feet and began systematically trying the keys in the lock. There were well over a dozen keys on the ring, and Daniel had little recourse but to try them one by one. With each failed attempt the door rattled on its hinges, and though Daniel made every effort to subdue the vibration of trying the lock, it was impossible to control.

Cox was growing worried. In their excitement, she was concerned they were making too much noise.

Not wanting to alarm Daniel as he worked the door, she put her back flat against the wall next to him and nonchalantly asked –

'Do you have this?'

Daniel, fixated on not losing his place on the order of keys being tested, nodded to her and mouthed some words silently to himself.

Cox crept out of the room and back towards the main chamber. She advanced to the double doors where they had entered the medical wing and pressed her ear to them. When she heard nothing, she delicately opened it and peered out, shining the flashlight low in both directions.

Nothing but the patter of water falling from the overhead piping.

Mindful of the hinges, she gently slid the door closed and surveyed the triage room again. Two more chambers were off of this one, aside from the room where Daniel worked the lock. She crept along the side of the room where the microscope leered on the table.

As she approached one of the exits her eyes fell onto the tangled mess of uniformed corpses. She knelt down beside the mound, frowned in disgust as she fished through it with the muzzle of her sidearm. She was delighted to be rewarded with another pistol, a Glock 17, and a couple clips of 9mm. The Glock was sticky with gore; she depressed the mag release and racked the slide a few times to clear any obstructions. Content it was in working order, she replaced the clip and tucked the weapon into the back of her waistband before continuing to sift through the debris.

* * *

Daniel was growing frustrated – *how many fucking keys do you need?* – but as the locking mechanism finally turned over, he knew the aggravation was well spent.

The hinge was well greased, and the door glided open without protest.

Daniel opened the flap to the canvas messenger bag and produced the matchbook from his pocket. He folded a match out and struck it. It flared to life and the pungent sulfur overpowered the closet air. In the flickering flame, the rows of bottles looked taller and the shadows they cast danced playfully.

This had it all.

Antibiotics, potent opiates and assorted painkillers, stimulants and suppressants; it was impossible to remember his prioritized list.

No matter.

Daniel thought back to his time as a student at UNB, where one of his professors taught him the importance of compartmentalizing.

When overwhelmed, divide and conquer.

As Daniel struggled with where to start, the match ran down and seared his finger tips. After the sudden staccato of the shock, Daniel laughed at himself and struck another match.

Let's try that again.

There was a large, heavy medical kit sitting invitingly on the counter. Its security seal was intact and the metal container was essentially latched.

Daniel started with that.

Next he loaded up with antibiotics, greedily stuffing his bag with bottles and vials of varying sizes as the tablets clattered about in their containers. With a broad selection of penicillin and non-penicillin variants he moved on to the morphine, Oxy and Percocet. He found EpiPens, Benadryl, Ventolin and Anadrol, beta blockers, cough suppressants, multivitamins, anti-inflammatories, analgesics, statins; a trove of pharmacological treasures.

This was a candy store.

* * *

Cox chuckled to herself privately, thoughts returning to her decision to enlist in the armed forces.

She flicked her wrist and expelled some gunk from off her sidearm.

This is not how the recruiter described it.

She rose from her knees and rolled her head back onto her shoulders, allowing the beam of the flashlight to fall to her feet.

She could hear Daniel rummage through the closet, pills and tablets rattling around in hard plastic containers as they were shifted about the shelves. When he had everything he deemed useful stowed away, he'd be back out.

She had time to kill.

Cox took a deep breath of the sour air, unfortunately quite accustomed to it.

She stepped over to the next door and pressed her ear against it.

She expected to be greeted by the same severe silence of the basement.

This time, however, she was rooted in place.

Something stirred within.

She strained her ears, tried to determine their number and approximate distance, but couldn't isolate the source.

Whatever it was, it didn't sound like the shuffling of feet.

Believing it to be the tormented throes of another half consumed corpse, wriggling about on the floor, she decided the best course of action would be to silence the thing before it attracted any more attention.

She prepared herself and inched the door open.

The room it revealed was much longer than she expected; the soldiers who defended this place must have retreated further in when they lost the triage area. Essentially, it housed more of the same; splashes of crimson and buckshot decorated the wall, bits of necrotic flesh lined the floor.

She had guessed right. Just opposite the door a ragged thing crawled toward her, dragging its paralyzed legs behind it. The ghoul was missing a significant proportion of its jaw and throat, its voice box torn out either by searing lead or snapping teeth. Feeling no threat from it, she allowed the flashlight to survey the room.

The breath was stolen from Cox's lungs.

Several infected stood outside a door at the far end of the hallway.

Some were shambling towards her.

Still more were struggling to rise from wherever they fell.

The ghouls must have heard their searching; they had awoken from their dreadful slumber but were unable to locate the source of their sleep's disruption. Muffled through the doors and the dim senses of undeath, they couldn't fully process her presence just outside the door. Without a clear prey signal, the ghouls merely shook off the dust as one might stretch their muscles after a long nap.

Now, however, they had much more appetizing stimuli.

She involuntarily opened her mouth to scream, but regained control with just enough time to stifle the sound.

The moment those at the head of column laid eyes on the abrasive light, they roared with bestial fury. The creatures lurched forward, incredibly fast considering their state of decay.

Cox stumbled back from the door as it scraped shut and turned to run.

All hope of stealth was abandoned now.

'*Daniel*,' she cried out midstride, '*we need to go!*'

It took Daniel a moment to process. He ran his arm along the shelf and swept as many bottles as he could into his bag before breaking into a sprint back to her position. Most of the bottles missed altogether, falling to the floor and skittering across the tile where they were either trampled or sent flying as he ran by.

By the time he was back in triage, Cox was full flight out the double doors, crashing hard into the wall before propelling herself on. Daniel thundered after her, the heavy messenger bag banging awkwardly into the backs of his legs as he struggled to keep up with the agile corporal.

The door Cox had just been inspecting swung open and a ghoul spilled through, tumbling to the floor.

Terrible cries called after them.

Daniel gulped the air, eyes fighting to adjust to the changing light as the flashlight pulsed between the corporal's strides.

The doors on either side of the corridor were being pounded on from within, their hollow echoes chasing after the intruders as surely as the ghouls behind them.

'*Wait!*' Daniel cried from somewhere behind.

She didn't pause.

She had to escape.

Cox ran with abandon. Her muscles screamed for oxygen as her legs pumped, the sound of the adrenaline coursing through her veins overpowering Daniel's thudding footsteps behind her.

Nearing the end of the corridor and the base of the stairwell, Cox turned her head to chance a look back.

He was making good time, laden as he was.

In that instant, she plowed into the figure of a man.

Cox cried out in terror; the impact of the collision sent the flashlight spinning into the air. Its harsh beam spun circles in the dark as Daniel struggled to catch up.

The ghoul was briefly knocked back by the impact, but it towered over her. Dazed by the blow, the corporal was off balance. The creature roared while its hideous hands mauled the air as it tried to bring an end to its terrible hunger.

The two grappled as the ghoul sought to envelop her. Her range of motion was impaired, her weapon arm partially pinned against her body as she fought for precious inches. The ghoul was slow, necrotic, and as she twisted and writhed under its bulk she managed to free her arm long enough to get two rounds off. The creature shuddered as the .45 devastated its sternum, the force of the bullets at that range pushing the thing back half a step.

The combination of the muzzle flash and the report from the pistol was disorienting; Cox's vision was awash in spots and colour. Impervious to such things, the ghoul's dead eyes flared and its jaw opened wide as it renewed the assault.

Cox managed to hit the thing in the shoulder as it closed the distance, taking off a chunk of flesh but succeeding only in causing the thing to rotate slightly.

Its course remained unaltered.

The two came together again. Considerably outmatched by the size and power of her assailant, the slender corporal was forced against the wall at the base of the stairwell. In the layer of gore beneath the stairs, her footing slid awkwardly as they battled.

The lusting jaws chomped the air mere fractions of an inch from her skin.

She could smell the imminent death from it.

The inevitability.

But not the blessing of finality.

An image flashed in her mind.

A picture of her, parched and insatiable, wandering these halls forever.

Her arms began to buckle and she cried out in hopelessness.

* * *

Sully and Isaac both froze.

'Did you fucking hear that?'

They were more than halfway up the left side of the gymnasium, but in the long and dreadful silence of the Armouries it was unmistakable.

That was gunfire.

Both were off like shots, hustling back to the main expanse.

No discretion now in the weight of their steps.

They broke hard along the wall, moving quickly to retrace their steps to where they had separated.

They weren't the only ones to have heard the disturbance.

Several doleful moans announced themselves throughout the chamber.

* * *

She had given up, resigned herself to the cruelest of fates.

She could feel the wicked breath as its disease licked at her flesh.

Suddenly, the weight was off her.

She was pulled from the wall and knocked from her feet, her vision returning only as she struck the soiled tile.

A grotesque column of ghouls marched towards her.

For good measure, Daniel delivered a kick to the head of the ghoul. Satisfied it had been sufficiently delayed, he bounded up the metal steps, taking two at a time.

She didn't hesitate.

She placed her hands before her, one on the tile and the other in a puddle of something she dare not think about, and pushed herself up from the floor. The line of ghouls emerged from the corridor mere steps behind as she rounded the base of the stairwell and followed suit.

Daniel was several steps back into the main chamber when Cox reached the double doors. The things behind clattered up the stairs, the jumble of their footsteps pounded off the catwalk grating. As she emerged from the basement dark and again felt the high ceilings and natural light, an overwhelming sense of relief flooded her as the adrenaline dumped.

She made it in a few short strides before she slipped and spilled to the floor. The Colt 1911 slid from her grasp, scraping a few feet before it came to rest against a half-eaten mess.

The tormented cries were getting closer.

They had almost crested the stairs.

Sully and Isaac saw Daniel emerge from the darkness at full stride a moment before; their pace quickened to converge with him near the entrance of the gymnasium when the corporal fell.

As she pawed at the ground, desperate to reach her weapon, Daniel rushed past her – back towards the terrible dark of the basement.

On her hands and knees, she crawled.

Her fingers finally found the familiar wood paneled grip of her .45; Cox rolled to her back to see Daniel barricading the doors closed with his body. The entire frame shook under the heavy assault from within as he desperately tried to keep the doors from coming off their moorings.

As Daniel struggled to set his feet and press his back against the doorway, he realized his error.

Seeing Daniel so committed, Isaac broke off from the wall and sprinted diagonally through the minefield of corpses. Sully needed to ensure Isaac didn't compromise his line of sight and leapt a few more steps along the wall and crouched, shouldering the rifle.

The creatures furiously pounded on the door.

Daniel lifted the strap of the messenger bag around his neck and threw it towards the corporal. It fell to the floor with a heavy thud, the top of the canvas bag opening and partially spilling its contents. A couple bottles bounced out, rattling across the floor.

He smiled meekly, to no one in particular.

The door shuddered again as the tide of hands and teeth crashed against it. Daniel was briefly knocked off the door and it opened a fraction of an inch before he threw his body against it again.

Still dazed, Cox battled to come to her feet and raise her weapon.

Isaac had another two dozen yards to cross, leaping over piles of human debris as he tried to close the distance.

'*Goddamnit…*,' Sully cursed under his breath as he raised the scope to his eye.

Another wave crashed against the door and its hinges ripped from the wall. Daniel was thrown from it, struck in the back of the head by one of the doors as they crumbled down. He was knocked to the floor and rolled onto his side, coming to his elbow before collapsing.

The flood of ghouls spewed from the darkness.

The .308 thundered.

* * *

Anders stopped mid sentence; the words were stolen from him.

He was just climbing out from the cab of a truck when the unmistakable *crack* split the morning air.

Terror filled Keeley's eyes.

Without a word, she broke off from their position and sprinted towards the entrance of the barracks.

* * *

The shot echoed for miles.

Madison, Emily and Jacob thrust themselves against the window and rustled the blinds.

They watched helplessly as Keeley darted across the yard.

'No, no, no, no…,' Jacob repeated, muttering in disbelief, hoping his denial would alter the outcome.

They had surely been noticed.

Anders crawled out of the cab and lowered himself down heavily onto the snow.

She had covered almost half the distance to the door.

He instinctively moved to join her, but as he came to the end of the vehicle he was hiding behind he paused for a moment. His unblinking eyes fell to his boots and he took several short breaths. He peered out from behind his cover and confirmed several shapes now shambled towards him.

They're all you've got, now.

He shuffled laterally a few steps and then broke into a run after Keeley.

* * *

The first ghoul exploded as Sully's devastating round struck it at the base of the neck, blowing it apart just above the center of its collarbone.

As it went down, three more took its place.

Cox's training took over and seized control of her movements. She loosed several rounds from the .45, each one finding its intended mark.

Daniel scrambled, his fingers digging into the polished floor as he fought to crawl away.

The .308 roared again and another ghoul burst.

Isaac surged as the hatchet begged for satisfaction.

Keeley sprinted into the room, eyes wide as they processed the scene.

Isaac hadn't noticed her entrance; he had only a dozen more yards to cross.

Sully loosed his last round.

Cox continued to fire into the crowd, hoping to suppress the sinister advance.

...there was just too many.

One finally shuffled through the gauntlet and found its mark.

Its weight pinned him to the floor as its pestilent jaws dug deep into his leg, tearing through the denim and rending his muscles.

Daniel howled in agony, wailing inhumanly as the creature gnawed his flesh.

'*Nooo!*' Keeley shrieked in horror, as much a sob as a scream.

More hands wrapped around his body.

Daniel cried pitifully as the feast continued, screaming out in terror as he was devoured.

He begged for death.

Isaac slowed, dumbfounded. The hatchet lowered at his side as he watched the vulgar display.

Sully replaced the box mag.

He shouldered the rifle and took aim.

He drew a deep breath.

He exhaled slowly.

At the base of the breath, he squeezed the trigger.

Chapter 27

'FUCK, WHAT DO WE DO?' MADISON LAMENTED.

Jacob's face tightened in thought.

Their options weren't good.

Something unspoken told Emily to go to the bedroom and look out the window there, survey the streets on the other side of the building.

She could hear Jacob and Madison debating their course of action, but she couldn't make out the words.

Emily stared at the church.

A trick of the eye.

The windows vibrated; the pattern of light striking the glass wavered momentarily.

Suddenly it burst, glass twinkling in the morning sun as it spilled into the street.

Emily's hand covered her mouth as she stifled a scream.

She began to tremble and shake, finally succumbing to a terrified sob.

Madison rushed into the room to find Emily pale and stricken.

As she moved to comfort her, she caught sight of the throng of corpses filtering out the church window. Emily buried her face into Madison's shoulder as Madison wrapped her arm around her.

The two huddled together as the column of ghouls began to advance towards the sounds of gunfire.

* * *

The howling stopped.

Feeling sick to his stomach, Sully recoiled from the aperture.

Keeley ran towards their downed companion.

Cox unconsciously took a step back and dropped the expended magazine from her .45.

Isaac snapped back to the present, realizing that in her grief Keeley hadn't recognized the futility of the situation. He bounded over the last few obstacles and intercepted her path, catching her with an arm around her waist and lifted her clear off her feet. He wrestled with her as she fought to get past him, arms outstretched and sobbing.

Several ghouls now knelt and joined in the meal, but the space about their dead friend was becoming crowded. As more ghouls poured from the stairway, some were becoming more focused on those yet living.

Cox slammed another clip into the .45. She snapped off a few rounds as she continued to backpedal.

Anders came in to the main chamber and recognized their dilemma.

'*This way!*' he cried, waving his companions back out to the yard.

Realizing they had lost any semblance of advantage, Sully dashed towards Anders.

Though Isaac continued to grapple with Keeley, her thrashing was calming and Cox was falling back to their position.

'We'll clear the exit,' Anders offered as he assessed their situation. Sully nodded to him as he ran past.

Anders and Sully turned from the chamber and fell back.

Sully darted through the winding corridor towards the entrance. As he rounded the final corner, a lone ghoul roared and raised its hands. Instinctively, Sully smashed its face with the butt end of the .308. The creature was sent spinning as its jaw was blasted off its hinge and crumpled to the floor. Anders threw his body against the riveted door and it swung open into the deceivingly cheerful daylight.

Any relief that either felt at being outside would be short lived.

A stack of ghouls, at least a dozen deep, staggered toward them from around the back corner of the barracks. A formidable line of hungry corpses shuffled through the streets from where they came.

Anders spun on his heels, trying to determine where to run.

A few more shots echoed from the chamber.

The nearest infected cried out and picked up speed as they were presented with the prospects of fresh meat.

Sully emerged from the darkness and skidded to a stop behind Anders.

Sully cursed under his breath; trapped between a rock and a hard place.

No doubt they were spotted.

As Sully scanned the horizon for options, Anders grabbed him by the sleeve and pulled him towards the derelict tangle of vehicles. Several ghouls broke off from the main mass and followed them. It would have been more but for the continuing shots from the .45 echoing from somewhere inside the structure.

Anders led them to a high backed transport, scrambled up the fender and into the bed. Sully threw the rifle up to him and Anders hauled the Irishman over the battered tailgate. The two fell back into the truck and into a pile of frost-covered corpses. Each shifted some bodies and sank into the ruin, concealing themselves as best they could beneath a layer of death.

Anders tightly shut his eyes and tried to count how many ghouls had broken off to pursue them. He replayed the moments as best he could in his head, trying to differentiate between the infected by whatever detail he could pick out.

His eyes snapped open as a pair of fists rapped against the tailgate; a burst of clarity in his otherwise chaotic thoughts.

When they emerged from the barracks…

They failed to shut the door.

* * *

Madison watched helplessly as the grim procession shuffled towards the barracks. Nose pressed to the wall, only her eyes crested the window sill.

Jacob had seen Anders and Sully dart in and amongst the vehicles but lost sight of them in the jumble of metal and meat.

Emily sat with her arms wrapped around her knees and stared vacantly at the wall.

As Madison studied the terrible parade mindlessly shamble about the streets, she couldn't help but remember the Apple Blossom festival back home. The whole community would all but shut down, surrendering the streets to tacky floats and relics of a time that stubbornly refused to submit. They would sit, year after year, gathered together on the lawns and watch the same sad, small town floats drift along the same predictable course.

As silly as it was, she couldn't help but feel the world would be sadder for it.

This was a very different parade.

Madison and Jacob had been staying out of sight, puzzling about what to do.

None of the options sounded plausible.

As the two continued their debate, Emily interrupted unexpectedly.

'We should leave them.'

* * *

Keeley was tiring and struggled less.

Isaac was dragging her away, back towards the entrance.

Cox continued to select her targets with care as she fell in beside the others.

'We need to go,' she barked between shots.

Isaac twisted Keeley around and ushered her towards the door with the corporal close behind. Most of the creatures that yet poured from the basement paused to join in the frenzy about Daniel; Cox had sufficiently thinned the rest. A few broke off from the feast to pursue them, but they were gaining some distance.

With only a few more yards to go, the first ghoul rounded the corner to the main chamber from where they had entered together.

Cox's .45 was up in a flash, blasting a perfectly placed round through the thing's forehead. With the proximity of the flash and the subconscious signal that their exit was now cut off, Keeley seemingly regained control of her body.

The dead now approached them from two sides.

'*Fuck*,' Cox cursed as she slammed her final clip in. She racked the slide on the Colt, 'I'm almost out.'

Sensing Keeley's change in demeanor, Isaac released his hold around her waist and considered their options.

They couldn't go back.

Ghouls continued to filter into the room, groaning and growling, lifeless eyes wild with hunger.

Isaac put his hands on the corporal's shoulder and shoved her into the middle of the chamber, towards the immeasurable remains.

'That's further in,' she protested.

Isaac glared at her; he didn't need the reminder.

'Well, there's nothing coming from *that* direction,' he retorted cynically.

Cox dropped the nearest ghoul as it lurched towards them, its frost-bitten flesh bursting under the percussion of the .45.

The trio waded into the sea of death, away from the grim familiarity of the entrance and pushed towards the far right end of the chamber. Isaac led them on, pausing occasionally to chop anything on the floor he thought had moved as Keeley traced his footsteps as best she could. He had no idea whether this direction was safe or suicide, but knew insofar as he and Sully had pressed along the offices they'd find no shelter there.

Their only chance was to push deeper.

Cox brought up the rear, choking back painful tears as she watched many of the ghouls pouring from the entrance jockey for position at the meal.

His sacrifice had kept them alive.

Even now, as his blood wet the tile, he was buying them time.

As she glanced over her shoulder she realized that not every ghoul in the chamber was content with fighting for the leftovers.

* * *

Madison turned from Emily and lowered her eyes to the floor.

'Look, they're not getting out from that,' Emily pleaded, appealing to her companions' better sense, 'we have a chance!'

Jacob left the room in disgust and went back to the front window.

His heart rate was elevated; he could feel every beat in his stitches.

He flicked a few of the blinds down and surveyed the yard.

'We warned them,' she sobbed, 'we *fucking* told them!'

Only a handful of ghouls had broken off to pursue Anders and Sully – the rest had mostly disappeared into the depths of the Armories.

'Madison, you know I'm right,' Emily continued, unabashed. 'They're all going to die. If we go after them, we'll die too.'

Madison ignored her and peered out the bedroom window.

Emily brazenly folded her arms across her chest, clearly annoyed that common sense was lost among her company.

Madison scanned both directions; the line had thinned out. A few ghouls staggered up the street but no more dead belched from the church.

She whispered to Jacob and the two plotted once more.

Emily hugged herself tightly and began to sniffle.

'We're not going to make it,' she lamented as heavy tears streaked her face.

Jacob cursed their vantage; their sight lines were limited.

He missed his hatchet.

They had only kept a handful of kitchen knives with them.

It would have to do.

* * *

They reached the back of the chamber.

As they neared the entrance to another dark corridor, Cox shifted to the head of the column and Isaac dropped back to the rear. Keeley was moving under her own power, but she was in a daze, eyes thick with fog and disillusionment.

Cox immediately noticed the same bundle of wiring tacked to the ceiling and set about tracing its winding path. Sidearm raised and at the ready, she led them through the blood soaked aisles as fast as they could manage in the dreadful darkness, always following the overhead web of wiring.

She was on autopilot now, mind trying to reconcile Daniel's sacrifice as an act of stupidity as much as selflessness.

Whenever a creature emerged, Isaac would leap forward and drive the hatchet into its head until it went limp, then fall back to his position.

Finally they arrived at a heavy set of doors with an uncharacteristically large cluster of wiring anchored to the ceiling as if it formed the center of a major intersection. Its fingers stretched outwards in all directions. The doors were reinforced metal, severe and imposing.

It looked important.

Cox pressed her ear against it and strained to hear anything at all.

The cool metal of the door kissed her ear mischievously.

The anguished sounds of their pursuit loomed in the shadows behind them.

'Is this it?' Isaac asked, trying to mask his fear.

In the distant light from the main chamber, Isaac and Keeley could make out several silhouettes as they bobbed and lurched towards them.

Their mournful chorus grew louder.

The distance was closing.

Keeley pressed her back against the wall, wishing she could sink into the cold concrete block.

When Cox didn't answer, he asked again, tone as sharp as the hatchet.

'Is this it, or do we keep pushing?'

Cox didn't reply. She removed her ear from the door and threw her shoulder against it. It scraped against the floor but didn't yield.

Isaac took a deep breath and brandished the hatchet as he stepped towards the advancing line of corpses.

* * *

Why won't they wander off?

Anders kept his eyes shut as tightly as he could as the creatures continued to beat the outside of the truck. The irregular drumming of their dead hands against the steel made it impossible to tell their number. Their voices were virtually indistinguishable, the same breathless sound of grating stone.

Anders felt as if he was suffocating beneath the weight of his camouflage. While the infected seemingly lacked the fine motor control required to climb, they clearly weren't interested in anything but their whereabouts. He considered fighting his way out, but each time he had nearly mustered the courage to do it, he pictured a ghoul cresting the tailgate just as he revealed himself.

So he waited.

Sully also grew restless, but in a different way. His stomach was in his throat and his breath felt shallow. He knew he had made the merciful choice, the choice he hoped anyone would make for him, but the sight of Daniel's body exploding through the aperture burned his eyes.

It wasn't getting any easier.

He lied still, hoping the terrible images would fade.

* * *

Cox reeled back and threw herself against the door again.

Isaac swung the hatchet in a wide and upward arc, burying the blade beneath the jaw of the nearest ghoul. He grabbed the creature by its collar with his free hand, taking a few steps back as he twisted the hatchet free.

He couldn't slow them enough.

The dead were almost on top of them.

Keeley stared at the blood soaked floors and gasped for air.

The crowd of ghouls was thick and several deep. Isaac had been able to pick off the few loners at the head of the column, but he now struggled for options as he retreated from their perverse line.

A bullet snapped over his shoulder and the face of a ghoul exploded, bits of bone and flesh burst onto the walls. The fallen ghoul delayed those behind it for a moment, and the once seemingly impenetrable front now had a gap.

Isaac seized the moment and rushed forward, hatchet spiking down and collapsing the skull of another. He gripped the hatchet with both hands and yanked it free as he bounded back a couple steps, out of reach of the prying hands that slashed the air at him.

Cox could see Isaac was almost out of real estate.

His arms were low at his side; exhaustion was claiming him.

She squeezed off another round into the crowd and crashed against the door.

It grinded open an inch, but refused to give. Something barricaded it closed from within.

Cox screamed in desperation and kicked the door.

The stroke echoed pitifully into the black corridors, drowned out by the coming tide.

Keeley straightened off the wall.

Isaac was backpedalling fast now; the ghouls' pace quickened.

Cox fired twice more before she launched herself against the metal a final time. It yielded beneath the weight of the blow but she found herself involuntarily following it in; her shin banged into something hard and she tumbled awkwardly into the gloom.

Before she could regain her senses, she was under attack.

A uniformed ghoul was on top of her in an instant. She fought to keep the jaws from finding her flesh, but the sudden ferocity had her on the defensive from the outset.

The absolute black of its eyes reflected the dark of the room as its teeth gnashed wildly.

As Cox squirmed beneath the creature, it shuddered violently, and its thrashing stopped. Its dead weight sagged on the corporal as she struggled to roll out from underneath it. A blade poked diagonally through its open mouth from where Keeley had driven her knife through the back of its neck, severing the brain stem. A thick morass of blood dripped down the blade.

Isaac's feet kicked and slid manically as he struggled to shift the filing cabinet back against the door. He had managed to sufficiently close the gap between the downed cabinet and the door to prevent a whole body from slipping through, but a tangle of hands and arms flailed between the few inches of space.

The infected roared outside.

Cox came up to an elbow and shirked the thing off of her.

Jesus Christ… twice in one day…

She kicked at the creature and shifted it a fraction of an inch, its head comically propped up off the floor by the blade yet protruding from its mouth.

Cox's gaze lifted to find Keeley kneeling over her. Isaac crossed the distance to them in a single bound, grabbed her by the shoulders and spun her to face him. Even in the dim light, Keeley could see the blood spatter dotting his skin and glasses, the fear of loss plainly written on his face. She met his eyes as he wrapped his arms about her.

Stunned, she halfheartedly returned the embrace.

He broke off the hug and scanned her, pushing the hair from her face and checking her for any visible cuts or scratches. Satisfied none of the blood on her was her own, he squeezed her shoulders warmly before returning his attention to the mounting throng eager to beat their way into the room.

The ghouls' primal, sorrowful wails continued as the inhuman crowd tried to squeeze through the narrow opening. The flesh of those at the front of the column was being torn by the edges of the doors as the line behind them surged and pushed, impossibly trying to cram through. Isaac swatted the ragged arms with the hatchet, but it wasn't sharp enough to take a limb off in a single whack; instead it left a brutal wake of tattered bone and muscle.

Cox's head swam. She was sitting up now, holding herself up with her hands behind her and staring at the bloodstained floor between her boots. Daniel's messenger bag hung heavy off of her, like a noose of weighted chain.

As she considered the strange spectacle unfolding around her, she was overcome with something unfamiliar.

Remorse.

None of them had a reason to save me.

Isaac's pace had slowed. His breath was labored and he retreated from the doorway. Jagged, hacked off limbs slashed at the air, their shattered bones poking through the flesh like vicious talons.

Isaac dropped to a knee, struggling to find his breath.

He was running on fumes, chest heaving beneath the exertion.

The filing cabinet slid open an inch as the frenzy of ghouls capitalized on the respite. The scrape of metal against the tile was a foreboding reminder of what awaited them.

Isaac threw his body against the filing cabinet at a point behind the door, just out of reach of the flailing arms, but it was too far off center to properly brace it. He pressed his back against the cold metal and set his feet as best he could, but he knew that from here he could only delay the inevitable.

The ghouls had claimed too much ground for him to shore up their defenses.

Seeing that Isaac was out of options, Keeley instinctively began to run to him before he shouted her down.

'*Stay there!*' he boomed.

His voice was threatening, but his eyes were unmistakably weak.

Chapter 28

ISAAC COULD FEEL THE WEIGHT OF THE DOZEN or more ghouls outside as their force was transferred through the door and ultimately into his heels as he dug them in. He was catching his breath, but the adrenaline dump had sapped his muscles.

Only a matter of time...

He looked longingly at his fiancée, his wife.

As the creatures continued to savagely beat the door just behind him, his thoughts turned to whether it would be kinder to end the game on his terms. The thought of their flesh being consumed, of forever roaming these cursed halls in ravenous undeath was too much to bear.

Hopelessness washed over him.

He succumbed to defeat.

He had failed her.

'How many bullets do you have?'

Cox didn't reply; only continued to stare into vacant space.

Isaac repeated the question, but the corporal still didn't turn to face him.

'Not enough,' was her grim response.

Isaac took a long breath and cleared his throat.

'Not enough for what?'

His tone was grave.

Cox's head turned subtly as she processed his intended meaning.

Keeley hadn't missed the connotations, either.

'Fuck that,' she spat as she ripped the knife from out the smitten ghoul and set about examining the room.

The corporal managed a grin from where she sat; the bag felt a little lighter.

The room was square with several tall windows that didn't admit much light despite being south-facing. Sparse shelving lined one wall with a makeshift workspace. The doors Isaac barricaded seemed the only entrance or exit. The bundle of wires along the ceiling coiled down into an industrial-sized gas generator that sat in the middle of the floor, partially concealed amid some blue tarpaulin that shrouded a series of bulky objects.

Keeley approached it cautiously. She looked over the generator, a massive construct, and ran her fingers along the various buttons and switches. She gingerly pushed the bundle of wiring aside and checked the connections; everything seemed to be in its rightful place. She grabbed the handle and pulled the recoil starter. Its draw was heavy; she needed to brace herself against it with her foot as she tugged with all her might. The pulley yielded and turned over.

The generator sputtered impotently.

It was bone dry.

She released her grip on the starter and allowed it to snap back loudly against the casing.

Undeterred, Keeley continued to search about. The rigid tarpaulin crackled as she threw the plastic back, disturbing a layer of gray dust that swirled in the shafts of dull light cast from the windows.

Her eyes widened excitedly as it revealed a series of barrels.

More specifically, barrels of petrol.

She tilted some of the containers and could tell from their weight that several yet had fuel within. Possibilities were running amuck through her thoughts, but she hadn't any idea how to action them.

'*Holy shit*,' she started, 'corporal?'

Consumed in her own thoughts, Cox didn't seem to notice.

'*Corporal*,' Keeley called out more insistently, 'corporal, I need you here!'

Cox barely heard a thing. She was replaying her near death experiences, imagining what would have happened to her had it not been for Daniel.

Or for Keeley.

Cox snapped back to reality.

In an instant she was to her feet and over to the barrels, assessing their options.

'Alright,' she began, rifling through the bag slung over her shoulders.

A daring smile flashed across her thin lips.

* * *

Jacob led them into the yard.

They took cover behind some type of military transport. They had lost sight of Anders and Sully between the wreckage, but several creatures pounded the tailgate of a vehicle some twenty yards ahead.

Their continued interest in the back of that truck could only mean one thing.

Jacob peered out, careful to not be spotted as he assessed their options. He counted four ghouls, keenly aware of the possibility that stragglers yet approached.

Emily whimpered somewhere behind him; Madison didn't make a sound.

If it was only four, their odds would be decent; surely they could nab two by surprise. But threats unseen and uncounted, as well as untested companions, were wildcards that could easily tilt those odds against them.

Jacob gritted his teeth.

The flesh around his stitches tightened from the tension.

He described the scene by whisper to his companions and outlined the plan.

They could get a little closer before being forced into attack. They would rush the dead, hit them as one. They'd thin the gathering in one shot, and then need to deal with the melee afterwards.

Everything would hinge on timing.

Summoning what confidence he could, he led them on.

* * *

Isaac was in a daze and continued to pay little attention to his surroundings.

In his despair, he was virtually oblivious to the room beyond the steady blows against the door.

One of the creatures had almost slipped through. The metal edges of the door had stripped away much of its exposed flesh as fully a third of its body had forced through the gap. Isaac had mangled its arm in his earlier foray; the grayed tissue flapped about the bones of its forearm as the ghoul stabbed and parried the air, desperate but unable to reach its prey.

Cox raised the sidearm and fired one round into the thing's head, causing it to explode against the door behind it. The report of the sidearm in such closed quarters caused Isaac to wince in pain, but brought him back into the moment.

The corporal kicked over a half empty barrel of petrol, spilling its slick contents all over the floor. The dark pool of gasoline spread out wide as it gushed from the barrel. She uncapped another and Keeley helped her tip it over.

She had almost forgotten the smell of petrol.

Isaac watched as she unwound a spool of gauze and formed a makeshift fuse, running the length of it away from the barrels back towards him and the doors.

Cox reached into the bag and pulled another small item from it.

'You're going out that window and hook back up with the others. I'm going to hold this door until you're clear, then I'm going to light the fuse.'

She paused for a moment.

'I'll be right behind you.'

Cox lifted the strap of the messenger bag weightlessly over her head and passed it to Keeley.

Isaac and Keeley exchanged worried glances.

'You don't need to do this,' Keeley offered as she donned the bag.

'Yeah,' the corporal replied flatly, 'I really do.'

Keeley was at a loss for words.

Cox produced the Glock from the back of her waist line and plunked down next to Isaac. She pressed her back hard into the filing cabinet and pulled the spare mags from her pocket.

Cox held the sidearm by the barrel, offering its handle to Isaac.

Finding new strength in his companions, Isaac shed his hopelessness; he steeled himself and took the weapon and the spare clips.

'Thank you, corporal,' he began before he added, '... don't be long.'

The corporal nodded.

Isaac and Keeley immediately set about trying to pry open one of the windows.

Cox pressed her back firmly into the filing cabinet and watched them work the glass, feeling the reverberations of the assault against the door filter through her body. After they determined the window wouldn't budge, Isaac pushed Keeley back and began smashing the hatchet's blunt end against the tempered glass, causing it to splinter and crack with each strike.

As a section of glass finally gave and daylight poured through the hole, the pace of Isaac's blows quickened until the entire window shattered outwards into the morning sun.

Isaac cleared the shards away from the sill and scanned the yard. Satisfied it was clear, he turned to face the soldier that had taken his place. He nodded to her once before turning to offer Keeley a boost through the window.

Cox set her feet and braced against the cabinet.

The crowd outside continued to pile on, and the door was being forced open.

'Jennifer,' the corporal said softly, 'it's Jennifer.'

Neither Isaac nor Keeley immediately registered the response. They simultaneously paused and turned back to her, perhaps seeing her now for the first time as a person, as just another survivor.

Though tears welled in the corporal's eyes, her determination shone through.

'Jennifer,' Isaac repeated solemnly.

Keeley smiled to her before she added the name, herself.

'Jennifer,' she paused, 'we'll see you soon.'

* * *

They had crossed to their next cover point without attracting any attention.

Jacob's chest heaved as he steadied his breath.

He peered around their concealment and his heart sank.

With this new angle, a fifth and sixth ghoul were now visible.

The pieces had changed around him, but the initial plan was still the best he could come up with.

He looked at the shabby kitchen knives with contempt.

* * *

The immediate vicinity was clear.

As Isaac landed from the window, he grabbed Keeley's hand and brusquely pulled her along behind him. The force of his grip jolted her muscles uncomfortably.

No telling what opposition they'd encounter; he wouldn't risk separating, even by inches.

They neared the corner of the building and Isaac leaned out to survey the yard. He couldn't get a solid read on it; from this approach the vehicles were all stacked up differently than he remembered.

Nevertheless, he knew it was a lot of ground to cover to get back to the apartment where the others camped.

He trusted the Glock but didn't want to use it.

Isaac retracted from the corner and cursed under his breath.

The barracks were set in a wide open space that stretched out to the Bay, with an almost certain probability of infected nearby.

They'd need to obscure the possibility of sight lines in the distance.

They'd need to seek shelter in the tangled mess of vehicles.

* * *

She had watched them climb from the window with a satisfied smile as she turned over the tiny object in her hands.

It was the matchbook Daniel had collected from the Good Doctor.

She bent a single match before she plucked it, closing her eyes and feeling the rhythm of the creatures pounding just outside.

Her eyelids were heavy.

She sat in contemplative silence as she forced herself to relive unpleasant memories.

At last satisfied they had been afforded sufficient time to clear the vicinity, she struck the match carefully. She admired the tiny flame as it burst into life between her fingers.

Jennifer wondered if she'd really have time to escape the room.

Or if she even meant to.

She forced the thoughts and protests from her mind.

Unable to stifle the laugh that pierced her, she lit the fuse.

* * *

Keeley struggled to keep her feet as Isaac yanked her along.

They quickly crossed the distance to the assembled wreckage.

Somewhere ahead Isaac could hear the unmistakable sound of ghouls as they beat against something metal. He and Keeley kept low as they crept between the derelict vehicles, flitting between the ruins until they were overlooking a truck that had attracted significant attention. Several ghouls pounded their fists and scratched futilely at the transport, as if trying to reach whatever treasures lay within.

Isaac put his back flat against their cover and looked skywards.

He guessed they were about half the distance to the apartment across the street. These creatures were occupied, and they could likely go around. But there was no telling what lay beyond. Furthermore, something was obviously drawing the interest of the ghouls gathered here.

With only a knife and a sidearm between them, Isaac anxiously wrung his hands about the Glock.

* * *

It was time to move.

Jacob and Madison slipped out from their corner with Emily close behind.

Their steps were unsure at first but gathered strength as they advanced towards their quarry.

Only a few steps out…

* * *

The concussion from the blast shattered every window in the room, the glass littered the yard beyond as the fireball consumed all the available oxygen present. A billowing plume of black smoke poured through the openings, blotting out the sun as the flames devoured the brick structure in destructive orange light.

* * *

Emily's pace slowed instantly.

The deafening thunder of the explosion reverberated all around them.

Jacob and Madison pressed on, but the ghouls' focus had been drawn. The decaying creatures turned from whatever they had cornered in the back of the truck, their eyes flaring at the sight of new prey.

They had lost the initiative.

Jacob managed to drive his blade home into one as Madison tangled with another. Stricken, Emily was several paces back as the ghouls' line retorted. Jacob had ripped his blade free and squared to his next target, but Madison struggled to wrench her knife from out the skull of the one she had dispatched. The limp creature was dead weight and she dragged it back with her as she tried to twist free.

Three ghouls converged on her as she fought to retrieve her weapon.

'*Here!*' Jacob shouted at the creatures, but his attempts to draw their attention went unanswered.

Recognizing a human voice, Anders and Sully each scrambled to free themselves from beneath the corpses that concealed them.

Unable to recover the blade, Madison allowed the corpse and the knife embedded within to fall to the snows as she hastily backed away. Eyes wild with hunger, the infected jaws greedily snapped at the air as their rotten hands reached for her.

Jacob knew he was cut off.

'*Help her!*' he cried at Emily, but she stood only as a statue.

Isaac and Keeley couldn't see between the jumble of twisted vehicles.

'Stay close, watch our back,' Isaac ordered Keeley, and he rounded the corner of the vehicle and with the Glock raised.

Keeley gripped her blade tightly and followed immediately behind.

Madison continued to backpedal, her features clearly betraying her panic.

Preoccupied with his pleas to Emily, Jacob had to split his attention between her and the ghoul he circled with. It lunged and the two grappled briefly before they tumbled to the snow, his knife slipped between the collarbones of the creature and angled harmlessly downward into its chest cavity. Jacob surrendered his grip on the knife and fought hard to keep the clawing hands at bay as they rolled on the ground.

Isaac and Keeley rounded the vehicle and came out parallel to where Madison was falling back.

In the truck, Anders was first to emerge. His eyes stung with the sudden change in light, but regardless he leapt from the tailgate and into the melee. Bolstered by support from Isaac and Keeley, he sped towards Madison. Sully squinted his eyes against the light reflecting off the snow and tried to determine his target.

Isaac squeezed off three rounds. The first dropped the ghoul nearest, the second and third struck the next in line in the shoulder and jaw respectively. The creature shrugged off the shot to the shoulder, but the bullet that caught the jaw blew half its mandible off. The remnants of its jawbone barely clung on; what broken teeth survived snapped weirdly while a devastated tongue lashed and licked its ruined mouth.

Isaac cursed himself under his breath; Anders was too close now to risk another shot from this angle.

Anders grabbed the remaining ghoul by the collar. He spun the creature about and ran it head first into an adjacent vehicle. It crumpled facedown to the snow. He lifted the creature and slammed its face into the fender of the truck, collapsing one of its cheek bones and shattering its front teeth. The ghoul writhed and squirmed beneath the assault and Anders struggled to maintain control of the thing. Keeley ran to help him.

Sully shouldered the rifle.

'*Get down!*' he yelled to Madison, who instinctively dove beneath the nearest vehicle.

The ghoul with the hanging jaw fell to the snow and pawed after her. Madison's fingers bled as she desperately clawed at the ground, digging her nails into the snow and ice to pull herself on. The ghoul managed to find a grip on her ankle, its fingers snaking around her boot as it yanked itself towards her. Instinctively, Madison kicked at the broken face and hands of her pursuer, stomping at its nose and fingers. Bone and cartilage crushed beneath her heel, but without a pain response the ghoul maintained its vice-like grip.

The two locked eyes as the creature licked its tattered lips and hissed.

Madison screamed as the thing suddenly exploded, its body shuddered as the balance of its skull burst from the heavy blow of the .308.

Anders smashed his ghoul's face into the vehicle a final time before he forcefully pinned it to the ground. Keeley drove her knife into the base of the creature's neck, angling it upwards into the brain as Anders kept the creature subdued.

Sully hopped from the truck and Isaac rushed past to where Jacob battled with the ghoul. Its teeth continued to snap and gnash. Unable to find a clean shot, Isaac lowered the Glock and delivered a strong kick to the ribs of the creature. The strike did little actual damage, but it did knock the ghoul off balance – Jacob seized the opportunity to roll the ghoul off of him and he now found himself on top. He cleared the arms and fumbled for the hilt of the blade. Isaac stomped on its head once before Sully brusquely pushed him aside and brought the butt end of the rifle crashing into its skull.

After the second blow, the skull collapsed and the creature went limp.

Jacob sat back on the ghoul's stomach and gasped for breath. His head swam but he managed to pull the kitchen knife out from the corpse.

Keeley wrapped her arms around Madison's shoulder as she slid from beneath the vehicle and helped her up. Tears welled in the corners of her eyes, but otherwise she seemed none the worse for wear.

Emily stood, useless. Anders checked her over.

She quivered at the sight of him and the violence he had wrought.

He wrapped his arms around her and laughed.

'Thank you,' he bleated in accented English, 'I *knew* you wouldn't leave us!'

Emily managed a stunned smile as she returned the embrace.

Keeley noticed something subtle in Madison but couldn't place it.

Anders thought he caught something fleeting as well, but he didn't care. He was too relieved to not be trapped in the back of that truck.

Jacob shakily came to his feet; Isaac gave him a hand.

'We need to go,' Sully stated flatly, 'we're exposed here.'

'We made a lot of noise,' Jacob agreed, 'coulda heard that for miles.'

'Jennifer,' Keeley begged, 'the corporal… we have to wait for her!'

Several incredulous pairs of eyes fell on Keeley as she recounted an abridged version of events.

'… would she have survived that?' Madison asked.

Isaac's expression turned grim; Madison didn't miss it.

He didn't speak.

'Fuck her,' Anders spat, either unable or unwilling to hide his disdain.

Sully nodded his agreement.

'Good riddance.'

Keeley was stunned by their apathy; her mouth hung open to protest only to have the words escape her. Isaac considered their options but thought it best to not alienate the only survivors he knew yet stood.

He reached for Keeley's hand.

'Come on… let's go.'

She stared back at him.

'*Where?*' she stammered, already feeling the sting of their betrayal.

Isaac surveyed the ruins of the barracks and the pillar of smoke and flame pouring from it.

The moans of the dead, real or imagined, echoed from within the structure.

Emily huddled into Anders.

Jacob and Madison looked expectantly.

Sully cycled the action on the .308.

'Anywhere but here.'

Epilogue

SMOKE CONTINUED TO BLACKEN THE SKY.

Quinn lowered the binoculars and passed them back to the spotter without looking at him. The explosion earlier in the day echoed through the vacant streets, stretching out for miles. He could swear he yet heard traces of it, bouncing between the empty buildings of the Uptown.

From the nest, Quinn surveyed the grounds beneath him.

It was only a matter of time.

The explosion would have called out to everything nearby.

A great and terrible dinner bell.

When the hordes come…

If the walls were tested, they would fail. They didn't have the manpower.

As Quinn went to rise, the soldier saluted him.

Consumed in thought, Quinn scarcely noticed.

As the salute was lowered, Quinn recognized something in the soldier.

Something he felt he had lost.

Determination.

Unflinching, unyielding determination.

Quinn studied the man for a long moment.

Regretting his earlier indiscretion, Quinn turned square to the spotter and offered his hand in genuine admiration.

* * *

Quinn had hidden as many survivors and as much material as he could fit in the nests before ordering the rest to hole up in the upper floors of the civilian quarters. He pulled his men from the shooting platforms and ordered no shots be fired until absolutely necessary – loosely defined as when the walls were overrun and the infected were in the complex. He had emptied the armories and distributed bullets, weapons and whatever other gear they could muster as equally as possible. None were to be outside except runners, and even then only until the dead were in sight of the spotters.

They would try to wait it out.

Any who wanted to leave in advance of the pending siege were welcome to.

If the walls were compromised, the chain of command would be unreliable. Each man and woman who remained – soldier and civilian alike – would need to make their own decision on whether or when to break and flee. Quinn retained a small group with him in the command module, to guard the radio and the vital equipment of the infirmary. He'd also have the option of sending a runner between posts if he determined the site was lost.

Andrew was feverishly running through his script over and over, desperate to raise someone.

Anyone.

The plan was as good as it was going to get.

Satisfied his assets were deployed as best he could muster, Quinn produced some paper from his desk.

As she watched Quinn begin to write, Lynn chewed her nails and her leg shook nervously.

It was possible the ghouls would find no incentive to stop their march at the Coast Guard site, so long as they found no stimulus that overpowered their initial instinct. It was possible, if they were lucky.

Luck had been in short supply.

* * *

The door to the command module swung open.

Quinn raised his eyes to meet the intruder, but he didn't need to ask for the report.

The infected army had crested the hill; it now descended towards them.

Their path to the source of the explosion and the plume of smoke would take them right outside the gate.

Behind the soldier and through the door Quinn could see a huddle of terrified faces, each looking to him for direction.

Quinn placed his pen on his desk. He stared intently at the pages.

An honest assessment of their struggle.

His final report.

Their eulogy.

Satisfied he had told their story without whitewashing the details, he carefully placed the pages inside a manila folder and positioned it prominently on his desk.

* * *

They trudged through the forest.

The snow was uneven; occasionally they would slip and plummet into the slush and grime beneath. With feet soaked and spirits low, the mutinous silence between them deepened.

They abandoned the city with little true direction, knowing only they had to leave that forsaken place. They walked through the night, putting as much distance as they could between them and the bitter memories of the Uptown.

Their salvation would be somewhere beyond its borders.

As the troupe stopped to rest, Keeley looked around at their company.

Emily nestled into Anders; the fair-skinned foreigner had his arm wrapped around her shoulders. Though his face was scarred and his jaw hung awkward, his boyish good looks did little to hide the fact he was yet a kind-hearted soul beneath. They'd made fast friends – a reflection on Anders' personal magnetism, she supposed. Keeley's mind drifted to the moment she had seen him in the courtyard, his hood removed, how battered and broken he had been. So overwhelmed by the memory, Keeley didn't notice he had caught her staring. He smiled and shot her a wink before returning his attention to Emily.

Jacob was unsteady; his face was pale and he shook visibly. He sat on a log, hands on his knees, struggling to keep himself upright. He had obviously overexerted himself. He needed rest now, more than any of them, but they couldn't spare the time… and he knew it.

He would fight through it.

Madison checked over Jacob's stitches and frowned. They had torn again and were seeping. She did what she could to clean and pack them before she set about filling a canteen with the cleanest bits of snow she could find.

Isaac worked his knife into a tree, seemingly intent on something. Keeley didn't yet know how to react to Isaac. At times he was familiar, at others he was a complete stranger. She had always cursed his pragmatism when they argued. He was logical to a fault, often missing the 'bigger picture' by relying on it so heavily. She knew now he was capable of terrible things, but perhaps that capability had kept them alive this long.

There was always a duality in men, but she couldn't yet reconcile the two.

Sully sat with his back against a tree. His eyes were closed as he leaned his forehead into the barrel of the .308. His breath came deep and rhythmic, almost pensive. Keeley couldn't know for certain what thoughts plagued him, but she could guess. She hoped he could keep it together.

Gruff as he was, goddamn if he wasn't reliable.

Keeley gripped the strap of the messenger bag tightly. They had an incredible supply of medicines, but that alone wouldn't keep them alive.

Or safe.

She wondered if such a thing even existed anymore.

'Anyone hungry?' Isaac asked.

He wedged a chunk of rotten wood away and motioned to the gash in the tree. Several small grubs wriggled within. It would be far from appetizing, but they had little choice. They would need to conserve what little canned food and water they had left. They needed to scavenge on the move, and though none could truly afford to miss the calories, the thought of eating whatever the hell those were proved too much for most.

'Best not to pass up the protein,' Isaac urged as he popped one of the larvae into his mouth.

He turned away so the others wouldn't see his disgust. The road would be long.

CPSIA information can be obtained
at www.ICGtesting.com
Printed in the USA
LVOW08s1706110417
530416LV00004B/789/P

9 781773 024677